MARCHES

J. S. F.

MARCHESTER ROYAL

BY

J. S. FLETCHER

AUTHOR OF

THE ROOT OF ALL EVIL,
EXTERIOR TO THE EVIDENCE,
THE AMARANTH, CLUB, ETC.

GROSSET & DUNLAP
PUBLISHERS   NEW YORK

MARCHESTER ROYAL

PRINTED IN THE UNITED STATES OF AMERICA

CONTENTS

I: THE TWO TELEGRAMS

MARCHESTER ROYAL

CHAPTER I

The Two Telegrams

OF ALL the crowd of highly respectable legal practitioners who tread the pavements of Chancery Lane and its adjacent purlieus about ten o'clock of a morning, day in and day out for at any rate ten months of the year, none were ever more clockwork-like in regularity and punctuality than Mr. Matthew Deckenham, solicitor, of Old Buildings, Lincoln's Inn.

Being of a very modest and retiring nature, as befitted a bachelor gentleman, who, at the time this story begins was well over fifty years of age, Mr. Deckenham never gave way to such foolishness as boasting or vaunting, but he was certainly once known to have declared with much force and fervour, not to say with absolute conviction, that if there were a more punctual man than himself on the face of the earth he would like to meet him and shake him heartily by the hand.

In truth, Mr. Deckenham, who as I have already said, was a bachelor, and, therefore, free of all the troubles with which married men are sadly too familiar, was a very model of rule and of order. He lived in an old-fashioned house in Mecklenburgh

Square, wherein his grandfather and his father had lived before him, and from this house he set forth for his offices in Old Buildings every morning at precisely fifteen minutes to ten o'clock.

He crossed Guilford Street at one appointed period, Theobalds Road at a second, Holborn at a third—the porters at the old gateway through which he turned into the Inn would rather have set their watches by his appearance than by any clock in the neighbourhood. Precisely as the clock struck ten he entered his private office, laid aside his overcoat, his gloves, his hat, and his neatly folded umbrella, and having seen that his necktie was quite straight, sat down at his desk and rang the bell for his head clerk and the letters.

It was the sixth day of May, in the year 1896—a beautiful spring morning, giving promise of all that was good until the eventide should fall over London.

Mr. Deckenham, as he came from his house, admired the trees in Mecklenburgh Square; a few minutes later he found himself almost rapturous over those in Gray's Inn Gardens. There were women and girls selling flowers by the kerbstones in Holborn; he gazed at the fresh blossoms with much pleasure, being a little of a horticulturist himself. But he allowed none of these peeps and glances at trees and flowers to interrupt his usual method of procedure—if anyone had been very curious on the point and had taken the trouble to do so they might have ascertained that Mr. Deckenham took exactly the same number of steps between his house and his office—and at the precise moment he turned into the Inn, climbed the staircase in the corner on the left-hand side, and let himself into his private office with his private key. A moment later and the clerks heard his bell.

The head clerk, who was too well acquainted with his employer's habits to keep him waiting for even the fraction of a second, and who accordingly always had everything in readiness, answered Mr. Deckenham's summons with a celerity which would have done much credit to a quick-change artist. He was at Mr. Deckenham's elbow with his sheaf of letters before the tinkle of the bell had died away.

"Good morning, Matthews," said Mr. Deckenham in his usual gracious manner. "A beautiful morning; in fact quite summerlike. And what have we this morning, Matthews?"

"There's nothing of any great importance, sir," replied Matthews. "At least, there's only that matter of Slingsby v. Carpenter. But here's a telegram just arrived for you, sir—it hasn't been delivered two minutes—you'd meet the boy as you came upstairs."

"I did meet a telegraph messenger as I ascended," remarked Mr. Deckenham, as he took the buff envelope and cut it open with an old-fashioned paper-knife, "and I wished, Matthews, that the authorities would endeavour to teach such lads that it is not necessary to stamp, or to whistle, or to—merciful Heavens! Matthews! Matthews——!"

The head clerk, who was looking through his papers, turned at these horror-stricken exclamations, to find his employer staring wide-eyed, white-cheeked, at the flimsy scrap of paper which rustled and shook in his trembling hands as quaker grass shivers in the wind.

"What is it, sir—what is it, Mr. Deckenham?" he exclaimed.

Mr. Deckenham let the telegram fall on his desk and groaned. He pointed to it with a shaking finger, and Matthews, obeying the mute command, picked it up and read it.

"Lord Marchester is dead. Come here at once. Most urgent.

"Saunderson."

The head clerk's face was very grave as he laid the telegram down again.

"Dear, dear, sir, that's very bad news!" he said. "And so sudden. Why, his lordship was here only the other day!"

"To be precise, last Tuesday, Matthews," replied Mr. Deckenham, who was now recovering from his shock. "And that he must have been in his usual robust health the day before yesterday is certain from the fact that we had one of his characteristically cheery letters from him yesterday morning."

"So we had, sir," said the clerk. "Dear me! Sudden seizure I should say, sir—apoplexy, no doubt. Sad; only twenty-eight, his lordship, I believe, Mr. Deckenham?"

"Twenty-seven," replied Mr. Deckenham. He jumped to his feet with more than his usual alacrity. "Well, I must go at once, Matthews—I can just catch the ten-twenty at King's Cross. You must attend to everything in my absence; no doubt I shall return this evening. Let Slingsby v. Carpenter wait, and, if it's urgent, do you yourself decide."

And, struggling into his overcoat, and laying hold of hat, gloves, and umbrella, Mr. Deckenham, with a hurried farewell to his head clerk, burst out of his private door, and went scurrying down the stairs in as undignified a fashion as that of which he had just complained as a characteristic of telegraph messengers. He ran rather than walked across the pavement and through the old gate, and the porter, who happened to be looking out just then, scratched his head and asked himself if old Deckenham had suddenly heard of his elevation to the Bench.

As good luck would have it, there was an empty hansom cab coming along Chancery Lane at that moment, and in two seconds Mr. Deckenham was inside it, and was being driven in the direction of King's Cross as rapidly as the traffic would permit.

Usually a very placid, though a somewhat fussy man, Mr. Deckenham on this occasion fumed and fretted, and once when the cab got into what seemed to be an inextricable mess at Holborn Town Hall, he felt a decided impulse to use strong language.

But Mr. Deckenham had just easy time when he jumped out at King's Cross, and he rewarded his cabman liberally. Hurrying to the window of the first-class ticket office, he booked himself for Marchester Royal, and was going away with his ticket and his change in his hand, when he heard a voice behind him, and felt a light tap on his shoulder.

"Wait a moment, Mr. Deckenham; I daresay we're bound on the same errand."

Mr. Deckenham turned sharply and confronted a man who might have been a soldier in mufti, or a cricketer in ordinary attire, or a professional instructor of gymnastics *minus* his usual paraphernalia—a tallish, broad-shouldered, well-set-up man of from thirty to thirty-five, with a bronzed face, keen, blue eyes, a dark-brown moustache with a touch of reddish gold in it, and a strong determined chin. He wore a smartly-made, well-fitting suit of dark blue serge, and his straw hat was circled by a band of dark blue. Well booted and gloved, and carrying a smart walking-cane, this person made a fine figure of a man, and some of the ladies' maids, waiting about for their mistresses, regarded him with admiration. As for Mr. Deckenham, he regarded him with open mouth and widening eyes.

"Inspector Skarratt!" he exclaimed.

Inspector Skarratt nodded, smiled, disclosing a set of beautiful white teeth beneath his military-looking moustache. He turned to the ticket window.

"First single Marchester Royal, if you please," he said.

Mr. Deckenham gasped. Marchester Royal! What did they want with this man, one of the sharpest, most astute men from Scotland Yard, at Marchester Royal at this juncture? Could it be that— a deadly fear came into his mind and turned him sick at heart—could it be that——

"Come along, Mr. Deckenham," he heard Inspector Skarratt saying. "We'll have a compartment to ourselves. Just let me get some newspapers—it's a long journey into Yorkshire."

Mr. Deckenham, moving as in a dream, seemed to realise nothing very definite until he found himself viz-à-viz with his companion in a compartment from which a guard had kept all other passengers away. It was not until the train had rumbled through the tunnels north of King's Cross that he recovered the full use of his scattered wits. Then he bent forward towards Inspector Skarratt, who was turning over a pile of newspapers and magazines, and spoke, with a world of wonder and suspicion in his voice.

"What on earth are you going down to Marchester Royal for?" he asked.

Inspector Skarratt shook his head.

"That I couldn't tell you, Mr. Deckenham," he replied.

"Couldn't tell me?"

"No, I couldn't tell you.   Because, you see, I don't know myself," answered Inspector Skarratt.   "I shall know, I suppose, when I get there."

"Then you have been sent for?" asked Mr. Deckenham.

Inspector Skarratt smiled.

"It's not very likely that I should be going there if I hadn't been sent for, Mr. Deckenham," he replied.

Mr. Deckenham continued to stare at the detective, who, on his part, continued to turn his newspapers over.

"Who sent for you?" he demanded at last.

"Who sent for you?" asked Inspector Skarratt, with a breezy laugh.   "Come, Mr. Deckenham, there's no need for old friends like you and myself to beat about the bush.   I don't know why I'm wanted at Marchester Royal, unless it's another burglary like the one I was concerned with there two years ago, which, as you know, turned out a complete success for the burglar or burglars.   That's what I'm supposing it is.   All I know is that we had a very urgent telegram early this morning asking us to send the cleverest man we had at command at once, and mentioning me for preference.   So off I came.   Seeing you at King's Cross there, and knowing that you're Lord Marchester's solicitor, I naturally came to the conclusion that you were going down, too."

Mr. Deckenham's eyes almost bulged out of his head, and he stroked his knees nervously with his hands, which trembled a little.

"I expect it is another burglary," said Inspector Skarratt half carelessly, as he unfolded and glanced over another newspaper.   "You see, they've a lot of heirlooms in that house, and it's a great temptation to the gentlemen with whom business brings me in contact. Don't you think so, Mr. Deckenham?"

Instead of replying to this question, Mr. Deckenham suddenly slapped his knees so violently that his companion looked sharply up from his newspaper.

"What's the matter?" he exclaimed.

"God bless me, man!" said Mr. Deckenham. "There's something wrong—very wrong! Was that all that the message to Scotland Yard said—all?"

Inspector Skarratt stared at the solicitor and noticed his agitation.

"All?" he repeated. "Yes—that was all."

Mr. Deckenham leant forward until his face was very near the detective's. His voice sank to a whisper.

"Lord Marchester's dead!" he said. "Dead!"

Inspector Skarratt frowned and stared.

"Dead!" he exclaimed. "Dead!"

"He's dead," repeated Mr. Deckenham. "See here," and he drew the telegram from an inner pocket and handed it across. "And since they've sent for you—why, I'm afraid there's something wrong—very wrong!"

Inspector Skarratt took the crumpled scrap of paper and read it over slowly, another frown making puckers beneath his eyebrows. He handed it back with a decisive nod.

"And I don't think you're far wrong, Mr. Deckenham," he said. "Yes—there's something wrong. If his lordship had died a natural death there'd have been no need to send for us. He hasn't been ill, has he?"

"He was in my office in Lincoln's Inn last Tuesday in as good health as a young man of twenty-seven could wish to enjoy," said Mr. Deckenham, shaking his head. "And I had one of his usual cheery letters —he was always breezy in his correspondence—yesterday morning. Of course, Inspector, it may have been a natural death—apoplexy, perhaps?"

"No, sir," replied Inspector Skarratt stoutly. "In that case they wouldn't have wanted our services. We shall probably find that it's murder."

Mr. Deckenham shuddered, and put out a hand as if to ward off the fatal word. Inspector Skarratt nodded his head.

"You'll see," he said with quiet persistence. "Let's see—he wasn't a rich man, was he, Mr. Deckenham?"

"No," answered the solicitor. "He was not. Four thousand a year at the outside. It was more than enough for him. He had very simple tastes."

"And unmarried?" said Inspector Skarratt.

"In my opinion," replied Mr. Deckenham drily, "he never would have married. He was not a marrying man, sir—like myself."

"And who succeeds?" inquired Inspector Skarratt.

"His only brother, Mr. Gerald Wintour," answered the solicitor. "It will be a change for him!"

"Why?"

"Because he's been very poor," replied Mr. Deckenham. "You see, the family never has been wealthy, old as it is—this is the fifteenth baron. Mr. Gerald had only a younger son's portion, and the late peer could never help him very much, because he was bound to keep up the place. And unfortunately," he added in a lower tone, "they never got on very well together, those two—never openly quarrelled, you know, but they'd no similarity of tastes. The late peer—dear me, to think I should be calling him that!—was all for horses and dogs and field sports—Mr. Gerald has always been a bookworm and a student."

"Mr. Gerald ever do anything?" asked Inspector Skarratt.

"He is a barrister of the Middle Temple," replied Mr. Deckenham. "But I question if he has ever earned enough to pay the rent of his chambers. A nice fellow, but somewhat reserved and gloomy—what I should call a broody man. However, he's Lord Marchester now. God bless me, Inspector. I wonder whatever news it will be that we shall find awaiting us!"

Inspector Skarratt's handsome face become stolid and enigmatical, and he shook his head.

"I'm afraid it will not be good news, Mr. Deckenham," he said. "I shouldn't be hurrying northward unless something had happened."

And then, being an omnivorous reader, he turned to a magazine, and Mr. Deckenham, doubting and wondering and surmising, tried to read the *Times,* and was thoroughly unhappy until at three o'clock in the afternoon they found themselves on the little platform at Marchester Royal, and were met by the dead peer's steward, Mr. Saunderson, whose countenance showed signs of great anxiety and concern. Mr. Deckenham drew him instantly aside, Inspector Skarratt close in attendance, and whispered a question. Mr. Saunderson's face quivered as he replied:

"His lordship was found in the library at seven this morning—murdered!"

II: MR. SAUNDERSON

CHAPTER II

Mr. Saunderson

THE effect of the steward's announcement upon the two men to whom it was made illustrated the difference in their respective character and temperament.

Mr. Deckenham, man of law though he was, and well accustomed to all manner of distressful matters, could not repress a groan of horror at the dreadful news—he had known the dead man ever since the latter was breeched, and had always cherished an affection which was almost parental for him and his bright, breezy ways. He thought now of him lying dead—slain by the hand of some assassin—and groaned again. The tears welled up into his pale blue eyes, and he drew out his handkerchief and blew his nose violently.

The effect upon Inspector Skarratt was quite different. His bundle of newspapers and magazines under one arm, his smart walking-cane dangling from his disengaged hand, he heard the news without moving a muscle of his face, and merely nodded his head when Mr. Saunderson pronounced the fatal word. Then he turned sharply, and looking about him, said:

"Is there anywhere near where we can go for half-an-hour and hear what you can tell us, Mr. Saunderson? And we can get some food at the same time. Beyond a sandwich or so neither Mr. Deckenham nor myself has had anything to eat since we left King's Cross—we'd no time at York."

"I had thought of that, Inspector," replied Mr. Saunderson. "I knew that you could not stop at York longer than was necessary to catch your train, so I have ordered a hot lunch to be ready for the three of us at the 'Marchester Arms' close by, in a private room. It will be ready now, so we will go across, and then, after we have lunched, I will drive you to Marchester Royal—it's a good three miles' drive, as you're both aware, gentlemen."

Mr. Deckenham, full of memories, nodded his head mournfully. Inspector Skarratt nodded his in quite a different way.

"Do the people in the neighbourhood know of this yet?" he inquired, as they walked across an open space between the station and the little hotel, above the doors of which the arms of the Barons of Marchester were emblazoned. "Or have the local police kept it quiet up to now?"

"No announcement has been made so far, Inspector," answered Mr. Saunderson. "It was considered best to keep the matter quiet until the afternoon or evening."

"I suppose they've moved the body?" said Inspector Skarratt. "They always do."

Mr. Saunderson stared at the detective in surprise.

"Why, of course, sir!" he said, almost indignantly. "His lordship's body was most reverently disposed as soon as possible. You wouldn't have left it lying where it was found, I'm sure?"

"Then don't be sure," retorted Inspector Skarratt. "For I should. You oughtn't to have touched it or anything about it until I came. Ha! I wonder when we shall get a bit of commonsense in this country? They manage things better in France. If this had been in France they'd have had a cordon of police drawn round that body as soon as it was discovered, and they wouldn't have let foot or hand near until an expert arrived! That's what I'm always having to contend with. And I remember your local police— I'd enough bother with them when I was down here about that burglary two years since."

"Well, sir, you didn't solve the mystery of that!" retorted Mr. Saunderson. "You did no better than they did."

"Gentlemen—gentlemen!" said Mr. Deckenham. "Come, we are, as it were, in the presence of the dead —do not let us—er—squabble."

"I don't want to squabble," said Inspector Skarratt. "I want a good wash, and a good dinner."

"The latter," said the placatory solicitor, "I am sure Mr. Saunderson will give you."

"Plain Yorkshire fare, Mr. Deckenham—plain Yorkshire fare!" said the steward. "We do our best, sir, in these regions, but of course we are not up to London kickshaws. It's a bad business, this, Mr. Deckenham," he continued, as Inspector Skarratt went off to wash and left solicitor and steward alone in the little parlour wherein they were to dine. "Do you think this chap will be able to do anything to unravel it—the local men haven't a clue, so far."

"If he can't, there isn't a man in Scotland Yard who can," replied Mr. Deckenham with decision. "He's the smartest man they have, and that's not saying a little nowadays, sir."

"Well, he didn't do anything in the matter of the burglary," remarked Mr. Saunderson. "He was a dead failure there."

Mr. Deckenham smiled faintly.

"How do you know he was?" he said. "He said to

me as we were coming along that he'd got a very strong clue to that business, and that he was almost confident of bringing it to a satisfactory conclusion. He——"

At this moment the subject of their conversation returned, and was immediately followed by a plump waiting-maid with very red cheeks and very bright eyes, who bore in and set upon the table a noble sirloin of beef, smoking hot, which she presently supplemented with one bowl of mealy potatoes and another of stewed celery. After placing a foaming jug of ale and a decanter of whisky in the centre of the table, she blushingly retired, and Mr. Saunderson, having mumbled a short grace, laid hold of the carving-knife and fork and gazed appreciatively at the sirloin.

"It's a beautiful undercut, gentlemen," he said. "I chose it out of the butcher's shop myself as I came through after breakfast, and brought it along in the trap with me. There's gooseberry tart and a custard to follow, and a ripe old Cheshire cheese after that— I hope you'll make good dinners."

"I have always known you as a most hospitable host, Mr. Saunderson," said Mr. Deckenham, "and you have provided most bountifully. I wish that this sad event had not gone far to spoil my appetite."

"It hasn't spoilt mine," said Inspector Skarratt. "I'm hungry, Mr. Saunderson, and I shall enjoy your hospitality, I can assure you. I don't believe in letting anything interfere with my appetite. You can't work on an empty stomach. How do I know that after getting to Marchester Royal I mayn't be at work for twenty or thirty or forty hours without the chance of getting more than a mere snack?"

"I think the Inspector is quite right," said Mr.

Saunderson. "Come, Mr. Deckenham—we can't bring the dead back by starving ourselves."

"And now just run the facts over, will you, Mr. Saunderson," said Inspector Skarratt, when his own and the steward's knives and forks were in full play, and poor Mr. Deckenham was endeavouring to summon up enough appetite to do justice to the delicately carved slice of undercut on his plate. "Just the main facts, you know—no details."

Mr. Saunderson was a big man—a man of heavy frame, heavy countenance, heavy jaws. Those jaws at this moment were working steadily at Mr. Saunderson's dinner, and that their owner was enjoying the process was evident from the expression of satisfaction in his eyes and the hearty smacks of his somewhat too sensuous lips. He looked like nothing so much as a highly-respectable cow chewing her cud, unashamed, unconscious, and as he dubitated a moment on Inspector Skarratt's request, he rolled his eyes—which were much too small for his large, heavily-featured face, and much too closely set together—towards the ceiling in the same fashion in which bovine animals roll theirs at feeding time.

"Just the main facts," repeated the detective.

Mr. Saunderson made an end of a mouthful of roast beef.

"Well, of course, gentlemen," he said unctuously, "it's not quite the thing, I suppose, to talk of these things while one sits at meat, and with that I'm sure Mr. Deckenham there'll agree, but time presses, and you can't afford to be over squeamish. Let me give you another slice, Inspector."

"And rather more fat, if you please, Mr. Saunderson," replied Inspector Skarratt. "It's a prime piece of beef."

"In that, sir, you're right," agreed the steward solemnly. "It is a prime cut—as I've already remarked, I chose it myself, and I've a very shrewd idea, gentlemen, as to who fed that beef. But that's neither here nor there just now. The main facts of this sad occurrence—well, Inspector, they form what we country folk call a very simple tale. I can give you my Bible oath, gentlemen, that all was as right as right can be at Marchester Royal last night at half-past nine of the clock, for I was in the house myself. I had occasion to see my Lord on rather important business, and I called after I knew he'd finished his dinner. He sent for me into the billiard-room—there was his lordship and Mr. Gerald playing pyramids, and—"

"Is Mr. Gerald Wintour staying down there?" inquired Mr. Deckenham, looking up from his scarcely-tasted beef with some surprise.

"The Honourable Gerald Wintour that was, the sixteenth Baron Marchester that now is," said Mr. Saunderson, "has been staying at Marchester Royal for the past fortnight—I've had the honour of conversing with him—his lordship, as he now is—several times."

"Go on, Mr. Saunderson," said Inspector Skarratt. "You found Lord Marchester and his brother in the billiard-room at nine-thirty last night. Well?"

Mr. Saunderson helped himself to another slice of beef.

"Well, Inspector," he continued, "of course his lordship—I'm referring to his dead lordship—asked me to sit down. He was always very nice to me, his lordship—always. You know what an affable, free-and-easy young gentleman he was, Mr. Deckenham, don't you?"

"At all times—at all times!" sighed Mr. Deckenham.

"And, of course, you know his late lordship's hearty ways," continued the steward. " 'Hullo, that you, Saunderson?' he says, as soon as I got in. 'Sit down and have a whisky-and-soda and a cigar.' So I sat down, of course, and Jarvis, the under-footman, who was marking for them, he gave me a drink and a smoke, and I watched my lord and Mr. Gerald playing. 'Any business that's urgent, Saunderson?' says my lord after a while. 'Well, it is rather urgent, my lord,' says I, 'or else I shouldn't have intruded upon your lordship at this hour.' 'Oh, all right!' he says. 'Just wait till we've finished this game, and then we'll talk.' And they went on playing, and I sat and smoked my cigar and watched them. Dear me— to think of my lord as I saw him then, a fine, healthy young man, all life and fire, and to think of what he is now—yes, it's quite true that Bible saying about death being in the very midst of life, it is indeed! Try a slice of the outside, Mr. Deckenham—perhaps you'll like it better than the undercut."

But Mr. Deckenham waved a polite refusal.

"Go on, Mr. Saunderson," said Inspector Skarratt.

"Well, gentlemen, when the game was over, my lord came sauntering up to me, his cue in his hand, and lighted a cigar and got himself a drink, and sat down beside me in an easy-chair as friendly and sociable as we three are just now—he was always that way with me, Mr. Deckenham, as, of course, you're very well aware, having known us both so long. 'Now, then, Saunderson, what's it all about?' he says in his pleasant way. 'Get another whisky-and-soda, and then we'll talk.' And so, of course, we did our bit of business."

"How long did it take to do?" inquired Inspector Skarratt.

"How long? Perhaps a matter of twenty minutes," replied Mr. Saunderson. "It was the case of those tenants down at Marchester Common, you know, Mr. Deckenham—you sent in your written opinion about it a week or so since."

"Yes, yes, I remember very well," said Mr. Deckenham.

"Did the brother stop in the room all the time you were talking?" asked the Inspector.

"What, Mr. Gerald—that is now the sixteenth baron?" said Mr. Saunderson. "Oh, certainly, Inspector! There was no reason why he should go out —there was nothing private about the business. He stopped at the billiard-table, knocking the balls about —practising shots, you know. I'm a bit of a billiard player myself," concluded Mr. Saunderson, with a burst of confidence.

"Are you?" said Inspector Skarratt. "So am I— I'll play you a game one of these days. Well, go on, Mr. Saunderson, if you please."

"I think this would be a favourable point whereat to have the beef removed and the lighter things brought in," said Mr. Saunderson. "I see you've finished, Inspector, and as for Mr. Deckenham, his appetite seems to have left him. Try a little whisky-and-soda, sir—you're looking anything but well."

"Thank you," said Mr. Deckenham. "You're very good. It is early in the day for spirituous refreshment, but perhaps the occasion may warrant it. I have been much upset, Mr. Saunderson, much upset by this sad news."

"Ah!" said the steward, as he helped Mr. Deckenham to what the latter considered a rather liberal potation. "You may well say that, sir. If you'd seen that handsome young gentleman——"

Inspector Skarratt drummed his fingers on the table until the blushing waiting-maid had removed what Mr. Saunderson called the "heavies," and replaced them by the "lights." As soon as he had got a plateful of stewed gooseberries and custard before him he repeated his formula.

"Yes? Go on, Mr. Saunderson."

"Well," continued Mr. Saunderson, helping himself very liberally to the "lights," "of course, after I'd finished my business there was nothing for me to stay for, and I left the gentlemen to their amusement, both of them bidding me good-night in the most affable manner—which was always a characteristic of the family, as Mr. Deckenham knows. Now, of course, as you both know, gentlemen, my house is just on the edge of the Park at Marchester Royal, and thither I repaired as soon as I had left his lordship—his late lordship. I was in bed by half-past ten o'clock, and slept the sleep of the just until seven o'clock this morning, which is my usual hour for rising. I had just attired myself, and was about to go downstairs to breakfast—I always breakfast early, Mr. Deckenham—when I heard what is commonly called a commotion in the lower regions, and presently my housekeeper, Miss Mercer, came rushing upstairs to tell me that a groom had run across the park to tell me that my lord had been found in his library—dead. And not only dead, but shot! Shot! Murdered!"

"A little more custard if you please," said Inspector Skarratt, passing his plate across the table. "It's a very good custard, that. Well, go on."

"I went—as fast as my legs could carry me," said Mr. Saunderson. "I arrived at Marchester Royal, and was taken to the Study. The poor young gentleman was lying on a couch near the window opening on to the terrace—quite dead. In fact, Dr. Ollivant said he'd been dead some hours. There was a bullet wound——"

Mr. Deckenham pushed his chair back and rose from the table. He betrayed considerable agitation. He stretched out both hands.

"Inspector!" he said. "Is there any need for further——"

Inspector Skarratt swallowed his last spoonful of the excellent custard and helped himself to the merest mouthful of cheese. He, too, rose to his feet and threw his napkin on the table.

"Not the slightest, sir," he replied. "I've heard all I want to hear, just now. Whenever you're ready, Mr. Saunderson, I am. How long will your dog-cart be?"

Mr. Saunderson, looking somewhat surprised at this abrupt termination of the proceedings, answered that the mare and trap should be brought round at once, and he presently departed to the stable-yard to give orders.

"I am terribly distressed—terribly distressed!" said poor Mr. Deckenham, when he and Inspector Skarratt were alone. "What do you think, Inspector—what do you think?"

Inspector Skarratt shook his head. He smiled—and the smile was grim.

"That's a big question, Mr. Deckenham—as you ought to know," he replied at last. "I've no doubt I've got a difficult case before me—a very, very difficult case. But there's one thing I shouldn't be surprised about. It wouldn't surprise me if we find that the man who killed Lord Marchester was the so-called burglar of two years ago!"

III: SIR THOMAS BRAYE

CHAPTER III

Sir Thomas Braye

M R. DECKENHAM was so much astonished at hearing this pronouncement of opinion that he remained lost in thought and in wonder until the waiting-maid came to inform him and his companion that Mr. Saunderson was waiting for them in the yard of the hotel, and would be glad of their presence.

"Not a word of that to Saunderson, if you please, Mr. Deckenham," said Inspector Skarratt, as they went down a long, sanded passage towards the rear of the house. "I could trust you with any secret of mine, because I know you—I wouldn't trust Saunderson—he's a bit too oily for me."

"Dear, dear!" said Mr. Deckenham. "Now, do you know, he never struck me in that light. But this is a sad world, Inspector."

"It's a queer world, and there are some queer folk in it," said Inspector Skarratt.

Then they emerged upon the stable yard and found Mr. Saunderson awaiting them, and already seated in his conveyance. Like many men of his size and weight, he affected a governess-cart and pony, and as neither was of any great dimensions, Inspector Skarratt looked on both with some evidences of disfavour on his countenance.

"It'll take us some time to get over to Marchester Royal in that," he said. "Hadn't I better get a dog-cart and a fast trotter? I ought to be there as soon as ever I can."

Mr. Saunderson scowled. His face was not pleasant when he scowled—there were heavy lines about his face and eyes which indicated temper.

"You can do what you like, sir," he said, "but if you can find a faster trotter than this pony of mine within five miles, I'll buy you a new hat. You jump in and sit alongside of Mr. Deckenham there, and I'll have you in Marchester Royal inside of thirty-five minutes."

"Oh, all right—I beg the pony's pardon!" said Inspector Skarratt. "I was only thinking of what it had to carry—you're a good eighteen stone yourself, Mr. Saunderson, and I'm fourteen, and Mr. Deckenham I should set down at ten, so there's forty-two stone for you, and the trap as well."

"Never you mind, sir," said Mr. Saunderson, who had an uncomfortable idea that the Inspector was chaffing him. "You'll see, come up Roger!"

That Roger was an uncommonly game little animal was very soon made evident. He fell into his stride as soon as he got off the cobble-paved stable-yard, and went rattling away down the hill to Marchester at a pace which surprised the Inspector, who hastened to make the *amende honorable*.

"You're quite right, Mr. Saunderson," he said. "He is a good 'un—You've something to be proud of there."

Mr. Saunderson smirked with satisfaction, and then gave a solemn wink.

"I know a good thing when I see it, sir," he said. "I bought that pony twelve months since for five pounds. He was skin and bone—look at him now! That's what care and attention to good raw material can do."

The improved pony went rattling into Marchester village, and Mr. Deckenham, who knew the old place as well as he knew Mecklenburgh Square and Lincoln's Inn, looked about him with mingled feelings of pleasure and pain. Nothing ever seemed to change in Marchester—certainly nothing had changed during the thirty years in which he had known it. No house had been built; no house pulled down.

There were the same comfortable farmsteads, set in the midst of orchards and gardens and stackyards; there were the same little cottages with their yellow walls and red-tiled roofs and little windows, gay with flowering plants; there was the same old, majestic church, with its high, square, embattled tower and its famous Norman porch; there, overlooking it, rose the great elms which some folk considered Marchester's chief glory.

Nor was there any change, so far as Mr. Deckenham could see, in the little details of the village. That seemed to be the same old woman who sat in the sunlight at her cottage door, knitting; those seemed to be the same old men who leant over the wall of the pinfold, talking about bygone days; those seemed to be the very same ducks sailing up and down the pond under the willow trees. No—there was little change here.

"It's a grand old village," sighed Mr. Deckenham half unconsciously.

"You're right, sir," said Mr. Saunderson, "there's no finer village in Yorkshire." He sighed in his turn. "It looks very peaceful this afternoon, gentlemen, but it'll not be so peaceful to-night when the news is out, and I suppose it can't be kept back any longer, Inspector?"

"No, I'm sure it can't," answered Inspector Skarratt. "Why, of course, the Coroner will want to begin his inquiry to-morrow, and there'll be the jury to summon to-night."

"He was very popular in the village, was my lord," remarked Mr. Saunderson. "Very popular, although it wasn't all his property, more's the pity."

From Marchester village to Marchester Royal the road rises slightly, and the pony, having rattled over one half its journey at a more than usually smart pace, settled down into a steadier one. Presently, coming to a rather sharp hill, it dropped into a walk, and Mr. Saunderson remarking that a merciful man is merciful to his beast, said that they would get out and walk a couple of hundred yards until they came to the top.

Thus walking, they approached the entrance to what was evidently a private park—a pair of handsome stone pillars, between which was set a massive gate of wrought iron, which had recently been gilded and ornamented with a coat-of-arms. There was a neat lodge within these gates; it had recently been painted and renovated, and it and the ornamental garden in front of it looked very spick and span and formal, as did also the gravelled carriage-drive, which wound away from it beneath an avenue of chestnuts. Something about the gates in their grandeur of gilt, the lodge, in its glory of flowers, and the drive in its prim properness, suggested wealth.

As the three men came abreast of this place, a lady and a gentleman, both on horseback, were coming through the gates, held open for them by a respectable looking old woman, who dropped a deep curtsey as they passed. The gentleman took no heed of this salutation; the lady rewarded it with a pleasant nod and a sweet smile.

Inspector Skarratt, who, from sheer habit, always saw anything within range, made a rapid inspection of these two equestrians. The gentleman, very correctly attired in the riding costume affected by country squires, was a short, podgy person of presumably sixty years of age, with a very red, choleric face ornamented by mutton-chop whiskers, now snow-white, whose sole expression in face and figure, was one of great pomposity—he bestrode his horse as though he had been some Cæsar returning to Rome after an epoch making victory. Something about him brought the first beginnings of a smile to Inspector Skarratt's usually grim, soldier-like face; he was reminded of a visit to a circus in his boyish days, when he had seen a monkey riding a horse.

But Inspector Skarratt felt no inclination to smile when he looked at the lady who rode by the side of this pompous little gentleman. He was a great admirer of female beauty, and he said to himself that he had rarely seen a more beautiful woman than this. Tall, exquisitely shaped, her dark blue riding habit showing off her beautifully rounded figure to perfection, she looked a young goddess in modern costume. He caught but one glimpse of her face as she turned it for a second in his direction; he was conscious of a pair of deep violet eyes; of a complexion of roses and lilies, of a wealth of hair, the colour of old gold, coiled in great masses beneath the smart bowler hat. A dream of fresh English beauty! Inspector Skarratt felt his heart jump.

The equestrians turned down the hill towards Marchester; Mr. Saunderson lifted his hat as he passed, and received in return for his salutation and those of his companions a curt nod from the pompous person and a gracious bow from his companion. Mr. Saunderson laughed—the laugh had a decided sneer in it.

"Who are those?" inquired Mr. Deckenham. Mr. Saunderson laughed again—this time with an added sneer.

"Those are what the folks hereabouts call 'Nowt and Nobody but for Brass,'" he replied. "That's the great Sir Thomas Braye, and his daughter Miss Margaret, the new tenants—or rather proprietors of Marchester Abbey, yonder. Faugh!"

"So that is Sir Thomas Braye?" said Mr. Deckenham. "Of course, I knew who had bought the place, but I had never seen him, although he has been there —why, it must be quite a year, eh?"

"More," said Mr. Saunderson laconically. "Fourteen months."

"He seems a little—pompous?" said Mr. Deckenham.

"Pompous! I should think he was pompous!" exclaimed the steward. "I believe he thinks all the world belongs to him. I'm sorry for his daughter— she's as sweet and nice a girl as ever lived, and how she ever came to be his, I can't think. It must have come from her mother."

"Who is this Sir Thomas Braye, then?" asked Inspector Skarratt as they took their seats again in the governess-cart. "He wasn't here of course, when I was down here two years ago."

"Why, Inspector, I can soon tell you who he is," said Mr. Saunderson, "for I happen to know all about his history. He's a retired carpet manufacturer from Blackford, in the West Riding, and a man of considerable wealth—according to some people in a position to know, he's a millionaire, and I shouldn't be a bit surprised if that were true—he's certainly tremendously wealthy. They say that he began life as a

common operative in one of the Blackford Mills, and
worked his way until he began to manufacture for himself—well, nobody would think any the worse of him
for that, but unfortunately, he's so blown out with
conceit and so pompous, as Mr. Deckenham just said,
that there's no bearing with him. With the daughter, of course, it's totally different. She's been edu-
cated in London, and Paris, and Germany, and I should
say that the old man married a good deal above him
—Miss Margaret, at any rate, is a lady. I'm sorry
for her, I am, indeed."

"Why?" asked Inspector Skarratt.

"Why?" said Mr. Saunderson. "Why, because
she'll find it as lonely here as she would in a convent!
The country folk about here'll never have anything
to do with them. They all know, bless you, that old
Braye made his money in carpets; that he can't speak
decent English! that he talks about nothing but himself and his money, and that he only got his knight-
hood because he happened to be mayor of Blackford
the year that the Queen went there to open the New
Town Hall. Oh, of course, they'll be ostracised—
no matter how nice the girl is, nor how wealthy she is.
In some parts of England they wouldn't be, but the
county families round about here are very old, and
very exclusive, aren't they, Mr. Deckenham?"

"Oh, yes, yes!" replied Mr. Deckenham. "Very
exclusive indeed."

"I can tell you a good story about Sir Thomas
and old Lady Beaudevere, who, of course, as Dowager
Marchioness of Beaudevere, is the acknowledged
leader of Society in these parts," continued Mr. Saunderson, with a chuckle of great satisfaction. "Of
course, when they came to the Abbey, nobody called
on the Brayes. They went hunting, but people used

to stare at them so—you know how they can stare,
Mr. Deckenham, that sort, at what they think their
inferiors!—that presently the girl gave it up though
the old man brazened it out to the end of the season.
Well, whether or not it was that Sir Thomas got des-
perate I don't know, but it's a fact that when they'd
been here about six months he got into his brougham
one afternoon and drove to Lady Beaudevere's place
and sent in his card. You can guess what happened,
Mr. Deckenham!"

Mr. Deckenham sighed and nodded.

"I can't," said Inspector Skarrat. "What did happen?"

Mr. Saunderson laughed—the laugh with a sneer
in it.

"Why," he said, "this is what happened. Lady
Beaudevere sent her butler back with the card, and
this message, which, in the presence of several people
in her drawing-room, she charged him to deliver, word
for word; 'Her ladyship is not in need of new carpets
at present, and when she is she will get them from her
usual tradesman!"

"Did the man deliver the message?" asked Inspector
Skarratt.

"It would have been as much as his place was worth
if he hadn't!" answered Mr. Saunderson.

"And what did Sir Thomas do?" inquired Inspector
Skarratt.

"Do? Drove away with all the flunkeys smiling
at him!" said the steward.

"I'm sorry to hear that," said Inspector Skarratt.
"He's a pompous-looking little frog, but I wish he'd
had more grit. I'd have hit that butler if he'd been
twice as big as myself. And as for your old frump
of a Marchioness—why, I say she was a bigger cad

than Sir Thomas could possibly be! Bah!—you make
me sick!"

"You do not understand, my dear Sir," began Mr.
Saunderson. "The——"

"I don't want," said the Inspector brusquely. "I
wish that pony of yours would get on as fast at the
end of his journey as he did at the beginning."

However, at that moment the pony turned a corner
and revealed the ancient, moss-grown entrance to
Marchester Royal, and beyond it the famous avenue
of elm trees for which it is celebrated, all the world
over. At the farther extremity of this, half a mile
away, they could see Marchester Royal itself—an
ancient Elizabethian house of red brick, the front of
which was almost entirely obscured by ivy.

"We've only been thirty-three and a half minutes
now, Inspector," said Mr. Saunderson, consulting his
watch as they rattled up the drive. "We shall do it
easily."

Inspector Skarratt made no answer. His handsome face had become very grim and set; it looked like
the face of a general who is just about to give battle.
As they emerged from the drive and came in view of
the house, he regarded the latter and its drawn blinds
with a long, steady look. This, one of the most beautiful places in England, was the scene of a mysterious
murder with which he was there to deal! There was
a small group of men in the entrance hall when the
governess cart drove up—some local police, the Coroner, the Chief Constable, some servants. All eyed
the great London detective curiously as he went up
the steps with Mr. Deckenham. His set face and
drawn brows kept them silent.

The old butler came forward, beckoning to Mr.
Saunderson.

"Mr. Ger—I mean his lordship—wants to see Inspector Skarratt instantly," he said. "I was to take him to him as soon as ever he arrived."

"Lead the way, then, if you please," said Inspector Skarratt.

He showed no sign of the presence of the others, but followed the old butler along halls and corridors which seemed strangely gloomy until they came to a room which he remembered as being the dead man's study. The door opened and closed behind him; he found himself in the presence of the man whose fortunes had so strangely changed within a few hours. And for one moment Inspector Skarratt, in his sharp fashion, studied the new Lord Marchester's face. A handsome man, with a very sad expression, he said to himself—tall, dark, clean-shaven, with very large, lustrous eyes, a firm mouth, a resolute chin—barrister all over, said Inspector Skarratt. The two men looked at each other.

"Good-day, Inspector—I am glad they have sent you. This is a most mysterious affair—as mysterious as it is terrible."

"From what I have heard of it, my Lord, I quite agree with your lordship."

The other seemed to wince. He trifled with some object on the table before him, and looked up suddenly.

"For the time being please don't address me by any title, Inspector. Call me Mr. Wintour. You will understand?"

"Quite so, sir."

"I put everything into your hands—see the local police. I—I am afraid I have not much faith in them, though they have done their best. The inquest is fixed for to-morrow, here. Perhaps by then you may have discovered—something. You will find me here whenever you want me. Everything has been arranged for your comfort while you are here."

"I thank you sir. May I ask a question?"

"Certainly—a hundred."

"Have you any clue—any suspicion?"

"None whatever!"

Inspector Skarratt bowed and withdrew. Outside, in the corridor, he paused for a moment, as if he meant to return to the room which he had just left, but he suddenly went off towards the entrance-hall.

"Something on his mind!" he said to himself. "Something on his mind! What?"

VI: THE INQUEST IS OPENED

CHAPTER IV

The Grotto in the Wood

INSPECTOR SKARRATT, once settled down to work, worked quickly and silently. Within ten minutes of his leaving the new Lord Marchester in the study, he had gathered the surface points of the case together. And those points, he said to himself, were very simple indeed; rarely, he thought, had he known or heard of a more simple case. He summarised it briefly in his notebook, thus:

1. The library at Marchester Royal is a long, low-ceilinged apartment on the ground-floor of the east wing, of which it runs the entire length.

2. It is lighted by eight French windows.

3. Over these windows curtains are drawn at night.

4. Each curtain is in two pieces; the material is an old silk, or brocade.

5. These windows open upon a terrace which over-looks an Italian garden, beyond which is a thick pine wood.

6. In front of the second window—going from left to right—is a broad couch, or settee, without back, placed close to the curtains.

7. On this, the face turned towards the interior of the room, the body of the murdered man was found lying.

8. On examination, the window directly behind the body was discovered to be unfastened; all the other windows were properly secured.

9. No sound of any shot was heard by anyone in

the house, but the library is some distance from any other apartments in general daily use, and it is the custom for the household to retire early.

10.   The dead man, however, used to sit up rather late, and had a trick, as the butler says, of wandering about the house and the terrace and the Italian garden long after everybody else was in bed.

11.   There is a body of evidence to show that it was a usual custom of his to throw himself down on this particular settee.

12.   The last person who saw him alive was Christopher Parvis, under-footman, who left him alone in the billiard-room at half-past ten o'clock, Mr. Gerald Wintour having said good-night to his brother and retired to his own apartments in the west-wing of the house some five or ten minutes previously.

13.   The person who discovered the dead body was Emily Marsh, housemaid, who went to the library in pursuance of her duties at seven o'clock in the morning and at first thought his lordship was asleep there.

14.   The bullet had been fired at close quarters.

15.   There were no finger-marks on the framework or glass of the windows behind the settee; no foot-marks on the terrace without, which is asphalted.

16.   No one had heard or seen any suspicious person or sound.

These were the rough surface notes which Inspector Skarratt first made. When he had completed this, his preliminary investigation, he invited the Chief Constable to a private conversation, and asked the old butler, Mountford, to show them into a room where they could be quiet. Mountford, without a word, conducted them to his pantry, a snug and comfortable apartment, remote from the rest of the house.

"You'll not find a quieter room than this, gentlemen, in all Marchester Royal," he said. "Double doors, you see gentlemen—I keep silver in those safes, and that's the strong room. Nobody'll interrupt you here, gentlemen, as long as you like to stay in the room. Now, is there anything I can get you before I leave you to your talk—a little refreshment, now?"

The Chief Constable said that after such a hard day he would like a whisky-and-soda. Inspector Skarratt answered nothing, but lighted his favourite briar pipe. The old butler bustled about with decanters, and glasses, and soda water bottles, and setting a box of cigars on the table, left them to themselves. The Chief Constable mixed himself a drink and helped himself to a cigar, and, having taken a hearty pull at one and a long draw at the other, sighed heavily.

"This is a strange case, Skarratt!" he said.

"It is a strange case," agreed Inspector Skarratt.

"Do you make anything of it?" asked the Chief Constable.

"Not yet," replied the Inspector.

"Do you think you will make anything of it?"

"Can't say—so far."

The Chief Constable blew out a big cloud of blue smoke, and watched it rising in fantastic spirals towards the ceiling.

"I think I could do something myself," he said half-querulously, "if I only had the faintest ghost of a clue. But bless me if I can see any clue!"

"Just so," assented Inspector Skarratt.

"You see," said the Chief Constable, taking another generous pull at his whisky-and-soda, "you see, Skarratt, it isn't as if we knew of anybody that bore him a grudge. There wasn't a more popular young man in all the countryside—take my word! I can remember him, of course, ever since he was a mere lad—he came into the title, you know, as a minor—and I can assure you that he has never at any time had what you might call bother with tenants, or tradesmen, or neighbours, or anybody. A heartier, simpler, more unassuming young man, you couldn't meet."

"Just so," said Inspector Skarratt. "I've seen that for myself."

"Then what motive could anybody have for murdering him?" asked the Chief Constable, in a tone which suggested that the culprit had done him a personal injury. "Eh, what motive?"

"Ah!" said the Inspector. "That's just what we've got to find out."

The Chief Constable shook his head dolefully.

"I'm sure I don't know how it's going to be found out," he said. "I can't see a single ray of light on the subject. There's one thing certain—it wasn't robbery. I examined the body myself—they didn't touch it till I got here, of course—and all his valuables—I mean what he'd usually carry—were on him. Watch and chain, two or three fine rings, a gold cigarette-case, several sovereigns—a common thief would have had those if he'd taken nothing else."

"This was no common thief, nor burglar either," commented Inspector Skarratt.

"Well, that's what I say," said the Chief Constable. "Then—where's the motive? It wasn't out of revenge—it wasn't for robbery—what was it for? It isn't even as if anybody would gain by his death."

Inspector Skarratt looked askew at the Chief Constable. Then, slightly smiling under his moustache, he helped himself to a very weak mixture of whisky-and-soda, and re-filled his well-seasoned pipe.

"Well, you can hardly say that, you know," he said presently.

"Say what?"

"Why, that no one benefits by his death."

The Chief Constable turned on him sharply.

"There is one person benefits considerably by his death," said Inspector Skarratt, gently.

The Chief Constable looked his question.

"His brother," said Inspector Skarratt, still more gently.

The Chief Constable started and frowned.

"Oh, that's nonsense!" he exclaimed. "Of course, Mr. Gerald gets the title and the estates and all that, but then that was to be expected—oh, it's nonsense, Skarratt!—if you'd lived in this district as long as I have you'd know that the Wintours are like What-d'ye-call-um's wife, above suspicion."

"I didn't say that I was suspicious," said Inspector Skarratt. "I merely said that Mr. Gerald Wintour benefits considerably by his brother's death. That's a fact."

The Chief Constable drank off what remained of his whisky-and-soda, and getting up from his easy chair replenished his glass. He seemed ill at ease.

"It would be a bad thing to ventilate a theory of that sort, Skarratt," he said. "It's a poor work interfering with great families."

"Who spoke of interference?" said Inspector Skarratt. "You made a statement, and I traversed it—that's all. And I was right. Here, let's get on to something more practical. What are you proposing to do? Of course the Coroner will open his inquiry to-morrow, but you and your men will be doing something. What will that something be?"

"Well," answered the Chief Constable, in the tone

and manner of a man who very much dislikes being questioned on a matter about which he himself is not very clear. "My notion is to look for that revolver."

"What revolver?"

"The revolver with which the crime was committed, to be sure!"

"You think it may be somewhere about, eh?" asked Inspector Skarratt.

"My experience," replied the Chief Constable, "based on a good many years' observation, is that in these cases the murderer's first instinct is to get rid of the weapon with which he committed the crime. I've got some of my men examining the grounds now, and I'll have more to-morrow."

"You might as well give them all telescopes and set 'em to work trying to find out how many mountains there are in the moon," said Inspector Skarratt. "The man who did this—or the woman—is far too clever to leave a revolver lying about. There must be four square miles of woodland in this park—do you intend to dig it all up, inch by inch?"

"I'll have a proper search made of the grounds, all the same, Inspector," said the Chief Constable. "I'm not going to give up theories——"

"I don't believe in theories very much," said Inspector Skarratt, drinking off his whisky-and-soda, and rising. "Well, of course, you'll do what you think best."

"And what shall you do?" asked the Chief Constable.

"I? Oh, I shall just hang round for the present, and keep my eyes and ears open. There's nothing else that I can do," replied the Inspector. "Of course, after to-morrow we may want further assistance from the Yard. In that case——"

"Oh, in that case I suppose we shall have to have it!" said the Chief Constable, not over graciously. "But from what I've seen of the case I don't believe that all Scotland Yard put together will ever solve this matter. I'm sure I can't make head or tail of it—there's no motive."

"Well, I'm going to have a look round," said Inspector Skarratt. "I shall see you in the morning."

And leaving the Chief Constable to refresh himself still further if he were so minded, the Inspector left the butler's pantry and went out of the house to stroll about the grounds and think over the facts which he had gathered up so far. Crossing the Italian garden he caught sight of the new Lord Marchester walking up and down with Mr. Deckenham. They were in earnest conversation, and the Inspector was turning off in an opposite direction when Lord Marchester, raising his head, caught sight of him and beckoned him to approach.

"I suppose you have come to no conclusion, arrived at no theory, Inspector?" he said.

"None, sir."

"You think it a mysterious case?"

"I think it a most mysterious case, sir. If your brother had any enemies——"

"Oh, I don't think my brother ever made an enemy in his life! What do you say, Mr. Deckenham?"

"I am quite sure his late lordship never had an enemy in this world," said the solicitor with emphasis.

"Sometimes," said Inspector Skarratt, with the air of one who advances a proposition with respect, "sometimes, gentlemen, people have enemies of whom they know nothing and whose enmity they never suspect."

Lord Marchester who had walked along with his

eyes fixed upon the ground, raised his head and regarded the detective with great attention for a long
moment.

"Yes," he said. "I quite agree with you, Inspector.
I believe that to be an indisputable truth. At the same
time I cannot conceive how any living soul could
cherish any feelings of enmity against my brother.
What is being done at present, Inspector?"

"Well, sir, the chief constable is endeavouring to
find the revolver. He thinks it would be thrown away
or hidden immediately after the commission of the
crime."

Lord Marchester smiled.

"And do you agree with him?"

"Frankly, no, sir. I think that whoever committed
the crime was clever enough to dispose of the weapon
much more effectively."

"And what are you doing?"

"At present, nothing, sir, beyond observing and
thinking. I shall be able to do more after the inquiry
to-morrow," answered Inspector Skarratt.

Lord Marchester nodded, turned to Mr. Deckenham, and resumed his walk and his conversation with
him; Inspector Skarratt went off in the opposite direction. He left the Italian garden and passed into the
pine wood beyond. There was a quiet path in it
along which he had often strolled when staying at
Marchester Royal at the time of the burglary two
years since. He turned into this, and walked slowly
along, deep in thought. He knew very well that
he was face to face with one of the biggest problems
which had ever been presented to him in the course
of his professional career.

At the farther extremity of the pine wood, where a
low fence separated it from the park, Inspector Skar-

ratt halted.   There was a stile there, and he leant
over it, looking across the green expanse before him.
Immediately opposite, at a distance of some forty
or fifty yards, was another pine wood also entered by
a stile.   And as he looked across he saw a woman's
face outlined against the trees of this second pine
wood, and with his detective instinct instantly aroused,
he slipped down behind the hedge, and, looking
through the branches, watched.

A woman appeared at the opposite stile—a young,
active woman, who, resting the tips of her fingers on
the top bar of the stile, looked round about her on all
sides.   Then she bent down for a second by the left-
hand post of the stile.   What she did Inspector
Skarratt could not see.   Another second and she was
up again.   She came over the stile and advanced carelessly across the intervening space.   Inspector Skarratt noiselessly slipped into better cover and watched
her.

"A Frenchwoman—and a lady's maid," he said
to himself.

The woman—a typical Parisienne—came along
humming a gay tune.   She climbed the stile over which
the detective had just been leaning, and went along
the path which he had just traversed.   He knew that
there was a right of way along that path almost as
far as the Italian garden—at a point one hundred
yards from there one turned off into another path
which led to the high road.

Inspector Skarratt waited until the woman had disappeared in the distance; then he leapt over the stile,
ran across the grass, leapt the other stile, and bent
down to examine the post over which the woman had
leant.   And there in one of the holes into which the
bars of the stile fitted loosely, he found a folded paper

—a mere scrap. It bore nine words—in a woman's handwriting.

"To-night—ten-thirty—the grotto in the wood."

Inspector Skarratt looked about him when he had restored this missive to its hiding place. His practised eye quickly detected a vantage point from which he could see without being seen, and in another minute he was safely ensconced within it. And there, stolid and patient, he waited, watching, for a good hour.

At the end of that time Lord Marchester came strolling, deep in thought, from the opposite wood, approached the second stile, got over it, took the note from its hiding place, read it, put it in his pocket, and, crossing the stile again, went off across the park, apparently as unconcerned as when he came. When he was in the distance Inspector Skarratt emerged from the holly bushes which had sheltered him, and went back to Marchester Royal.

That night, after a particularly good dinner, and a fine cigar, which he was careful to finish before he left the house, Inspector Skarratt slipped out of Marchester Royal very quietly. He knew the grotto in the wood; he also knew how to conceal himself so that he could overhear anything said there. And so it came about that at half past ten he heard first a light step—a woman's—a heavier step—a man's—close by him—and then whispers which, in the weird silence of the woods, were clearer than loudly-spoken words.

"Gerald!"

"Margaret!"

V: LOVERS

CHAPTER V

Lovers

IN spite of his many fervent assertions to the contrary, Inspector Skarratt was a very sentimental man. He could be cold and keen as steel, hard and unyielding as adamant in the exercise of his professional duties, but if he were a detective by calling he was still a man of flesh and blood, and he had a great feeling for and admiration of the opposite sex. And realising now that he was playing the part of eavesdropper at a meeting of lovers, who, judging from the way in which they merely pronounced each other's names, were something more than ordinarily enamoured of each other, he felt himself blush to the very roots of his hair, and wished, for the lady's sake, that he were a thousand miles away.

"This is one of the nasty things of the profession," declared Inspector Skarratt to himself. "I hate this sort of business! However, I've got to go through with it. Margaret? That's the name of the old buffer's daughter that we saw this afternoon. Now, I wonder what's going to come out of this?"

It appeared to Inspector Skarratt that the first moment of the meeting between the lovers was spent in silence in each other's arms—he certainly heard the unmistakable sound of a kiss. Then Lord Marchester spoke.

"You are quite sure you are safe, Margaret?"

"Oh, yes! Leonie is watching for me. I have

always been safe so far, Gerald. What is this dreadful news about your brother? Is it true that—that——"

"It is only too true, dear. He is dead—and, so far as we can judge, murdered. Deliberately and cruelly murdered."

Inspector Skarratt heard clearly the girl's exclamation of horror.

"But that is terrible!" she said. "Who can have done it?"

"We have not the faintest idea," replied Lord Marchester wearily. "I don't believe poor Gervase had an enemy in the world. Still, as Skarratt very wisely said this afternoon, one sometimes has enemies without being aware of it."

"Who is Skarratt?"

"A detective from Scotland Yard, a very clever, intelligent man."

"Will he try to find the murderer?"

"Why, yes, of course. But the thing, to my mind, had been planned with such diabolical cleverness, and there is such entire absence of anything in the shape of a clue, that I fear the cleverest detective living would find it difficult to trace the culprit."

The girl uttered another exclamation of horror. Then, after a brief silence, she said:

"Gerald, won't this make a great difference to you?"

"Yes, of course, all the difference in the world. I succeeded to the title and estates. I don't pretend, dear, that I'm indifferent to that—I'm not so foolish as to be blind to the material advantages of both—but I am honest when I say that I wish they had come to me in any other way. It made me sick when the servants and the people who came to the house to-day began—but never mind. Don't let us talk of that

just now. Margaret, I spoke to your father yesterday
—as you wished me to."

"Yes?"

"Has he told you of it?"

"So far, no. But he has been in a very irascible
temper all day—indeed, he has scarcely spoken to me
at all."

"He is a hard man, your father, Margaret. And
something seems to have soured him. He heard what
I had to say with impatience, and replied with contempt. I put it to him plainly that we loved each other
and meant to be true to each other for always, and
that neither of us cared greatly for riches as long as
we could live in reasonable comfort. At that he
simply sneered, and made some insulting remarks as
to the position of younger sons, which I bore for
your sake. And then he said one or two things which
I wish he had not said."

"What were they, Gerald?"

"Well, he said: 'If you'd been your brother, the
peer, poor as he is with his beggarly five thousand a
year, I might have listened to you, for you'd have had
at any rate a good old title to give my daughter. As
it is, you're nothing but a fortune-hunter.' That hurt
me, because it was not true."

Inspector Skarratt heard the sound of another kiss.

"Never mind, dear," said Margaret Braye, "my
father is very—well, peppery. And he thinks that
the people about here treat him very rudely, as indeed
they have done. Even your brother, who had such a
reputation for kindness, used to pass him with a cool
stare. And—well, naturally, he feels it. Even a
retired tradesman has some feelings, Gerald."

"I know—I know," said Lord Marchester hastily.
"I hate all that sort of thing, as you know, Margaret,

but it isn't my fault if the people round about here treat your father in that way. Naturally, he must feel it."

"He not only feels it, but is beginning to resent it, and to speak vindictively about it," said Margaret. "He frequently threatens what he would do if he had any of these people in his power, and that's not good to hear. You told him everything, Gerald?"

"Yes, I told him that we had met in London, and in Paris, and that we had promised ourselves to each other."

"I meant to tell him all that myself to-day, if I had only found the opportunity, but he has given me none. Perhaps I have been wrong in not telling him before. But——"

"Yes, dearest?"

"I have never been happy at home, Gerald. If my mother had only lived——"

Inspector Skarratt felt his heart grow very sentimental indeed. He respected the silence which followed Miss Braye's last words.

"Margaret! Now that things are as Fate has made them——"

"Yes?"

"I do not think there will be any further opposition from your father."

There was another silence.

"No, I suppose not," said Margaret at last, "but the worst of it is that, after what he said to you about what might have been if you had been your brother, you will feel that you have no more respect for him. With all his faults he is a very sensitive and observant man, and if he had been more kindly received by the people about here, he would have shown himself in a very different light."

"For my part, I shall think no more about that," said Lord Marchester. "We must let all this sad business about poor Gervase tide over, and then I will speak to him again."

There was another pause—then the girl spoke again.

"Gerald dear, tell me—did you love your brother?"

Inspector Skarratt heard Lord Marchester sigh very deeply. It was a full moment before he answered Margaret Braye's question.

"It is a very difficult thing to answer such a question, Margaret," he said at last. "Difficult, because the word 'love' in such a sense is hard to define. I know what I mean when I say that I love you—I know what it meant to love my mother, the very little that I knew of her. I certainly did not love my father—he was cold and unsympathetic to me, and I had much more fear than admiration for him. As to my feelings for poor Gervase—well, he and I never had, I think, even ordinary brotherly affection for each other. You see, we were always so different—so different that we might not have sprung from the same parents. The difference extended, as you know, to our very physical appearance—he was fair, I dark. All his life he cared for nothing but horses, dogs, his guns, sport; I, on the other hand, was always a bookworm and a student. I question very much whether Gervase ever read anything but the sporting papers and magazines, and occasionally a hunting novel. So that, you see, there was no similarity of taste between us, and where there is no similarity of taste between two people there can be little affection. No, truthfully, I cannot say that I loved him as brothers, I suppose, should love each other—I cannot honestly say that I had any affection for him."

"But you were always good friends?" Margaret asked.

Inspector Skarratt listened eagerly for the answer to this question—to him, whatever answer was coming seemed to be of great importance. And again Lord Marchester hesitated.

"There again," he said at last, "there again I find it difficult to answer your question, Margaret. Perhaps I am too precise—I like to use words only in their exact sense. I cannot think that Gervase and I were good friends, because I don't believe that—in the real, true sense,—we were friends at all. We were merely acquaintances—just as much and as little acquaintances as the men one meets at one's club."

"But you never—quarrelled?"

Inspector Skarratt listened still more eagerly. Something was convincing him that the new Lord Marchester was a stickler for truth—perhaps too much of a stickler. And this time the answer came quickly —without hesitation.

"Oh, never, never, not even as boys—except, perhaps, as all boys will, over mere trifles. As men, certainly never. We were always on the best of terms —as acquaintances. Of course, as men, we saw comparatively little of each other. Whenever he asked me down here it was tacitly understood that we never interfered with each other. I used to spend most of my time in the library; he was out and about all day. We always dined together in great amity, and we invariably spent the evening in the billiard-room—it was, I think, the one bond between us that from boyhood we were both passionately fond of billiards, and became experts at the game at a very early age. Poor Gervase!—we were playing billiards last night!"

There was another pause and a long silence, and then Margaret said:

"Gerald, haven't you the remotest suspicion as to who killed your brother? Not the remotest?"

"I have not even the ghost of a suspicion, dear. To me it is an absolute mystery—a thing unbelievable that anybody should want to kill him."

The girl made no answer, but in a moment or two she spoke again.

"I must go now, Gerald," she said. "I do not want to keep Leonie waiting too long. I hope—I hope we are at the end of these stolen interviews—I have never liked them, dear. And yet I suppose we could not help ourselves."

"I have liked them as little as you have, Margaret. Come, I will go with you as far as the Abbey bridge —you are sure you will be safe then?"

"Oh, yes—I always have been!"

Inspector Skarratt watched the two figures, arm in arm, fade away into the darkness amongst the trees. He waited until there was no possibility of their hearing his footsteps or the cracking of a dry twig, and then he turned and went swiftly in the direction of Marchester Royal. He had an idea that he would like to see Mr. Saunderson before retiring for the night.

The steward lived in a very comfortable house on the edge of the park about half a mile from the pine wood beyond the Italian garden. There were lights in the lower windows as Inspector Skarratt crossed the trim lawn, and he saw the substantial figure of Mr. Saunderson outlined against the white blinds. The steward himself opened the door in response to the detective's knock. He was in dressing-gown and slippers, but was evidently not preparing to retire immediately, for he had just lighted a large cigar, the particularly fine odour of which stole out into the rose-coloured porch.

"Good-evening, Mr. Saunderson," said Inspector Skarratt. "I thought I'd just come to see you for a minute or two. May I come in?"

"Oh, it's you, Inspector, is it?" said the steward. "Come in, come in, sir—I couldn't see who it was at first. Come in and have a drop of something and a cigar—I'm just taking a little refreshment myself before going to bed. It's been a very trying day, this, Inspector, a very trying day indeed," he continued, leading the way into a very comfortably appointed dining-room, where a spirit-case and cigars were set out beneath a shaded lamp. "Yes, a very trying day, and I'm sure one can do with something. Now, help yourself, Inspector, do—there's whisky, and there's gin, and there's rum in the case there, but if you prefer brandy I've some old French cognac in that sideboard that's as perfect as it's ancient. And light a cigar and make yourself at home."

"Thank you—I'll take a glass of whisky-and-water," said Inspector Skarratt, helping himself, and picking out a cigar. "I'm a very abstemious man as a rule, Mr. Saunderson, but I like a good glass of whisky at the end of a day's work, and I think mine's about over for this day. Your good health, sir."

"Your very good health, Inspector. I expect you've made nothing out yet?"

Inspector Skarratt shook his head.

"No," he said, "I've made nothing out so far."

"Well, it's a queer business," said the steward. "I saw Sergeant Mathers just now—I've just come from the house—and he tells me they can't find a single clue."

"Just so," said Inspector Skarratt.

"If anybody had had a grudge against him, now," said Mr. Saunderson. "If any tenant, or anything of that sort, had quarrelled with him, one could have understood it. But he never got cross with any of 'em; as a matter of fact, he was too easy-going with all of 'em. I know this much—he was the most popular man of his family within memory."   . . . .

"What sort of man was his father?" asked Inspector Skarratt.

Mr. Saunderson pointed to an oil painting which hung over his fireplace.

"That's the fourteenth Baron Marchester," he said. "Gervase his name was, like his son's, now murdered. The eldest son has been called Gervase for I don't know how long—ever since Charles the First's day, anyway. What like man was he? Well, he was one of that sort that like to be on top—a trifle overbearing, you'll understand."

"You were steward to him, I suppose, Mr. Saunderson?"

"Yes, sir, and so was my father before me. We've been connected with the family a matter of over sixty years," replied the steward.

"Did either of the two sons resemble their father?" asked Inspector Skarratt. "I don't mean physically, of course, because I can compare them myself—I mean in character, temperament, and so on."

"Why, oddly enough, Inspector, I can't say that they ever did," answered Mr. Saunderson. "He was a sort of mixture of the two. He was fond of hunting, he was also fond of books. He liked a day amongst the pheasants—famous pheasant shooting on this estate, sir—but he was just as happy in his library. He was an energetic magistrate, and they said he was well up in the law—in that I suppose, the new lord follows him. An all-round man, sir, he was—but arbitrary, very arbitrary, just as arbitrary as his eldest son was easy-going."

"And what was his wife like?" asked Inspector Skarratt.

"His wife, sir, was the Lady Anne Gilbert, third daughter of the sixth Earl of Wrottesford," replied Mr. Saunderson. "A sweet lady, Inspector, of a somewhat pensive mood. She died at what one may call an early age—she was little over thirty. The new Lord Marchester resembles her very closely in appearance, and, from what I have seen of him, in temperament also. Dear, dear me—this is a strange world!"

"It's a bit queer!" agreed Inspector Skarratt.

He stayed chatting with the steward for half an hour longer; then, remarking that they would most likely have a busy time next day, he bade him good-night, and set off at a sharp pace across the park. He had learnt something that night, he said to himself —what bearing had it on the case?

He was pondering this over as he approached the house, when one of the local police suddenly stepped out of a shrubbery by the side of the carriage-drive, and accosted him.

"Inspector Skarratt, sir? I was coming out to look for you—we thought you might have gone down to Mr. Saunderson's, sir," he said. "Sergeant Mathers wants you."

"Anything fresh?" asked Inspector Skarratt.

"Yes, sir. We've found the revolver."

IV: THE GROTTO IN THE WOOD

CHAPTER VI

The Inquest is Opened

INSPECTOR SKARRATT said nothing on receiving this important piece of information. He walked on in silence; the local man walked at his side.

"Where is Sergeant Mathers?" asked Inspector Skarratt at last.

"He is in a room which they have given him for a sort of office, sir, close to Mr. Mountford, the butler's room," answered the man. "He told me, if I found you, to ask you to go to him there."

"All right!" said Inspector Skarratt abruptly.

He strode sharply away, leaving the local man somewhat huffed at his taciturnity, and entering the house by a side entrance, made his way to the room just indicated to him. Sergeant Mathers and one of his men were bending over some object on the table.

"Well," said Inspector Skarratt, as he closed the door behind him. "I hear you have found something."

Sergeant Mathers turned a triumphant face upon him.

"Aye, the Chief was telling me just before he left that you laughed at his theory, that a murderer always tries to get rid of his weapon as soon as he can, Inspector Skarratt," he said. "I'm thinking you'll have to acknowledge the Chief was right."

"Shall I?" said Inspector Skarratt. "Well then, I shalln't. What have you found—your man outside said *the* revolver. He meant *a* revolver—which makes all the difference."

71

"Oh, you're so particular!" said the sergeant sulkily. "It isn't a revolver at all—it's a pistol. But I'll bet that's what did it, revolver or pistol."

He and his subordinates drew back, and the sergeant motioned the detective towards the object at which they had been looking. Inspector Skarratt drew near the table and looked at the thing lying in the white light of the brilliant lamp.

An old duelling pistol!

"What do you think of that?" asked the sergeant. "It wasn't made yesterday, that wasn't, Inspector Skarratt."

Inspector Skarratt made no reply. He took the pistol into his hands and examined it with care. It was a beautiful piece of workmanship; the barrel damascened in gold; the stock richly inlaid in the same metal. And on the side of the stock was a small gold plate bearing the name of a famous Italian gunsmith and the date—*fecit* 1776.

"Where was it?" asked Inspector Skarratt.

Sergeant Mathers turned to his man—a country constable who was obviously swelling with pride and importance.

"Tombleson, there, found it," he said. "Tell the Inspector how you came across it, Tombleson."

Tombleson drew himself up as if he were in the witness-box and spoke in the witness-box style.

"In accordance with instructions received I was examining the garden outside the terrace which is outside the libr'y where the deed was committed it struck me had anybody examined the pots of flowers on the balustrade of the terrace I began to examine them myself when I came to the one immediately opposite to the window where the murder was committed I found that there weapon thrust into the mould and the mould scratched over the butt-end of it and having taken it out of the mould brought it to Sergeant Mathers and reported matters in due course."

"And very clever of you, my lad," said Sergeant Mathers admiringly, "and I'll see that your conduct's duly reported in the right quarter."

Inspector Skarratt, who had been thoughtfully examining the pistol, now laid it on the table again.

"You don't know if Lord Marchester is in the study?" he asked.

"I believe his lordship is there with Mr. Deckenham, the lawyer," answered the sergeant. "They were there a quarter of an hour ago."

"You haven't told him of this discovery?"

"No. I was just going to do so," said Sergeant Mathers.

"Don't," said the Inspector. "Don't say a single word of it, neither you nor your men, until the inquest to-morrow. If any of your men know, let Tombleson here go out and warn them."

The sergeant hesitated.

"Well, I don't know, Inspector," he said. "You London gentlemen always want your own way so much. Why shouldn't I inform his lordship at once?"

"I'll tell you why, Sergeant Mathers," replied Inspector Skarratt, speaking very slowly, and with emphasis. "Because I want you, or Tombleson, to produce that pistol at the inquest to-morrow. It'll make a sensation."

The sergeant had certain dramatic instincts in him; he suddenly foresaw grand possibilities. His face betokened a new sense of the situation.

"All right, Inspector," he said. "We'll do as you suggest. Tombleson, just run out and warn everybody not to say a word. I wonder what that inquest will bring out, Inspector?" he said, when Tombleson had left the room.

"Aye, so do I, Sergeant!" said Inspector Skarratt laconically.

Marchester Royal next morning was busier than it had ever been since its ancient, ivy-clad walls first rose from the ground. The news of the murder of its popular young proprietor had by this time spread all over England, and folk of every degree, officials, police, pressmen, the merely curious, the merely idle, came flocking to its gates, most of them kept back by the cordon which now surrounded house and park.

In the house itself everything was bustle and activity; the Coroner for that particular district of the county was a fussy individual who appeared to instil into his immediate subordinates and satellites something of his own fussiness. Inspector Skarratt, quietly watching things, wondered when they were really going to get to work with the enquiry, which was held in the great oak dining-room, around which were ranged the portraits of all the dead and gone Barons of Marchester.

There was so much coming and going; so much whispering between the Coroner and his officer; the Coroner and Mr. Deckenham; the Coroner and a solicitor who appeared on behalf of the police; the Coroner and another legal gentleman who had received telegraphic instructions from the Treasury. He wondered if they were ever going to begin. But at last, a jury being duly formed of twelve highly-respected farmers, tradesmen, and labourers of the district, each and all of whom looked uncommonly grave, a commencement was made.

The jury went off to perform the gruesome task of viewing the body, and came back sadder visaged than ever. Then the Coroner began his address—he was long-winded and prosy, and took full advantage of the occasion to relieve himself of a long string of platitudes. He spoke of the dead man's virtues and qualities, of his good heartedness, his popularity with all ranks and classes, of his ancient lineage, and of his sad death. It was all very appropriate and very necessary, no doubt, but it made Inspector Skarratt yawn, because he knew all that sort of thing by heart.

Looking round him as the Coroner went on with his turgid sentences, the Inspector was suddenly aware of a slight commotion or sensation at the end of the room where two folding-doors gave entrance to the hall. He looked in that direction and saw that the policeman in charge of the doors had just admitted Sir Thomas Braye, who, hat in hand, was tip-toeing into the room and looking about him for a vacant seat. Sir Thomas was not alone—following closely upon his heels, very red of face, very self-conscious of the eyes turned upon him, was a young rustic, dressed in his Sunday best, whom Sir Thomas was obviously leading.

"That means—something," said Inspector Skarratt. "Or I'm a Dutchman! But what?"

Somebody found seats for Sir Thomas Braye and his companion, and they subsided into them and folded their arms. Sir Thomas looked round the room with hauteur, the Sunday-suited youth, after gazing for some time into the crown of his hat, summoned up sufficient resolution to look elsewhere, and finding that nobody was taking the slightest notice of him, became peaceful and at ease.

The Coroner's weary droning came to an end at last, and a flutter of excitement went round the room when he announced that he should first call the new peer, as the deceased's next-of-kin, for the purpose of identification.

Heads were raised, necks craned forward as Lord Marchester stood up at the table where the Coroner sat. He was very pale, and looked worn and haggard, as if he had had little sleep the previous night, and his voice sounded tired as he gave his evidence in answer to the coroners' bland questions.

Yes, he was the Right Honourable Gerald Wintour, Baron Marchester. He identified the body which he had just seen as that of his brother, the Right Honourable Gervase Wintour, his predecessor in the title. His brother was twenty-seven years of age and unmarried. He was a justice of the peace and a deputy-lieutenant.

"When did you last see your brother alive, Lord Marchester?"

"At about twenty minutes past ten the night before last."

"Where was that?"

"In the billiard room here. We had been playing billiards together all the evening since dinner, and at the hour I have just mentioned I felt tired, and as we had just finished a game I said good-night to him and went to my own rooms."

"You never saw him alive again?"

"No!"

"When did you next see him?"

"I was fetched to the library about half-past seven next morning—yesterday morning—and found him lying on a settee, placed by the second window from the left-hand side, quite dead. I saw at once that he had been shot through the brain, and that he was quite dead—had been dead for hours."

"Then I suppose you sent at once for the police and medical assistance?"

"Oh, yes, at once! I telephoned to the Chief Constable at Market Fordham, and to Doctor Richmond in the village."

"I do not want to ask you any unnecessary questions, Lord Marchester, but can you think of, or suggest, any motive for this crime?"

"I cannot."

"Your brother had no enemies?"

"None that I know of. He was a most popular man —always and everywhere."

The Coroner bowed in token that he had no more to say. But the legal gentleman who represented the Treasury had a question or two to ask.

"Was your brother in his usual health and spirits on the evening of which you have just spoken, Lord Marchester?"

"Oh, yes! He was in very good spirits, and his health was always good."

"He had nothing to trouble him—no worries?"

"I should say, knowing him as I did, that he had not a care in the world."

"Please do not take this question in any wrong sense—were you and he on perfectly good terms?"

"Perfectly good terms. We never had a disagreement in our lives,—unless it was as mere boys, over boyish trifles."

No one else showing any disposition to ask him further questions, Lord Marchester sat down, and Christopher Parvis, the under-footman, was called. The questions put to him were few and simple.

"When did you last see your late master alive, and where?"

"Night before last, sir, in the billiard-room."

"What time was that?"

"As near as I can remember, sir, about half-past ten."

"Did you leave him in the billiard-room?"

"Yes, sir."

"What was he doing?"

"Just knocking the balls about, sir."

"Did he tell you to go to bed, and that he would turn out the lights?"

"He did, sir."

"Had he ever done that before?"

"Oh, many a time, sir! He used to do it nearly every night."

"His lordship seemed in just his usual health and spirits?"

"Oh yes, sir—he'd been just the same all the evening, laughing and joking with Mr. Gerald."

Mr. Parvis stood down, and Emily Marsh, the housemaid was called forward. She was obviously still suffering from the effects of the shock of her discovery and had plainly wept much. She dissolved in tears as soon as the coroner began to question her, and had to be accommodated with a chair and a glass of water. Fortunately, there was little need to keep her for any length of time. Her evidence was simple. In pursuance of her duties she entered the library at half past seven o'clock the previous morning. Although the curtains were drawn across the windows the room was full of light. She was astounded to see her master lying fully dressed on the settee by the second window—as she thought, asleep. She was hesitating what to do when she suddenly saw blood.

"And what did you do then?"

"I screamed, sir, and ran to tell Mrs. Page, the housekeeper."

Questioned, she said that she saw nothing unusual in the room except the dead man. The furniture was all in its place; the window curtains were not disarranged; there was no sign of any scuffle. If she had not noticed the blood-stains on the sofa and the carpet she would have left the room thinking that her master had gone off to sleep there the night before.

The Coroner called the doctor next—Dr. Charles Richmond who said he was a Fellow of the Royal College of Surgeons, and a Fellow of the Royal College of Physicians. He gave evidence to the effect that he was telephoned for at twenty minutes to eight the previous morning, and that he arrived at Marchester Royal about forty minutes later, bringing the village constable with him in his trap. He was met by Mr. Gerald Wintour and the butler, who took him at once to the library. There he found the body of the late Lord Marchester, who was quite dead. He judged that he had been dead at least nine hours. He had been shot through the brain from behind—and the weapon had certainly been held within a few inches of the head when it was discharged. The injuries were of a terrible nature, and death must have been instantaneous. No, it was literally impossible that the wound could have been self-inflicted—literally and absolutely impossible. The dead man was lying on his right side, with his right hand and arm under him. When the shot was fired he had probably rolled over a little—very little—towards the right. Under no conditions whatever could he have discharged the weapon himself in such a position as to cause the death wound.

And now came the first tangible evidence of the crime into which the Coroner and jury were inquiring. The Coroner opened a small cardboard box which lay before him and took from it an object which those close by saw to be a shapeless piece of lead.

"You and the police found this flattened against the wall in a direct line with the dead man's head?"

"Yes."

"You believe it to be the missile which caused his death?"

"Without doubt. It is a leaden bullet which must have been discharged from a very old-fashioned pistol —that is, in my opinion."

"Stand aside, for a minute, if you please, doctor. Call William Tombleson . . . Tombleson, in the discharge of your duty you were last night searching the ornamental flower vases on the terrace outside the library windows?"

"I was, Sir."

"And concealed in the vase opposite the second window you found a pistol?"

"Yes, sir."

"Produce it."

Tombleson, swelling with pride, dug his hand into the breast of his tunic and drew forth the duelling pistol. For a second he held it up as if to exhibit it—the next instant it was snatched from his hand by Lord Marchester. His voice, hoarse and strained, fell on a suddenly hushed crowd like a premonitory note of evil.

"Why, that's mine! It was my father's. And it has been stolen from my rooms in Jermyn Street!"

VII: THE INQUEST CONTINUES

CHAPTER VII

The Inquest Continues

OF all the people present in that crowded room, Inspector Skarratt was probably the only one who heard Lord Marchester's excited exclamation with imperturbability. Inspector Skarratt from long experience, was always expecting the unexpected; he had been certain that the inquest would bring something out. Here it was!—not, perhaps, quite what he had thought it might be, but something of importance. He folded his arms a little more closely, and watched in silence.

But upon the rest of the people a curious effect was produced. A murmur and a buzzing arose, as of bees suddenly disturbed in their hive. Men turned and stared at each other with wondering faces. In many faces it was plain to see that their owners had suddenly developed an idea, or a thought, or a suspicion.

Mr. Deckenham sat staring at the pistol as if he were fascinated; the legal gentleman who represented the Treasury sat trifling with some papers; Mr. Saunderson shaded his fat face with his hand as if he were in church in an attitude of devotion. Even the Coroner forgot his usual fussiness and became somewhat human. He raised his hand, deprecating this sudden buzz of talk and whisper.

"Silence, gentlemen! Do you say, Lord Marchester," he continued, amidst a sudden hush, "do you say that that is your pistol?"

Lord Marchester, who still remained standing near

the policeman, examining the pistol which he had snatched from his hand, turned excitedly towards the Coroner.

"Most certainly I do!" he replied. "It has been stolen, as I said just now, from my rooms in Jermyn Street."

"Stand aside for a few minutes, Tombleson," commanded the Coroner. "Now, Lord Marchester," he continued, when the policeman had taken his seat again, "it will perhaps be the wisest plan if you tell us at this stage what you know about this pistol, which you say is yours and has been stolen from your rooms in London."

Mr. Deckenham rose somewhat diffidently.

"I am not quite sure whether his lordship should—" he began.

But Lord Marchester waved the solicitor aside.

"I am not only too willing to tell you anything I can," he said, "I confess I am utterly astonished, bewildered at the sight of this pistol. If it is really the weapon with which my brother was shot, then there is some diabolical mystery attaching to the whole matter which I cannot guess at. This pistol, sir, is one of a brace which has been in our family for well over a century. They were manufactured by a famous Italian gunsmith, as you see from the date, in 1776, and there is a tradition that an ancestor of mine used them, or one of them in a duel fought in Lincoln's Inn Fields, about 1780, in which he killed his man. On my twenty-first birthday, these pistols, amongst other things, came into my possession, and I have since had them in my rooms in Jermyn Street, where this one should certainly be at this moment. It has been stolen."

You are quite sure that that is one of the

brace of which you have spoken, Lord Marchester?"

"Absolutely sure!"

"Where did you keep these pistols?"

"They were kept in their own case, which stood on a bureau in my study."

"Was the case locked?"

"No—it opened by a spring—a very simple affair."

"When did you last see the case open with the pistols in it?"

Lord Marchester shook his head.

"Oh, I can't say! Several months ago, I should think."

"You can't remember the exact occasion?"

"No, I can't. Stay—I remember showing the pistols to some friends who were spending the evening with me about the beginning of November last. I think that must have been the last occasion on which I opened the case."

"I suppose anybody who entered your rooms could have opened the case and taken a pistol out?"

"Oh yes,—anybody!"

"You don't think it possible that you are mistaken in identifying this pistol as one of yours?"

"Oh I am sure this is mine—positive!"

The legal gentleman from the Treasury rose.

"I am about to suggest, with a view to no misunderstanding on that point, that a telegram should be at once despatched to some person who can examine the case. I suppose you have a servant at your rooms, Lord Marchester?"

"Oh, yes, and I will write out a telegram for him at once! But you will find that what I have said is correct—this is one of my brace of duelling pistols, and it has been extracted from its case in Jermyn Street."

When the telegram had been written out and despatched, Mr. Deckenham wished to ask Lord Marchester a question or two.

"Does your lordship receive many visitors at your rooms in Jermyn Street?"

"No—comparatively few."

"Do you keep any record of them?"

"No."

"Do you keep a diary?"

"Yes—but in a very perfunctory fashion."

"You do not enter up in it the names of people who come to see you?"

"Sometimes I might—sometimes not. Anything of importance I should enter—anything trivial I shouldn't."

"Of course, you never transacted any business at your rooms?"

"Oh, dear me, no—I have chambers in Brick Court."

"Therefore no one but friends and acquaintances would be likely to call at Jermyn Street?"

"Quite so."

Mr. Deckenham sat down and the Coroner looked perplexed.

"I don't see that we can pursue that matter any further just now," he said. "There seems to be no doubt that this pistol, found by Constable Tombleson last night in close proximity to the scene of the murder, is Lord Marchester's property, and has within the last six months, according to his evidence, been abstracted from his rooms in London. I think I will hear Tombleson again as to the actual discovery of the pistol—now, constable, tell us plainly how you came to find this weapon."

Tombleson drew himself up into his stiff police-court-witness-box attitude, and cleared his throat.

"In accordance with instructions received I was examining the garden outside the terrace which is outside the libr'y where the deed was committed it struck me had anybody examined the pots of flowers on the balustrades of the terrace I began to examine them myself when I came to the one immediately opposite to the window where the murder was committed I found that there weapon thrust into the mould and the mould scratched over the butt-end of it and having taken it out of the mould brought it to Sergeant Mathers and reported matters in due course."

The Coroner picked up the pistol and looked it carefully over.

"Of course you cleaned the pistol? The barrel would be full of mould?"

"Yes, sir, it was. Sergeant Mathers and myself cleaned it."

"It seems to be in very good repair for such an old weapon," said the Coroner.

Lord Marchester rose again.

"I forgot to say just now that since I last saw it that pistol had been in the hands of a gunsmith," he said. "The lock has been put in thorough repair."

The Coroner continued to examine the pistol.

"This weapon was not at any great depth beneath the soil?" he asked, turning to Constable Tombleson.

"No, sir,—it was just pushed into the mould—it's very light mould in that pot, sir—and the earth scattered over it, like. I felt it as soon as I put my hands on top of the mould, and drew it out at once."

The Coroner turned to Dr. Richmond and handed him the pistol.

"Look at this pistol, if you please, doctor. Do you

think it likely that the flattened bullet which you and the police found was fired from it?"

Dr. Richmond took the pistol and examined the bore.

"Yes, sir, most certainly. Personally, I should not have the slightest doubt that this is the weapon from which the bullet was discharged. You will observe that the bore is considerable—one that would throw a bullet of some size."

"That would account for the extensive injuries to the deceased's head?"

"Exactly. A bullet fired from a weapon like this would have very shattering effects—as it had in this case."

"From your point of view, then, you consider it a very probable thing that this is the weapon with which the murder was committed?"

"Yes. If it was not with this pistol it was with one of exactly similar, or very similar character."

The Coroner nodded and Dr. Richmond sat down again.

"I don't know how far we can go to-day, gentlemen," he said, looking at the twelve anxious-faced jurymen. "Of course, the police are investigating this matter, and I understand that in addition to the admirable talent which we possess in our local force there is an Inspector of great ability present from Scotland Yard. However, we may as well go as far as we can, and there are one or two matters I want to deal with. In cases like this the first thing one seeks for is motive. Now it may—probably will—be the initial feeling of everybody on first hearing of this dreadful calamity that the murderer's motive was robbery—it is only two years since, as we all know, that a burglary took place in this very house, which resulted in the loss of an extremely valuable family heirloom. In this case robbery does not seem to have been the motive, and it will be as well that we should establish that point at once, so I propose to take the evidence of the Chief Constable, who examined the deceased nobleman's body and clothing, and of Mr. Mountford, the butler, who looked over the house to see if robbery had followed the murder. We will have the Chief Constable first."

The Chief Constable said that he was summoned from his house at Market Fordham by telephone at ten minutes to eight o'clock on the morning of the previous day. He immediately drove to Marchester Royal, and arrived at half-past eight. He was instantly conducted to the library, where he found the dead body of the late Lord Marchester lying on a settee. The present Lord Marchester, Dr. Richmond, the village constable from Marchester, Mr. Mountford, the butler, and Mrs. Page, the house-keeper, were in the room. At Lord Marchester's request he examined the dead man's clothing with a view to ascertaining if robbery had been the object of the murder.

The Coroner inquired how deceased was attired.

"He was wearing evening dress, with a dinner jacket."

"I suppose you examined his pockets in order?"

"Yes, one by one, making notes of what I found. In the left hand inside breast pocket of the dinner jacket, I found a notecase containing five five-pound Bank of England notes. In the right hand side pocket were two letters. In the left hand outside pocket was a gold cigarette case with a monogram in pearls; in the right hand outside pocket a gold match-box, similarly decorated. In the left hand pocket of the waistcoat was a gold watch, with a monogram in pearls and

diamonds; it was connected with the right hand pocket of the waistcoat by a plain gold chain which terminated in a gold charm. In the right hand pocket of the trousers I found four sovereigns and three half sovereigns; in the left hand pocket, four shillings in silver, three pence in bronze, and two small keys, fastened on a silver split-ring. In the shirt front was one diamond stud. There was a plain gold stud at the front of the shirt neck and another at the back. On the wrist of the left hand was a gold bracelet, having a medallion in the centre in which a lock of hair was set in a small crystal case. On the—"

One of the jurymen rose, his hand making a sounding board for his ear.

"I beg your pardon, sir—did you say a bracelet round the poor gentleman's wrist?"

The Chief Constable almost impatiently re-read his notes. The juryman dropped back in his seat with a mystified air. He had never heard of men who wear bracelets.

"On the third finger of the right hand I found a curiously-enamelled ring with a device on a shield; on the little finger of the same hand a plain gold signet ring. On the fourth finger of the left hand I found a gold ring set with one large diamond. All these valuables were in perfect order."

"It is very evident, gentlemen," said the Coroner, as the Chief Constable sat down, "very evident, indeed, that robbery was not the motive of this murder. It would have been an easy matter for the murderer to possess himself of these valuables—the sum total of which would amount to a good deal."

"Isn't it possible, Mr. Coroner, that the murderer might have been interrupted before he finished what he meant to do?" inquired one of the jurymen. "He

might have heard a noise and thought someone was coming. What about the noise of the shot—did no one hear that?"

"There is no evidence before us—and I may as well tell you that none will be forthcoming—that anyone did hear the sound of the shot," answered the Coroner. "It may seem strange that that is so, but it is a fact. Not a single person who was in the house that night has come forward to speak of having heard it, at any rate. You must bear in mind that this is a very large house, and that its interior walls are of great thickness. It is, as you know, in the form of an elongated H, and there is a considerable distance between the east wing, in which the library is situated, and the west wing, where everybody was sleeping on the night in question. The nearest person to the scene of the murder was Lord Marchester, whose rooms are at the juncture of the west wing and the main front— I am correct, I believe, in saying that your lordship heard nothing?"

Lord Marchester bowed.

"I never heard a sound," he replied.

"That, you see, gentlemen, shows that if robbery was his motive, the miscreant had no cause to fear disturbance," said the Coroner. "A few moments of waiting, and he would have known that the shot had not been heard. No, gentlemen, robbery was not the motive in this case—but we will strengthen the evidence on that point by hearing what the butler has to say. . . . Mr. Mountford, you have been in the service of the family for a great many years?"

"Yes, sir—five-and-forty years, man and boy."

"Naturally you know all about the valuables of Marchester Royal—pictures, old china, silver, and so on?"

"I do, sir—no one better."

"And when you became cognisant of this dreadful occurrence you made a hurried inspection of the house to see if anything had been taken?"

"Yes, sir, and have made a more careful one since."

"Do you miss anything?"

"Nothing, sir, with one exception."

"What is that?"

"A hunting-crop, sir, which belonged to the late Lord Marchester—I mean the present Lord Marchester's father. It used to hang in the library, but it is gone. I confess I had not noticed it for months."

"Oh, well, there is little in that! The deceased might have removed it. Thank you, Mr. Mountford. There is one question, however—had not the late Lord Marchester, into whose death we are inquiring, a valet—an Italian?"

"Yes, sir—Pietro Vasari. He had been with Lord Marchester for several years. But he has not been well, and my lord sent him to Whitby for a holiday last week. He is there now."

The Coroner nodded, and the old butler sat down and sighed deeply. The Coroner looked at his notes and his watch.

"I think I shall adjourn, gentlemen," he said. "I don't see what we can——"

There was a sudden agitation at the end of the room, and looking in that direction the Coroner and those who sat at the table saw Sir Thomas Braye, standing erect and pompous.

"Sir," said Sir Thomas, "in the interests of justice I desire to make a statement."

VIII: THE INQUEST CONCLUDES

CHAPTER VIII

The Inquest Concludes

SIR THOMAS BRAYE'S startling announcement, made in the rasping tones which cut the
heavy atmosphere like a knife, caused a sensation
which in its way was quite as great as that caused by
Lord Marchester when he snatched the old duelling-
pistol out of Constable Tombleson's hands. But it
had a different effect. There was now no buzz of talk,
no animated whispering, no movement of heads cran-
ing forward towards each other. Instead, there was
a dead silence. Every face was turned towards
Sir Thomas. He stood, more pompous and self-
consequential than ever, as if he were some dictator
facing a mob. There was pride in his eye—the pride
of wealth. There was disdain in his whole figure—
the disdain of the man who has himself been disdained.

Inspector Skarratt, watching this little scene out of
his eye-corners, saw quickly that Sir Thomas Braye
was not merely unpopular with one class but with all.

There were several men of the county family class
in the room—after giving the retired carpet manufacturer a cool stare, they gazed at the ceiling, or
the floor, or anywhere, and paid no further heed to
him. The farmer class, of whom there were many on
the jury, looked at each other, and exchanged significant glances—one man, thrusting his tongue in his
cheek, elbowed his neighbour and nodded towards
the important-looking little figure with an unabashed
smile of derision.

The prevalent tone of the assemblage towards Sir Thomas was plain to be seen—it might have been put into words, frankly brutal: "What does this fellow, not one of us, want to interfere with us for—let him go back to his carpets!"

The Coroner, a solicitor of Market Fordham, who expected nothing at any time from Sir Thomas Braye, but got a good deal out of the people who considered that unfortunate person quite beneath their notice, pushed his spectacles high on his forehead, and looked across the room at the interrupter with a glance which was more than half supercilious.

"I beg your pardon," he said. "What did I understand you to say?"

"I do not know what you understood me to say, sir," replied Sir Thomas with marked emphasis, "but I know what I said. I said, sir, that, in the interests of justice, I desire to make a statement."

The Coroner fidgeted with his papers for a moment.

"Well, of course, Sir Thomas," he said peevishly, "if anyone desires to make a statement which has anything to do with the case, I cannot refuse to hear it. I suppose your statement has something to do with the case?"

"If it had not, sir, I should not presume to make it," retorted Sir Thomas. "With all due respect to you, I am as well acquainted with legal procedure as any man in this court. I tender you my evidence in this affair."

"Will you please step up to the table?" said the Coroner, pointing to a place on his left hand.

Sir Thomas walked the length of the room with all the dignity of which his podgy little figure was capable. He went through the customary formalities with great solemnity. Yes, he was Sir Thomas Braye, knight, of Marchester Abbey, in Yorkshire, and a justice of the peace, and deputy-lieutenant of the West Riding of the same county, and a justice of the peace for the city of Blackford, and a life-governor of Blackford University, of which he was an honorary LL.D. The enumeration of all these grandeurs made most of those present stare and open their mouths, for they now heard of them for the first time, the majority of them, like all country people, needing several years in which to learn facts that might be learnt from a halfpenny newspaper. They gazed upon Sir Thomas as if, chameleon-like, he had changed since entering the room, and one man, nudging another, remarked in a whisper that "he must have something more than carpet-making about him if he were all them things."

The Coroner leant back in his chair and spoke somewhat wearily.

"Well, Sir Thomas," he said, "you are at liberty to make your statement. Of course, I haven't the least notion of what you are going to say."

If most of the people in that room shared the Coroner's feeling of ignorance and of wonder as to what Sir Thomas Braye had to say on this matter, there were two persons at least who had a very good idea as to what was coming. Without seeming to do so, Inspector Skarratt was watching Lord Marchester. Had their attention not been wholly engaged by Sir Thomas' dramatic intervention, no one present could have failed to see that Lord Marchester was extremely agitated. He had grown very pale; his hands trembled as they turned over some papers on the table in front of him; and he looked at Sir Thomas with a certain species of fear. Inspector Skarratt, knowing what he knew, guessed what was going on in the young man's mind.

Sir Thomas Braye faced the Coroner and the jurymen boldly—he might have been a Chairman of Quarter Sessions.

"What I have to say, sir," he began, "I say from a sense of public duty. I shall be compelled to say some very painful things—to trample upon some very sacred feelings—I shall have to spare neither myself nor those who belong to me. But, as a citizen, and as one who has played no small part in public affairs, I—"

Lord Marchester rose and bent forward across the table.

"May I put it to you whether this is worth while, Sir Thomas?" he said in a very low voice. "You surely do not mean to—"

Sir Thomas turned angrily to the Coroner.

"Sir, I claim your protection," he exclaimed. "I refuse to be interrupted by Lord Marchester, or anyone else."

"You must really not interrupt, Lord Marchester," said the Coroner. "Sir Thomas is entitled to speak without interruption."

Sir Thomas glared angrily at his interrupter, who, with a gesture of expressive despair at doing anything with the choleric little knight, sank back in his seat.

"I was about to say, sir, when I was broken in upon in this unseemly manner, that as a citizen and public man, I shall do my duty at whatever cost to my feelings, or those of my family. Sir," continued Sir Thomas, "I shall shrink from no publicity, and, therefore, I say at once that in what I have to say I am bound to introduce the name of my only daughter, Miss Margaret Braye."

A wave of excitement ran round the room—Lord Marchester hid his face in his hands, and Mr. Deckenham, sitting near him, heard him groan.

"A man who has only one daughter, sir," resumed Sir Thomas, "is naturally very proud and fond of her, and has a great and implicit trust in her. I trusted my daughter. I regret that that trust has not been justified. She has deceived me—she—"

Lord Marchester sprang to his feet with an angry exclamation. Mr. Deckenham laid a hand on his arm—the Coroner shook his head disapprovingly.

"I must ask you to control yourself, Lord Marchester," he said.

"It is only recently—in fact, within the last three days," continued Sir Thomas—"that I have discovered that for nearly twelve months my daughter has been secretly engaged to be married to this man, now, by the accident of his brother's murder, Baron Marchester. It appears that they had met in London, and in Paris; I have ascertained, too, this morning, from my daughter's maid, that they have met clandestinely here, and have kept up a clandestine correspondence, and—"

The Coroner interrupted Sir Thomas.

"You will pardon me, Sir Thomas," he said, "but we are not concerned with the love affairs of your daughter and Lord Marchester, unless they happen to touch on this inquiry."

"They do touch on this inquiry—in my opinion, my strong opinion, sir!" retorted Sir Thomas, with considerable acerbity. "But I will come to the point. Two days ago—the day of the murder—Lord Marchester, then Mr. Gerald Wintour, the Honourable Mr. Gerald Wintour, came to me and had the cool effrontery to tell me that he was engaged to my daughter, and that they wished to marry. I asked him what they proposed to marry on, and reminded him that he himself was a younger son, that I knew his family for their position was comparatively poor, and that, although he was at the Bar I questioned if he had ever earned fifty pounds in a year in his life. He admitted all this, and added the usual tom-fool sentiment about them being so fond of each other that a very modest income would satisfy them. I pointed out to him that my daughter already had an allowance which was double that of the income which he confessed to commanding, and asked him if he thought it a fair or a manly thing to take a girl from a home and a life of luxury to live on a beggarly five hundred a year? For I warned him solemnly that if she married him she should never see another penny of mine."

There was something so intensely vindictive in Sir Thomas Braye's voice as he uttered these last words that every man present felt a sense of nameless fear. He went on amidst a breathless silence:

"Now, sir, I come to the point. I used certain words to this young man which I will repeat to you as nearly as I can. I said to him:

" 'You've come to me, after treating me dishonourably, and ask me for my daughter, having nothing to give her but the prospect of a poverty-stricken life. If you had been your brother, with an old title to offer her, even though it is only backed up by what I call a mere pittance, you might have had some excuse. But for you, practically a beggar, to ask for her is an insult.'

"That is what I said, as nearly as I can remember to the Honourable Gerald Wintour, now Lord Marchester. And, having said it, I showed him the door, and told him he might be thankful that my footmen did not kick him out."

Again the fearful note of hatred, of vindictiveness; the men around gazed at Sir Thomas Braye with uneasy faces.

"Now, sir, I have said part of my say. I will say more—and I say it deliberately. I will take any consequences which may arise from what I am going to say. I believe that man sitting there killed his brother! I believe that what I said to him suggested it to him—no fault of mine. He thought that while he had no chance as Gerald Wintour, an almost penniless younger son, he would have every chance as Lord Marchester, a peer of the realm. He used his cunning—the cunning which stole my daughter away from me, and robbed me of her trust and affection—to slay his brother. He knew his brother's habits of sitting up, of wandering about, yes, of throwing himself on that very settee. I say I believe him his brother's murderer—and I ask you, Mr. Coroner, to call John Stevenson, who can tell you of something that he saw on the afternoon on which this man called on me with his cool impudence to ask me for what he had already robbed me of!"

There was a universal drawing of breath as Sir Thomas Bray concluded this impassioned indictment of the man who now sat with shaded face and rigid shoulders half turned away from him. Men looked wonderingly into each other's faces, afraid to speak. There had been something awful in the ex-carpet manufacturer's venomous harangue; they gazed with wonder at him, as, marching back to his seat, he seized the youth who had accompanied him by the arm, and half led, half pushed him to the table at which the Coroner sat.

"This is John Stevenson," he said. "Question him."

Then he went back to his seat, folded his arms, and gazing steadfastly at the Coroner, paid no heed to the wondering glances turned upon him.

The Coroner was obviously much disturbed and put out. But he went through the usual formalities with the youth, who was nervous and ill at ease, and began to question him impatiently.

"What is your name, and where do you live?"

"John Stevenson, sir. I live at Marchester Village."

"What do you do?"

"I am a woodman, sir, on Sir Thomas Braye's estate."

"Well, what do you know about this case?"

"Why, sir, I only know what I saw and heard. When I heard of the murder last night I felt bound to tell my master."

"Well, what did you see and hear?"

"Well, sir, day before yesterday, about four o'clock in the afternoon, I was at work in Beacon Spinney— at least I'd been working, but I was just then sitting down to have something to eat. I heard somebody coming along the path from the direction of Marchester Abbey, and presently up came Mr. Gerald there. I could see he was in a rare to-do; his face was all queer-like, and his eyes were awful. I kept still, 'cause I was where no one could see me. He was slashing at things, as he came along, and muttering to himself—awful. He stopped just where I was—there's a bit of a clearing there, and began walking up and down, with his head bent down and his hands pressed into his waist, like this. He stood just in front of me after a while—I wonder he couldn't

see me, though it's very thick thereabouts, to be sure—
and began feeling in his pockets. His face looked
—well, it wasn't nice to look at, sir,—angry-like.
Then he says:

"'Curse it, to think what a difference it would
have made if I'd been my Lord Marchester!'"

A murmur ran round the room—followed by a dead
silence.

"Go on," said the Coroner. "What then?"

"Then he laughed, sir, in a queer way, and slashed
at some nettles with his stick, as if he'd like to cut
them to ribbons, and then he lighted a cigarette and
went off towards Marchester Royal, still talking and
mumbling to himself."

"That's a perfectly true and accurate account of
what you saw and heard?"

"Yes, sir—quite true."

"Very well, you can sit down—unless Mr. Deckenham or Mr. Story there wish to question you."

But neither of the solicitors had any questions to
ask, and John Stevenson went back to his seat.

The Coroner hesitated, trifling with his notes.

"I think that as these things have been said about
Lord Marchester in public, he should have the opportunity of denying them if he wishes to do so,"
he said.

Mr. Deckenham lifted a deprecating hand towards
his client.

"I beg—" he began, rising to his feet.

But Lord Marchester waved him down. He looked
steadily at the Coroner.

"Everything that Sir Thomas Braye and John
Stevenson have said is quite true," he said quietly.

Amidst the succeeding buzz of voices the Coroner
spoke.

"I don't see that we can hear more evidence unless it's forthcoming," he said. "Is there anybody present who desires to give evidence?"

To everybody's intense surprise, two men, obviously labourers, rose together at the back of the court. After looking at each other for a moment, one man plucked up courage and spoke.

"If so please your honour, Mestur Crowner, me an' my neighbour, Bill Livesey here, can say summat, so long as we don't come to no harm," he said.

"Come up here—you'll come to no harm so long as you speak the truth," said the Coroner.

The two men came forward, fumbling their caps.

"Now then, who are you?" asked the Coroner as they approached the table.

"If you please, sir, my name's Stephen Bulmer, an' my neighbour's name is William Livesey."

"Where do you live?"

"Side by side of each other, sir, at Marlpit Lane Cottages—that's the other side o' Marchester Royal Park. We both work for Mestur Benjamin Sutton, of the Home Farm, sir."

"Very well—since you've offered yourselves, I'll swear you both, and hear what you've got to say. . . . Now, then, Bulmer, you first. What do you know of this matter?"

"Well, sir, the truth is this here. Me an' Bill here night before last went across to Market Fordham to sell some pigeons—we'm both pigeon-breeders, sir. Of course, it was latish when we left there, 'cause we hadn't left home till half-past six. When we got opposite Marchester Royal entrance gates we heard the stable clock strike half-past ten. 'Bill,' I says, 'they're asleep in the lodge, and they'll ha' gone to bed at the big house, 'cause they're early birds there,'

I says. 'Let's go up the drive and across that Eyetalian garden,' I says, 'it'll cut a mile off for us.'
'Agreed,' says he, and so we climb the gates and sets
off. Well, when we gets to the corner of the Eyetalian
garden we sees lights in the big room on the terrace.
'Keep under the terrace wall, quiet, Bill,' I says.
Well, we creeps along until we hears a sound—a window opening—and then we stopped. I peeped
through the railings of the terrace—so did Bill—and
we saw a man come out of one of the windows. He
half turned round when he'd got out, and then we
saw who it was—Mr. Gerald. He stood there for a
minute, and then he went off round the corner of the
house. And then me and Bill here, we scuttled across
and got into the Park. That's it, ain't it, Bill?"

And Bill, on oath, corroborated all that Mr. Bulmer had said.

The Coroner's summing up of the case—which he
now decided to close, leaving the police to pursue their
own investigation—was nebulous and vague. He
would say neither one thing nor another; he seemed
to be wavering between not merely two, but half a
dozen opinions. Finally, he dismissed the jury to
consider their verdict.

If Inspector Skarratt had been invited to give an
opinion he would have said that the twelve good men
and true would take all the rest of the day to arrive
at a verdict. But Inspector Skarratt did not quite
know the bucolic mind, the rustic habit of non-
committal. In twenty minutes, the jury, more stolid
of face than ever, were back, and the foreman delivered this verdict:

"We find that the deceased met his death by a
pistol-shot, which was not self-inflicted."

As the people slowly drifted away out of the room, Inspector Skarratt noticed that the big folk who were present went away without a word to Lord Marchester. He stood there alone—a suspected murderer.

IX: ENTER THE VALET

CHAPTER IX

Enter the Valet

THE room rapidly cleared. Somebody opened the French windows which gave upon the lawn, and a considerable number of those assembled in the dining-room went out upon the green sward and the trim walks, and stood in groups amongst the gay flower-beds, and borders, excitedly discussing the events of the day.

Here and there half-a-dozen men made rings round one or other of the jurymen, discussing the verdict; here and there a couple of jurymen walked together, going over the evidence again. Down the centre path, leading to the entrance gates, marched Sir Thomas Braye, his woodman following at his heels. He passed and was passed by others, and took no heed of anybody.

There were groups, too, within the dining-room. The Coroner was conversing in one corner with the Chief Constable and a local police-inspector; in another, Mr. Deckenham and the legal gentleman from the Treasury were in close consultation. And still Lord Marchester stood at the table, staring abstractedly at the papers and documents lying upon it; now and then he touched one or other of them; but in a fashion which showed that he was not conscious of his actions.

Inspector Skarratt, who had remained in his seat until the room had cleared, went up to Lord Marchester as the Inspector closed the door behind him.

"I wish you would give me a few minutes' conversation in the study, Sir," he said.

Lord Marchester started and stared at him. The proceedings of the morning had left their trace on his features, which were drawn and haggard.

"Oh, certainly!" he said mechanically. "We will go there at once. Come with me, Inspector Skarratt."

He turned to leave the room, and the Inspector was following him when he was called back by the Chief Constable.

"Where are you going?" asked the latter, as Inspector Skarratt approached him.

"I want to have a private conversation with his lordship," answered the Inspector. "We are going to the study."

The Chief Constable looked dubious.

"Well, I don't know," he said. "I—however, I trust to you not to let him out of your sight. After what we've heard I don't see that there's any other course than to arrest him."

Inspector Skarratt made no reply.

"What would you do?" asked the Chief Constable, somewhat anxiously. "Inspector Jenkinson here and myself think there's no other way."

"There are certainly things to answer and to explain," said Inspector Skarratt. "That's why I wish to have a talk with him."

"Well, he's in your charge, remember," said the Chief Constable.

Inspector Skarratt left the room. He went straight to the study, and found Lord Marchester standing in a thoughtful attitude on the hearthrug. He looked up as the Inspector closed the door behind him.

"Come in, Inspector," he said, in a tone which showed that his mind was occupied with something other than the matter immediately in hand. "You wish to speak to me?"

"I want you to realise, sir, the extreme seriousness in which the evidence given this morning has placed you," answered Inspector Skarratt.

Lord Marchester passed his hand over his forehead.

"Yes," he said. "Yes, I suppose it has—I suppose it has."

"I should like to discuss matters with you and to hear your side of the question," said Inspector Skarratt. "You have admitted——"

A knock came at the door, and Mr. Deckenham put his head into the room. He looked from one man to the other as if doubtful whether his presence were desired, or not.

"Perhaps I had better——" he began.

"No, come in, Mr. Deckenham," said Inspector Skarratt. "I thought you were engaged with Mr. Story, or I should have asked you to come with us. I was just saying to Lord Marchester that I want him to realise the extreme seriousness of the position in which the evidence given this morning has placed him."

"Yes, yes!" said Mr. Deckenham, advancing into the room, and carefully closing the door. "It is indeed a most serious position—I do not like the looks of the Chief Constable at all. I fear he will resort to extreme measures."

"You mean that he will arrest me on the charge of killing my brother?" said Lord Marchester, waking out of his apathy, and speaking excitedly.

"I very much fear so, my lord," answered Mr. Deckenham.

Lord Marchester looked at the detective.

"What do you think, Inspector Skarratt?" he asked.

"Well, my lord," replied the Inspector, forgetting

Lord Marchester's admonition for the moment, "I certainly think there are matters to answer. On the evidence of this morning there is what I think any magistrate would consider a *prima facie* case against you. Just let us consider what the points are—I tabulated them in my notebook in order:

"1.   The pistol with which there is litle reason to doubt the murder was committed is acknowledged by you to be your property.

"2.   There is no doubt that you benefit materially by your brother's death.

"3.   From his evidence it seems clear that your proposal to Sir Thomas Braye might have been very differently received if you had been in your brother's position instead of your own.

"4.   The remark which John Stevenson alleges you made before him—and which you admitted making—shows that you had that impression in your mind.

"5.   If the evidence of the two labourers, Stephen Bulmer and William Livesey, is correct you were seen coming from the library by one of the windows at about half past ten.

"You must admit, sir," concluded Inspector Skarratt, closing his notebook, "that these are very damning facts, which would amply justify the Chief Constable in causing your arrest.   Personally I should like to know what you have to say to them."

Lord Marchester threw himself into the elbow chair at the desk which had been his brother's and putting the tips of his fingers together, looked first at Inspector Skarratt, and then at Mr. Deckenham.   Something in his look convinced both of them that they were dealing with an innocent man.

"There is a good deal that I could say, Inspector," he said, "and I suppose I shall have to say it in another place—you may be quite sure that the authorities will see this out. Now, I tell you my own opinion of the matter—I think there is a certain amount of presumptive evidence against me, and I also think that I shall find it very hard to disprove some of it. But I tell you that I am not merely wholly innocent of my brother's death, but that, in spite of what John Stevenson certainly did overhear me say, I never even wished myself in his shoes! That remark was made in bitter irony, and more in contempt of a man like Sir Thomas Braye than anything else."

"Yes, I understand," said Inspector Skarratt. "Continue, if you please, sir."

"I will tell you both my position in the matter," said Lord Marchester. "It is now about eighteen months since I first met Miss Braye, who had just come of age. We met at the house of a common friend in London—we subsequently met often in London and in Paris. A great affection sprang up between us, and in due course we became engaged to be married. After careful consideration we decided that we would not yet inform her father of our engagement—perhaps we were wrong, but we had weighty reasons—one was that after taking up his residence here he considered himself neglected, and became extremely vindictive, not to say revengeful, against everybody in the neighbourhood—another was that at the end of twelve months I had reasonable hope of securing a very valuable legal appointment in India. The reason why I visited Sir Thomas the day before yesterday was that I had received the appointment that very morning."

"And you did not tell him of it?" exclaimed Mr. Deckenham, who now heard this news for the first time.

"I did not tell him of it because he gave me no chance to do so," replied Lord Marchester. "From the moment I had stated my business he poured out on me a flood of spiteful invective—you know what a ready flow of language he has—and refused to allow me even to speak. I was obliged to leave the house unheard—I do not think I said fifty words to him— and even then he followed me to his door and overwhelmed me with abuse in the presence of his servants. Naturally, I went away in a very resentful state of mind, and I was in a temper when the young man Stevenson saw and heard me. Had you heard the inflection of my voice in uttering the words he repeated, you would have known that I spoke in bitter contempt and irony of a man who let me see that a title would have made all the difference to him.

Mr. Deckenham nodded; Inspector Skarratt made a note in his book.

"Now, as regards the two labourers seeing me leave one of the library windows soon after half past ten," continued Lord Marchester, "that is perfectly true. During the course of our engagement, for reasons which you will readily appreciate, it has been absolutely necessary for Miss Braye and myself to correspond in what her father in his evidence called a clandestine manner—the fact is that he is one of those autocratic persons who believe that they have a right to interfere with any correspondence which may come to their house, whether it is addressed to themselves or not. When I came down here a fortnight ago we arranged a method by which we could exchange notes if need were—unfortunately we had to employ the services of Miss Braye's French maid, Leonie, who, I understand from what Sir Thomas said this morning, has now proved false to us."

"I should say, sir, that Sir Thomas Braye has frightened the maid into confession," said Inspector Skarratt. "That is the sort of thing he would do."

"Probably," assented Lord Marchester. "Well, the explanation of my being seen to leave the house by one of the library windows is this, and it is connected, of course, with the so-called clandestine correspondence—which was never more than a mere exchange of brief notes—between Miss Braye and myself. That evening, after leaving my brother in the billiard-room, I walked straight through the central corridor of the house—the one outside this very room—to the library, and there wrote a note to Miss Braye. While I was writing it the clock struck half-past ten. I let myself out of the library by one of the windows."

"Yes, sir—now *which* window," asked Inspector Skarratt.

"The last window on the right-hand side," replied Lord Marchester.

"Yes—please continue," said the Inspector, making another note.

"And I went straight to the place where these notes were deposited, left it there, came back, and entered the house by the window which I had purposely left open," continued Lord Marchester. "That is the real truth of that incident!"

"I should like to have some further information on two points," said Inspector Skarratt. "When you left the library, sir, were the lights burning?"

"They were."

"Where is the place where you deposited the note, sir, and how long were you in going there and returning?"

"The place is at a stile in one of the pine woods in the park, on a public footpath, and it would take an active walker say twenty-five minutes to go there and back."

"So that you would return, sir, at about eleven o'clock?"

"Just about that."

"You entered by that particular window again?"

"Yes, and closed it and bolted it after I had entered."

"Please attend closely to this question, sir. When you returned to the library were the lights still burning?"

"No, they were out. The room was in total darkness. I was not surprised at that, of course."

"Well, now," said Inspector Skarratt, who had been making copious notes, "according to the medical evidence your brother, sir, must have been shot between half-past ten and eleven o'clock—therefore, when you entered in the darkness you must have passed his dead body."

"It would seem so," assented Lord Marchester.

"You, I suppose, sir, simply passed straight through the library, and went to your own rooms?"

"Quite so."

Inspector Skarratt closed his notebook with a snap.

"It is very evident," he said, turning to Mr. Deckenham, "very evident that the murderer turned out the two lamps in the library. At any rate none of the servants acknowledge doing so, and I have seen no reason to doubt the word of any of them. My theory, sir," he continued, addressing Lord Marchester again, "is that the murder was committed by some person who was perfectly acquainted with your brother's habits; that your brother entered the library soon after you left it, threw himself down on the couch and fell asleep, and that the murderer entered from the window immediately behind the couch, shot him, turned out the lights, and made good his escape, placing the pistol in the ornamental vase as he left the terrace. Only one thoroughly accustomed to your brother's habits could have committed this crime."

"But—my pistol?" said Lord Marchester.

"Well, as regards that, sir, I want you to give me a note authorising me to examine your rooms in Jermyn Street, and particularly your diary," said Inspector Skarratt. "I want to know who has visited you during the past six months."

"After my brother's funeral you had better accompany me to town, and we will go carefully into the matter," said Lord Marchester.

Inspector Skarratt smiled somewhat enigmatically, and looked at Mr. Deckenham.

"I'm afraid that won't be possible, sir," he said, "I think that——"

At that moment a knock came at the door, and the Chief Constable and Inspector Jenkinson entered.

"That is what I thought," said Inspector Skarratt in a low voice.

The Chief Constable looked uncomfortable, but resolute and determined.

"I beg your pardon, my lord," he said, "it's really a very trying situation, but I have my duty to perform, and after the evidence we heard this morning I have no choice but to tell your lordship that you must consider yourself under arrest—the warrant will be here shortly. I'm sorry, my lord."

"Oh, I quite expected it!" replied Lord Marchester. "In the circumstances, it is the best thing to do. I am quite at your disposal."

"I think you might have left that over until after

the obsequies of the late peer," said Mr. Deckenham indignantly. "It is unseemly that——"

"I beg your pardon, Mr. Deckenham," interrupted the Chief Constable sharply, "but I hold myself to be as good a judge of unseemliness as you, and I am not going to be lectured by you. I have my duty to do, irrespective of rank."

"Yes—yes—you are quite right," said Lord Marchester. "What do you wish—what do you propose?"

"Well, my lord, I'm afraid we shall have to take you to Market Fordham, and then——"

The door of the study was suddenly flung open—a man entered and stood, silent, observant, on the threshold, surveying those before him with calm, steady glances. A medium-sized, muscular man, clothed in immaculate black cloth, and the finest white linen; a sallow-complexioned, black haired man, with coal-black eyes of a peculiar intensity, and an expression of great determination. And—unmistakably—an Italian.

"Well, gentlemen!" he said. "So my lord is dead—murdered? I did not hear of it until this morning—then I came, post-haste. And Mr. Wintour, his brother, is suspected of his murder? Ha! That, of course, is to be seen, is it not? May be, and may not be—justice will decide."

"I think you should remember that you are in Lord Marchester's presence," said Mr. Deckenham.

The Italian showed a set of gleaming white teeth.

"In Lord Marchester's presence!" he sneered. "That am I not, then! That late Lord Marchester, gentlemen all, was married—married to my sister, and the new Lord Marchester is her son—a handsome boy of five years old."

X: A SECRET MARRIAGE

CHAPTER X

A Secret Marriage

IF a thunderbolt had suddenly fallen in the midst of the five men who heard the Italian's announcement, made in an arrogant and overbearing fashion, which showed that he was secretly conscious of possessing some master card in this game, they could not have felt or shown more astonishment. The two police officials opened their mouths as if they never meant to close them again; Inspector Skarratt sank back in his chair with a curious click of his tongue; Lord Marchester half rose from his seat; Mr. Deckenham clapped his hand to his forehead, as if a sudden pain had shot through his temples. And the Italian, subtle-eyed, watched the effect of his communication with a smile, which showed his strong white teeth.

"Yes," he repeated, " a fine, handsome boy of five —my nephew."

Mr. Deckenham was the first to speak. He suddenly woke into something like activity.

"What do you say?" he almost shouted. "That the late Lord Marchester, your master, was married? Married?"

Vasari bent himself almost double.

"I said married, Mr. Deckenham," he answered. "I also said—married to my sister."

Mr. Deckenham took a very large pinch of snuff —anyone noticing him would have seen that his hands trembled very much.

"I don't believe it!" he said. "It's a fabrication."

Vasari's eyes gleamed, and an ugly look came into his face.

"On the contrary, Mr. Deckenham, as you will find," he said quietly, "I can prove the matter to you or to anyone, for I have all the papers and documents in my possession. I have something more than that too—something that you have not got, although you were family solicitor to my late employer."

There was something so confident, so cocksure, in the man's voice and manner, that the solicitor was startled. He took another pinch of snuff and faced the Italian again.

"What's that?" he demanded snappishly.

"His Lordship's will," replied Vasari.

Mr. Deckenham's eyebrows went up, and Mr. Deckenham's mouth opened.

"His will? His will? Why, he never made a will!"

"He made a will, and it is in my possession, Mr. Deckenham," said Vasari. "It is a perfectly good and valid will, and was drawn up by a highly respectable solicitor of Market Fordham. Oh, it is all in order like everything else."

"Show us it then," said Mr. Deckenham.

"At the proper time—after the funeral ceremonies," replied Vasari. "At present it is sufficient for me to announce to you—that is, to those of you whom it may concern—that my little nephew is the new Lord Marchester, and that I am his legally constituted guardian."

Mr. Deckenham was about to reply to this, but Lord Marchester stopped him. He looked at Vasari.

"It will be best at this juncture," he said quietly, "if you will tell us plainly what you mean. Give us some proof of the claim you advance—I cannot think you so foolish as to say these things without reason. We are entirely in the dark—if you really know what you say to be true, let us know also. Then we shall understand each other."

"I will do so with pleasure, Mr. Wintour," said Vasari. "I will tell you everything without reserve, and I assure you upon my honour, that I can give you the fullest proof that all I shall say is strictly true. If these gentlemen will be seated, and I may sit down, I will tell you the whole story—you may think it strange, but I have known stranger stories myself, for this I assure you is a strange world."

Inspector Skarratt watched this man with particular attention—it seemed to him that the valet was the most interesting personality he had met since his arrival at Marchester Royal. During his previous visit there, just two years before, the Italian was away on a long holiday in Italy—he met him now, therefore, for the first time. It needed little of the Detective's usual insight to know that in this keen-eyed quick gestured man he met a character and a force.

Vasari seated himself in a chair close to the desk at which sat the man whose claim to title and estates he boldly disputed. He drew out a cigar case.

"I shall smoke a cigar," he said, with all the easy assurance of a man who is confident of his ground.

"It is a somewhat long story—smoke, gentlemen." He passed the well-filled case round—no one responded to his offer. "What, you will not?" he said with a frown. "Very well, perhaps you will be glad some day to have the chance of smoking with Pietro Vasari."

"May we hear what you have to say," said Mr. Deckenham.

"Most assuredly, worthy Mr. Deckenham—I com-

mence," answered Vasari, putting himself in an easy
attitude. "You must know, gentlemen all, then, that
I became personal attendant to the late Lord Marchester seven years ago, just before he attained his
majority. We met in Paris under somewhat romantic
circumstances into which I need not now enter—
enough to say that he took a fancy to me, and I to him,
and we commenced a connection which was never anything but pleasant to both of us. I grieve, gentlemen,
sincerely, that the unfortunate affair of the night before last should have broken that connection, that
friendship, that relationship."

He paused to roll up the loose end of his cigar—Inspector Skarratt, watching him closely, saw that in
spite of his words the man cared nothing that Lord
Marchester had been murdered—there was a gleam in
his eye which betokened some strange sense of satisfaction at the position in which he found himself. He
was talking to those he addressed as if he were master
of the house they sat in.

"Soon after my lord attained his majority," he continued, "he and I set out for a long visit to Italy—
my native land, gentlemen. We went by way of
Paris, Marseilles and Monte Carlo, to Genoa and
thence to Pisa, Florence, and Rome, where we abode
for some weeks. From Rome we went south to
Naples. It was at Naples that my Lord met my sister
—now a widow."

Vasari paused a moment at this point, and sighed
deeply.

"It is strange, it is romantic, that such things should
be!" he said, in a reflective tone. "Sometimes I am
tempted to believe that there really is something which
arranges it all. For who could possibly think that
a great English lord should go all that long way to find

his bride in an unknown girl in a little Italian village?
But thus it came about—you must learn, gentlemen,
that my family resides in the village of Antignano,
which is a few miles out of Naples, on the other side
of the Heights of St. Elmo; my mother is postmistress
there till this day.   Agostina Vasari her name is, and
she is a Neapolitan of the Neapolitans.   Well, then,
what so natural when we had reached Naples, as that
being near to my native place and my people, I should
ask permission of my lord to visit them?   He never
refused me anything—my lord.   'Go Pietro,' he said.
'Go—make a holiday for a week with your people—
I shall amuse myself in Naples.'   And so I went
home to Antignano, which I had not seen for nine
long years."

The Italian's keen eyes seemed to melt at the recollection of his native land, and his countenance assumed
a dreamy look.

"Ah, how beautiful it was to see the well-beloved
place once more!" he continued.   "Yet there were
great changes, gentlemen, for my father was dead, and
my brother Filippo had lost his life at sea—drowned
off Capri in a sudden squall.   But most astounding
change of all I found in my sister Leonora, whom I
had left an awkward, not too well-favoured child of
eight years old, and now found a young goddess of
seventeen.   *Cospetto!*   I wish, gentlemen, that you
could have seen Leonora as I first saw her on my arrival at my mother's house.   Such eyes, such hair,
such a figure, and presence!   She was the most beautiful woman within fifty miles of Naples, and that is
saying a good deal.   There was not a young man in
Antignano who was not dying of love of her, and the
fame of her beauty had extended as far as Sorrento
in one direction, and of Capua in the other.   *Corpo di*

Bacco! What a beauty my little sister was at that time."

Vasari wagged his head in unaffected delight at these reminiscences. His pride in his sister was evidently sincere, simple, unaffected.

"But do not think, gentlemen," he continued, "do not think that Leonora encouraged any of the hundred young men who cast sheep's eyes at her. We are a proud family, gentlemen, for, although we have fallen somewhat in the world so far as position is concerned, we have noble blood in our veins, we Vasaris of Antignano, and can claim kinship with some of the greatest families· of southern Italy. No man had ever touched Leonora's heart, until my lord came across her path—then—ah, well, then——"

The Italian made an expressive gesture, and once more wagged his head and rolled his dark eyes.

"This way it was, gentlemen," he said, resuming his story. "During my week of vacation at my native place, Leonora and I walked much together in the neighbourhood. One evening—an evening of great beauty, such as is only possible in Italy, gentlemen—we were walking along the road which leads towards Soccaro along the hillsides of the high ground above Camaldollili, when we met suddenly and unawares, my master, Lord Marchester, who, it appeared, had been out riding in the country to the northward of Naples, and was then returning to that city. Naturally, on seeing me, he drew rein and addressed me, asking if I were enjoying my holiday, and how I had found my people, and so on. All the time he addressed me his eyes were fixed on Leonora; she, too, I saw, regarded him with attention, for he was, as you are all aware, a handsome and gracious youth. I presented Leonora to him as my sister—he spoke to her with a tone, gentlemen, which was pregnant with intense admiration. As for me, standing by I observed that he could not take his eyes off her, and for one moment—purposely, he lingered as long as he could, and his eyes were still seeking Leonora's when at last he bade us good-night. I was not surprised, gentlemen, when next day, he came to our house in Antignano. He had a plausible excuse for wishing to see me, but I knew very well that his real object in coming was to see my beautiful sister."

Vasari paused a little, meditatively rolling and unrolling the loose end of his long, thin, cigar. His reminiscences were evidently pleasing to himself—he smiled over them.

"You know, gentlemen, what the ways of young men are when they fall in love," he continued. "My lord was very impetuous, ardent and impulsive. It soon became evident that he was what you call head over-ears in love with Leonora—so evident, that after a consultation with my mother and my uncle and myself it became my duty to speak to him. I pointed out to him that we were a proud family, with noble blood in our veins, and that we should resent any trifling with the affections of Leonora in the strongest manner. I said that nothing could give me such pain as to leave his lordship's service and that I should be sorry to have to do so. Finally, I asked him what his intentions were as regards my sister, the apple of my eye. He replied frankly and unreservedly that he loved her, and desired to marry her, and requested permission to address my mother on the subject."

Mr. Deckenham interrupted Vasari's story.

"How long was this after he first saw your sister?" he inquired.

"How long?" said Vasari. "Possibly a fortnight, Mr. Deckenham."

"And possibly less," said the solicitor drily. "Well, proceed."

"I do not see that it matters whether it was within fourteen days, or fourteen weeks, or fourteen months," said Vasari. "That has nothing to do with what is an absolute, incontrovertible fact."

"That is just what we want," said Mr. Deckenham. "Give us the absolute, incontrovertible fact."

"Most certainly—as I have been doing, after my own fashion," answered Vasari. "The plain fact is that his lordship, having convinced my mother, my uncle Giuseppe Serafino Vasari, a saddler of Antignano, and myself of his good faith, proposed to and was accepted by Leonora, and married her a month later. That, Mr. Deckenham, is a fact which neither you nor anyone else, man of law or not, can possibly controvert."

"We'll see about that later on," retorted the solicitor. "Where did this marriage take place, pray, Mr. Vasari?"

Vasari smiled and shook his head with a knowing expression.

"Ah, Mr. Deckenham," he said, "if you have any suspicion that the marriage of my sister and the late Lord Marchester was not legally and validly celebrated, rid yourself of it, I beg! I took care of that, I, Pietro, the brother and protector of Leonora."

"I am not concerned with your part at all, sir," said Mr. Deckenham, testily. "I want to know if the marriage was valid, where it was celebrated, and where the proofs are."

"Very good," replied the Italian. "As to the marriage, it was celebrated no fewer than three times—

once before the civil authorities, once at the parish church of Antignano, and once at the English church in the Strada San Pasquale, in Naples. Oh, I saw that it was all correct! And as for the papers, they are in that safe, and I shall show them to you."

Advancing to a small safe which stood in one corner of the study, the Italian produced a bunch of keys, with one of which he unlocked the door. He took out a small packet of papers and turned to Mr. Deckenham.

"You are a man of honour and probity, Mr. Deckenham," he said, placing the packet in the solicitor's hands. "I freely intrust these papers to you for your inspection and Mr. Wintour's. You will find there the marriage certificates, the birth certificate of my nephew, the present Lord Marchester, and his father's will—five documents in all."

He placed the packet in Mr. Deckenham's hands and sat down again to smoke his cigar. Of all the men in the room he seemed to be the least concerned by what was proceeding.

Mr. Deckenham and the man who, until a quarter of an hour before, had believed himself to be Lord Marchester, went carefully through the papers. It needed little inspection of them to show that they were genuine, and that Vasari's story was true in every detail. Of the validity of the marriage there was no doubt. The solicitor turned with more anxiety to the will, which had been drafted by a local practitioner. It was brief, and in strict form. Proper provision was made for the widow, and five thousand pounds were bequeathed to Gerald Wintour. There were legacies for the servants, and all else was left to the testator's son, Gervase Benedict. Pietro Vasari— referred to in the will as "my faithful personal at-

tendant and friend"—and the widow were appointed
as executors and guardians of the young heir.

Mr. Deckenham handed the papers back to Vasari
in silence, but he nodded his head slightly as if to
express his concurrence with what the Italian had
said. For a moment he sat drumming his fingers
on the table; suddenly he turned sharply round and
faced Vasari with a piercing glance.

"Where is Lady Marchester, then?" he demanded.

"At her house in London," replied Vasari in his
blandest manner.

"Why did she not live here?" asked Mr. Deckenham.

"Since she came to England, six years ago," replied
Vasari, "her ladyship has been going through a long
course of education—it was my lord's intention to present her to Society this very year. She is now a
most elegant and accomplished woman. My lord
spent much time with her in town and on the Continent."

Mr. Deckenham rose. He looked weary; it seemed
to Inspector Skarratt that he had aged by ten years.

"Well," he said. "I wish the late Lord Marchester
had shown more confidence in me. Mr. Wintour, I
should like a few words with you in private."

The Chief Constable rose. He stretched out an
intervening hand.

"Excuse me, Mr. Deckenham," he said. "Mr.
Wintour is under arrest."

XI: ON THE TRAIL

CHAPTER XI

On the Trail

HEARING the Chief Constable make this announcement, Mr. Deckenham uttered an impatient exclamation.

"Dear me!" he said. "Surely you are not going on with that?"

"Pardon me, Mr. Deckenham," replied the Chief Constable with some hauteur. "I believe I am better acquainted with the nature of my duties than you are. After the evidence which we heard this morning, I have no other course open to me than arrest Mr. Wintour. I'm very sorry indeed that this should be so, but I can't help it. I shall have to ask you to accompany me to Market Fordham, Mr. Wintour— I have sent for the necessary warrant."

"Very well," answered Gerald Wintour. "I quite expected that you would do so. I shall be glad to get this matter settled. But may I not have a private interview with Mr. Deckenham?"

"Yes, sir, you may, but Inspector Jenkinson must remain in the room with you," answered the Chief Constable.

"We will go to the library, Mr. Deckenham," said Gerald Wintour. "We shall be quiet there, and Inspector Jenkinson can keep an eye on me while allowing us reasonable privacy."

The three left the study together; the Chief Constable, Inspector Skarratt, and Pietro Vasari remained. Pietro inspected the detective with interest.

"I suppose you are from Scotland Yard?" he suddenly inquired.

"Yes," replied Inspector Skarratt.

"Have you as yet formed any theory as to how my brother-in-law met his death?" inquired the Italian.

"No," answered the Inspector.

"It is a strange mystery," said Vasari, beginning to pace the room, and shaking his head. "I have just had the bare outlines of it from Mountford, the butler, but I cannot understand matters at all."

"I have been wondering, Mr. Vasari, if you could not give us some information which might help us," said the Chief Constable. "Was it within your knowledge that Lord Marchester used to stay up at night after the household had retired, and that he was in the habit of throwing himself down on the particular couch on which he was found lying dead?"

"Oh, yes, indeed!" replied Vasari. "His lordship did not sleep well the early part of the night, and he had a habit of wandering about the house, and especially about the library and the terrace outside. Yes, I have seen him lying on that couch late at night—he almost invariably turned out the lights of the library himself. Whoever shot him must have been infinitely well acquainted with his habits. That to me makes the crime all the more mysterious."

"You don't know of anybody who had any quarrel with Lord Marchester—any spite against him?" asked Inspector Skarratt.

Vasari shook his head.

"No, of a certainty," he answered. "He was most popular—as all know who knew him. No—I know of nothing of that sort. To be sure, when he was married to Leonora, my sister, there was a wild young fellow of Antignano, one Jacopo Rossi, madly in love

with her himself, who made foolish vows of vengeance
against the Englishman, but nobody paid attention to
them."

"You do not think that this man could have tracked
Lord Marchester down?" suggested the Chief Constable. "I have heard that your countrymen cherish
a grievance for a long time."

Vasari shook his head.

"No," he replied, "that is scarcely possible. If it
had been a question of vendetta, now, Jacopo would
have waited ten, or fifteen, or twenty years, even a
lifetime. But it was not, and could not be—there
was no blood feud. No, in that case it was simply
the ravings of an undisciplined youngster to whom
Leonora had never even accorded one glance of her
eyes. No—it is a mystery."

"You have opportunities of judging," said Inspector
Skarratt. "What is your opinion of the relations between the late Lord Marchester and his brother?"

Vasari spread out both hands and shrugged his
shoulders.

"They were simply indifferent to each other," he
said. "Pleasantly but coldly polite to each other—
just that, and no more. They were, you see, of such
different temperaments and dispositions."

"You wouldn't think it likely that Mr. Wintour
would murder his brother?" said the Chief Constable.

Vasari shrugged his shoulders again, and made a
grimace which showed his white teeth.

"Me?" he said. "How can I tell? I have seen
enough of the world, gentlemen, to believe the most
unlikely, the most unaccountable things possible.
There is many a man commits crime through some
irrepressible impulse—oh, I would not personally ex-

press an opinion on this matter, for or against Mr. Wintour. He was always polite to me."

"I suppose you are to be found here?" said the Chief Constable. "We may want some evidence from you as to the late peer's habits."

"Oh, I shall be found here," replied Vasari. "It will, of course, be my regular domicile until the young heir comes of age. I am going now to London to my sister, whom I shall conduct here to-morrow, with her son. After that, yes, you will find me here all the time."

"If you are driving to the station, Mr. Vasari," said Inspector Skarratt, "I should be obliged if you would give me a lift. I, too, am anxious to leave this afternoon. I shall return to-morrow or the day after," he added, turning to the Chief Constable.

"Oh, I shall give you a ride to the station with pleasure," replied Vasari. "I will go now and order the brougham to be in readiness within twenty minutes."

Inspector Skarratt had a few words with the Chief Constable, and with his permission repaired to the library to see Mr. Wintour and Mr. Deckenham. At the door of the library he met Mr. Saunderson. The steward's face was white and drawn—there were great beads of perspiration on his high forehead, and his eyes seemed to be staring at some far-off object. He started as he caught sight of Inspector Skarratt, and for a second glared at him as if he did not know him.

"Good-afternoon, Mr. Saunderson," said the Inspector. "How are you?"

Mr. Saunderson seized Inspector Skarratt by the elbow with a hand which was trembling very much, and led him into a quiet corner of the hall. He approached his mouth to the Inspector's ear.

"Is it true?" he said, in a hoarse whisper, "is it true—this that they are saying? That Lord Marchester was married?"

"I believe it is," replied Inspector Skarratt.

"And has left a son and heir?"

"Yes."

"And that the widow is that fellow Vasari's sister?"

"Yes."

"And it's all strictly legal and correct?"

"So Mr. Deckenham seems to think," replied the Inspector. "He has seen all the papers."

Mr. Saunderson's white face became almost purple. He seemed to lose control over himself; he lifted his right hand as if to call down the vengeance or the protection of Heaven; he stamped his foot upon the ground.

"That villain!" he hissed out at last. "Oh, that vile Italian scound——"

"Hush!" said Inspector Skarratt. "He's here." Vasari came hurrying across the hall. He caught sight of the steward and smiled—pretty much as a wolf might smile at a fat, defenceless lamb.

"Ah, the respectable Mister Saunderson!" said Vasari, his keen eyes sparkling, and his white teeth gleaming under his black moustache. "How do you do, Mister Saunderson? I shall have the pleasure of seeing you when I return from London to-morrow, and then, or on the next day, we will go into some little business matters, eh? Inspector Skarratt, I shall be pleased to drive you in a few minutes."

More than a little perplexed by the attitude and demeanour of these two men towards each other Inspector Skarratt made his arrangements for his temporary absence from Marchester Royal, and was soon driving away in the brougham with the man who was now its virtual master. The Italian leant back against the soft cushions with the nonchalance of a man who is readily adapted to altered circumstances.

"This has been a great shock to me, Inspector," he said. "And will have been still more dreadful to my poor sister, if she has heard the news, which, however, I doubt, for Leonora has never been a devotee of the newspaper. I telegraphed to her this morning that I was *en route*—it may be that it will be my mournful duty to break the fatal news to her."

"Your sister lives, I think you said, in London?" said Inspector Skarratt.

"Yes, Inspector, in a very handsome flat in the South Kensington district," replied Vasari. "She would shortly have come to Marchester Royal—it was on my advice that my lord, her husband, gave her a first-class education after her coming to England. She has had the best tutors and professors—she is now *une grande dame,* as if to the manner born, my Leonora. And at this juncture to have her husband snatched away from her by an assassin! What unhappiness, what ill-fortune! Ah, I do not congratulate myself on what I may have to do on my arrival, to-night, Inspector, for I am a tender-hearted man, and very fond of Leonora, who is the apple of my eye. Besides, I am just now not at all in good health."

"I heard that you had gone to the seaside for your health," remarked Inspector Skarratt. "Whitby, wasn't it?"

"Yes, Inspector, to Whitby. Have you ever visited Whitby?"

"No," replied the Inspector. "I have never visited any north-country seaside place—that is a pleasure to come."

"Whitby is a delightful town," said Vasari dreamily.

"Grey, romantic, typically northern. If you lived there always you would have a skin like a hide of a rhinoceros. It is, of course, nothing like our coast-towns in southern Italy, where all is sunshine, and light, and colour. But invigorating and healthy—*cospetto,* Inspector, I could have eaten and drunk all day long!"

When they reached the little station at Marchester it transpired that they were going in different directions. Vasari wanted a train for York, where he would catch the evening express for King's Cross. Inspector Skarratt wanted one for Hull, where he had important business.

"But you will be back again at Marchester Royal!" said the Italian as they parted. "You have not completed your work there?"

"I shall be back at the latest on the day after to-morrow," replied the Inspector. "No, I have not finished my business there yet—I am only beginning it."

Vasari nodded, and Inspector Skarratt crossed over to the down platform, and was soon on his way to Hull. His business there consisted of eating his dinner in the Station Hotel. Within an hour of his arrival, having dined well and comfortably, he stepped into a train, going northward along the coast-line—three hours later he stood on a wind-swept platform at Whitby.

It was then half-past nine—a fine though chilly and breezy evening. Inspector Skarratt, carrying his Gladstone bag, went out into the narrow main street of the old town, and began to look about him for hotels.

Coming to the end of Baxter Gate, where the salt-laden wind blew lusty and strong from the harbour, he found himself confronted by two hotels—the

"Talbot" on his left hand, the "Angel" on his right. He turned into the "Talbot" and sought the office.

"Have you a Mr. Vasari staying here?" he inquired.

"Mr. Vasari, sir? No one of that name, sir."

"Not been here during the last few days," said the Inspector.

"No, sir."

"Thank you," said Inspector Skarratt, and went away. "I suppose there'll be several hotels in the place," he said to himself. "I'll go through the lot if need be. Vasari's the sort of man who would be sure to stay at an hotel, and a good hotel—no boarding or lodging-house for him."

His quest ended, however, at the "Angel," into which he turned after leaving the "Talbot." No, Mr. Vasari was not there now, but he had been there for nearly a fortnight. See, there was his signature in the register.

"Ah, I'm sorry he's gone!" said Inspector Skarratt. "I'd hoped to have found him still here. When did he leave then?"

"Day before yesterday, sir."

"Day before yesterday? I thought he meant to stay till the end of the week. He did when I last heard from him," said Inspector Skarratt.

"Well, sir, he did leave rather unexpectedly; at least, he'd not said anything about going. He went off in the afternoon, just after lunch, by the 2:35 to York."

"Well, that's disappointing," said the Inspector, in a tone which suggested that Mr. Vasari was a very dear personal friend. "However, it can't be helped. I'll book a room, if you please—I shall only want it one night."

"Yes, sir," said the young lady to whom Inspector

Skarratt had addressed these seemingly innocent inquiries. "I can give you Number 11, sir—that's the room that Mr. Vasari had."

"Thank you," said Inspector Skarratt.

He went upstairs to Number 11 and washed away the dust of his journey, and then, returning to the coffee-room, enjoyed a comfortable supper. Over a good cigar and a glass of whisky in the smoking-room he meditated closely on the events of the day, and especially on the advent of Pietro Vasari on the theatre of operations, and on the startling news which he had made known. And finally, as he came to the end of his cigar, and the last drop of his whisky, he said to himself:

"Since he wasn't here, I wonder where he was that night. That's got to be found out."

Then he put the whole affair out of his mind, and went to bed and slept like a top.

But he was up very early next morning, and before seven o'clock was tramping up and down the old pier, drawing in long draughts of the keen North Sea air. He breakfasted at a quarter to eight, and before nine was in the train on his way to London.

It was half-past three in the afternoon when Inspector Skarratt got out of the express at King's Cross. He hailed a hansom and drove straight to Scotland Yard, where he had a long interview with certain of his superior officers. And that over he drove to Jermyn Street and sought out Gerald Wintour's chambers.

Gerald Wintour's servant admitted him on hearing who he was, and seeing the note with which his master had provided the Inspector. He looked uneasy and frightened, and Inspector Skarratt saw that he knew what had happened.

"I suppose you've heard the news?" he said.

"Yes, sir—I read it in the papers this morning. The inquest—and the arrest too. It's a bad job for my master, sir. What do you think about it?" asked the man anxiously.

"I don't know what to think, yet," replied Inspector Skarratt. "I shall know more after a while. I want to see your master's desk—he has given me the key of it, and full permission to look at his papers."

Left alone in Gerald Wintour's study, the detective first examined the case in which the duelling pistols were kept. Yes—one of the pistols was gone. He examined the other—it was an exact reproduction of that found at Marchester Royal, with the exception that the mechanism was out of order.

Inspector Skarratt unlocked Gerald Wintour's desk, and after some searching found the diary. He sat down and began to examine it, searching for the names of people who were mentioned in it as having called on its owner during the previous six months. Nothing suggested itself to him for a long time, but at last, under the date, April 7th of that year, he came upon an entry which put him on the alert;

"Vasari called about the Greuze—recommended him to try Agnews."

XII: MR. SAUNDERSON'S HOUSEHOLD

CHAPTER XII

Mr. Saunderson's Household

HAVING read this entry, which to him, viewed in the light of recent events, seemed to possess not a little significance, Inspector Skarratt rang the bell and summoned Gerald Wintour's servant to his presence. The man still regarded him with anxious eyes—the mere notion that he was closeted with a famous detective from Scotland Yard appeared to unnerve him.

"There are one or two questions I should like to ask you," said Inspector Skarratt. "If you can answer them it may be helpful to your master."

"I'm sure I should be glad to do anything to help him, sir," replied the man, with great earnestness. "Very glad, indeed!"

"Well," said Inspector Skarratt, "perhaps you can. Have you a good memory?"

"I think so, sir."

"Do you know Pietro Vasari, the Italian, who was valet to Lord Marchester?"

"Yes, sir—very well."

"You've met him often, I suppose?"

"Well, I couldn't say often, sir. During the three years I've been with Mr. Wintour, I've seen him occasionally. Sometimes I've taken a note from Mr. Wintour to Lord Marchester at Claridge's Hotel, when his lordship was in town, and I used to see Mr. Vasari then. Sometimes Mr. Vasari would come here with a note or a message from Lord Marchester to

Mr. Wintour, and of course I saw him on those occasions."

"Do you remember the last time he was here?"

The man thought for a minute or two.

"Yes, sir," he answered at last. "I do—quite well. It was somewhere about Easter, sir."

"Is there anything you remember that visit by?"

"Yes, sir. It was something about a picture which Mr. Vasari brought with him to show Mr. Wintour— a picture about a foot and a half square in size. I understood from what I heard about it that Mr. Vasari had discovered it in some second-hand shop or other, and wanted my master's opinion on it."

"Is Mr. Gerald Wintour an authority on pictures, then?"

"Oh, yes, sir—he's a bit of what they call an expert, sir."

"Where did they have their talk about this picture?"

"In this room, sir."

"Now, just try to recollect this—was Vasari left alone in this room at any time on that visit?"

The man answered this question without hesitation.

"Yes, sir, he was. Mr. Wintour had made an appointment with him for three o'clock, but just before that time Mr. Wintour was obliged to go out for half an hour, and he left word with me that Mr. Vasari was to wait in the study. Mr. Wintour was longer than he meant to be—Mr. Vasari was alone in this room nearly an hour, I should say."

"Very good—that's all on that point," said Inspector Skarratt. He took up the pistol case from the table before him and held it out to the valet. "Do you know what this is?" he inquired.

"Yes, sir,—a case of old pistols."

"You've seen them?"

"Yes, sir—I've seen Mr. Wintour take them out and show them to his friends sometimes."

"Lately?"

"No, sir—not for a long time."

"You've never opened this case yourself lately?"

"I never did open it, sir, at any time. I've dusted the case every day as it lay there on the old bureau, but I never even tried to open it—I always understood that there was some secret catch in the spring."

Inspector Skarratt opened the case.

"There!" he said. "You see there's one pistol gone. Now, can you remember when you last saw them both?"

The valet, after reflecting for some time, shook his head.

"Not exactly, sir, but it's a long time ago. Certainly not this side of last Christmas."

"You've never heard Mr. Wintour complain of the loss of one pistol?"

"No, sir."

"You read in the papers this morning what was said at the inquest about the pistol, didn't you?"

"Yes, sir."

"And you didn't try to open the case, then?"

"No sir, I came and looked at it and handled it, but I was then under the impression that it had a patent catch or lock."

Inspector Skarratt rose as if satisfied.

"Well, that's all I wanted to ask you," he said. "Of course you'll not breathe a word of what's passed between us to a single soul!"

"O, no, sir—you may trust me!" replied the man. "I hope you'll be able to clear my master, sir."

"I hope I shall lay hands on the right man," answered Inspector Skarratt.

Then he bade the valet good-evening and went away, carrying the diary and the pistol case with him. And as he walked towards Scotland Yard for another conference with his immediate superior, he said to himself that there were certain things he must find out—first, where did Vasari spend the night intervening between his departure from Whitby and his arrival at Marchester Royal; second, where, when, and by whom was the stolen pistol put in order; third, what were Vasari's antecedents before the late Lord Marchester engaged him? From which train of thought it may be gathered that the Italian was already an object of suspicion to Inspector Skarratt.

"I'll go down to Marchester Royal by the first express in the morning and see if anything further has transpired," he said to himself. "Vasari's sure to be back there later in the day."

If he had been able to see as far, Inspector Skarratt would have known that practically nothing had happened at Marchester Royal since his departure on the previous day. The dead body of the murdered man still lay in a darkened room awaiting burial; the servants still went whispering about the house, talking of the strange change which a few hours had wrought. Gerald Wintour was detained in the cells at Market Fordham, Mrs. Page was preparing rooms for the reception of the widowed Lady Marchester and her son, the dead peer's heir, of whose existence she had never dreamt. Mr. Deckenham, still perplexed and wondering, went in and out of the house, sometimes conversing with the local police, who were still pursuing their inquiries and investigations; sometimes talking to the old butler, who could scarcely believe the reality of the events which had just transpired. Nothing startling, nothing new of significance had occurred since Vasari drove Inspector Skarratt away to the station.

But a mile away, at Marchester Abbey, events had happened which, had they not been overshadowed by the great event, would have set the whole country-side a-talking much more than they did at the moment. Sir Thomas Braye, having lashed himself into a furious temper at the inquest, had worked himself up into something worse as he walked homewards— he walked so fast, and became so terrible in expression that the young woodman was devoutly thankful when he was dismissed.

"Somebody'll catch it when the old boy gets home," he said to himself, as he made off to his mother's cottage in the woods. "They will so!"

Sir Thomas went straight to his study when he entered his house, and after stamping up and down the floor for a few minutes rang the bell and bade his butler summon Mademoiselle Leonie to his august presence.

The French girl had already had one interview with the irascible and choleric little knight that morning, and had been wepeing ever since—she now appeared before the tyrant with red eyes and a woebegone expression which would have melted any heart but Sir Thomas's. She found him, however, sterner and more vindictive than ever. He treated her to a severe lecture, threatened her with all manner of pains and penalties, and finally throwing her some money in the presence of the butler, commanded that functionary to pack her out of the house, bag and baggage, within half an hour.

"Send one of the men with her to the station in the dog-cart," he roared. "And mind he sees her safely away by the London train. And do you tell

my daughter that I want to see her here at once—
at once!"

Margaret Braye entered her father's study with a
calm face. She looked the hot-tempered little knight
squarely in the eyes—anyone seeing them confronting
each other would have wondered to know that they
were really father and daughter.

"You sent for me, father?" she said in a quiet sad
voice.

"Sent for you!" exclaimed Sir Thomas. "Yes, I
should think I did send for you! I've packed that
lying hussy of a French maid out of the house."

Margaret bowed her head.

"It is your house, father," she answered.

"Yes, and by Heaven, I'll be master in it!" vocifer-
ated Sir Thomas. "No more lying and back-stairs
dealing and cheating for me—I'll stamp it out, miss,
I'll warrant you. We'll have an end of deceit, or I'll
know why."

"I am sorry if I have seemed to be deceitful," said
Margaret. "It seemed the only course to adopt, that
which you blame me for."

"Oh, it did, did it?" he sneered. "Oh, indeed!
Preferred to deceive an indulgent father to disappointing a scoundrel that's turned out to be a murderer,
eh?"

A faint glow of colour showed on Margaret
Braye's cheeks, and she drew a step nearer to her
father, and eyed him sternly.

"What do you mean?" she asked, in a low, in-
sistent voice.

"What I say. There's no doubt whatever that man
Wintour murdered his brother—no doubt!"

Margaret's finely-cut lips curled in a contemptuous
smile.

SAUNDERSON'S HOUSEHOLD 151

"That is sheer nonsense!" she said. "And you know it is."

"I know it's nothing of the sort," shouted Sir Thomas, banging the table by which he stood with his clenched fist. "Gerald Wintour will lie in the cells to-night, and he'll have the hangman's rope round his neck at York Castle within three months! And my evidence'll help to hang him! And now, you'll write him a letter throwing him off for ever, d'ye hear?"

Margaret stood staring at him for a moment.

"I shall not do anything of the sort," she answered quietly.

"You will!"

"I say I shall not!"

"But I say you shall!"

Margaret folded her arms and faced him sternly.

"And I say I shall not!" she replied.

They stood staring at each other for a full moment. Then the old man uttered a fearful oath and once more struck the table.

"Leave my house!" he almost screamed. "Leave my house! I'll have no ingrates here, even if they are my own flesh and blood. Go, I say, go—go!"

Margaret walked to the door. With her hand on it she turned.

"I take you at your word," she said. "Good-bye!"

She went upstairs to her own rooms, tearless, outwardly calm and collected. Looking out of her window she saw the departure of Leonie, who, having a very good idea of what was likely to occur, had taken the precaution to pack her trunks in the morning, and had fled as soon as the dog-cart could be got ready.

Margaret watched the dog-cart out of sight, and then, with a sad sigh, began to make her own preparations for departure. From a box-room she fetched two stout portmanteaux, and into them packed what she considered to be most serviceable—she had definite plans in her head as to what she intended to do, and did not trouble herself about taking away with her any of the fine gowns and costumes of which she was the possessor. If her father liked to have them sent after her, well and good; if not, she could do without them. She had a certain amount of money of her own, which had come to her from her mother, and she meant, after what her father had said to her, to remain independent of him.

When Margaret's preparations were made it was nearly evening. Determined to do nothing that could cause any of the servants to fall into disgrace, she resolved on removing her goods herself.

She went down to the gardens, found a wheel-barrow, and took it round to a side door which communicated with her own rooms by a staircase. A strongly-built, athletic young woman, she found no difficulty in carrying one of the portmanteaux downstairs and placing it on the barrow, with which she then set off across the park. There were some cottages outside the park gates which were on the Marchester Royal estates—at one of these she left the portmanteau with a woman, who was stupefied with astonishment to see her, while she went back for the other. And coming back on her second journey with the second portmanteaux, she met Mr. Saunderson, who was just passing the park gates on his way from the village to his house.

Margaret set the shafts of the barrow down and looked at the steward, who, full of astonishment, took off his hat.

"How do you do?" said Margaret. "You are Mr. Saunderson, are you not?"

"I am, miss," replied the steward. "At your service."

"I wonder if you can help me, Mr. Saunderson? I may as well tell you the truth, for everybody will soon know it. My father has turned me out of his house."

"You don't say so, Miss Braye!" exclaimed Mr. Saunderson.

"Yes, it is quite true, and I want to find lodgings for myself. I cannot leave this neighbourhood at present, because I understand that Lord Marchester, to whom I am engaged to be married, is charged with the murder of his brother, and of course I must remain near him. Do you know of anyone who would let me two clean, comfortable rooms, Mr. Saunderson? I have plenty of money—my own money."

Mr. Saunderson heard all this with mingled feelings. He had an itching love of sensation, and his ears tingled.

"Well, Miss Braye," he said. "I'm sorry to hear of a difference between you and Sir Thomas, for——"

Margaret Braye uttered an impatient exclamation.

"Never mind that, Mr. Saunderson, please," she said. "If you can help me——"

"Well, I'll tell you what, miss," said Mr. Saunderson, whose mind had been very active for the past few minutes, "there is only one house hereabouts that has proper accommodation for a young lady like you, and that's mine. Now I have two beautiful rooms—drawing-room and bed-room—which are never used, and you can have them with pleasure. I've also a very capable housekeeper, miss, who's a capital cook, and would look well to your comfort."

"Thank you," said Margaret. "I will accept your offer. What about terms, Mr. Saunderson?"

"Terms?" said the steward vaguely. "Oh—ah, well, we'll discuss the terms as we walk there—I suppose you'll like to go straight there, Miss Braye?"

"Yes, when I've left this portmanteau at the cottage, and made arrangements about sending it and another to your house," answered Margaret. "And I must leave the barrow at the lodge—you see, it isn't mine."

Half an hour later the steward ushered Margaret Braye into his drawing-room. It was growing dusk, and he lighted a lamp which stood on the centre table.

"Now, miss," he said, with hospitable tone, "if you'll be kind enough to sit down, I'll just fetch my housekeeper, Miss Mercer—she's perhaps a bit odd to look at, but she's a very capable woman, and a very good cook, as I've already remarked. I can assure you that she'll do all in her power to make you comfortable, as I shall myself."

"You are very kind indeed, Mr. Saunderson—thank you," said Margaret.

She sat down and looked about her. The room was well and tastefully furnished in old-fashioned style; there were some good pictures and a small collection of books—there was no reason why she should not be thoroughly satisfied with it so far as physical comfort was concerned. And, after all, she could not be lonelier there than she had been in the palatial grandeur of Marchester Abbey.

Mr. Saunderson returned, followed by a woman whom Margaret had never seen before—a woman of extraordinary appearance. The steward bowed to his lodger.

"Miss Braye," he said politely, "this is my housekeeper, Miss Mercer. You behold my entire household."

XIII: REMANDED

CHAPTER XIII

Remanded

MARGARET BRAYE looked at Mr. Saunderson's housekeeper with a feeling in which wonder, curiosity, and a species of fascination were mingled. Although she herself had lived in the neighbourhood for more than a year, she did not remember having seen Miss Mercer before—so curious a personality she would certainly not have forgotten. Now, having given her a polite greeting, she could not refrain from gazing at her as one gazes at something odd.

The housekeeper was a very tall woman, taller than Margaret herself, and she was as thin as she was tall —so thin that she might have been an articulated skeleton dressed in garments. Her face was almost fleshless, and her complexion the colour of old ivory —there was scarcely a trace of colour in her thin, tightly-closed lips. Her hair, rapidly turning grey, was drawn smoothly away from the centre of her forehead and confined at the back of the head in a tightly-plaited knot—it, like everything about her, from the plain, straight-lined black gown to the lace apron which she wore, was prim and formal. Nothing about her seemed alive but her eyes, which were dark and piercing—wells of fire in the placid surface of her parchment face. Margaret could not help wondering if the woman were quite in her right mind— there was something about her which seemed strange and uncanny.

157

"You will find Miss Mercer an admirable house-keeper, Miss Braye," Mr. Saunderson was saying.

"I hope I shall not give Miss Mercer any trouble," replied Margaret. "I am really very easily pleased, Miss Mercer."

A faint smile came to the housekeeper's thin lips.

"I will see that Miss Braye is perfectly comfortable," she said.

The woman's voice seemed to Margaret almost as peculiar as her appearance. The accent and intonation were perfect; it was, without doubt, the voice of a woman of culture and refinement. But it was as colourless as Miss Mercer's face; it sounded to come from a long way off; it was just such a voice as a well-bred skeleton might be supposed to have if a skeleton had a voice at all.

"Oh, I am quite sure you will!" said Margaret.

"Perhaps you would like to see your room?" suggested Miss Mercer, and led the way upstairs.

There Margaret found herself as comfortably lodged as she could desire, and her trunks presently arriving, she proceeded to unpack them, aided by the housekeeper, with whom, during the process of unpacking, she discussed certain arrangements. She was settling down very easily into her new surroundings, she said to herself, and though she was sorely grieved because of the estrangement with her father, she determined to face the situation boldly. Her object in life just then, she felt, was to do something to clear Gerald, and at any rate to be a comfort to him during this time of trouble. She began to wonder how she could get in touch with him.

"Do you think Mr. Saunderson is engaged?" she inquired of the housekeeper later on, when the latter came in to clear Margaret's supper-table. "If he is

REMANDED 159

not I should like to see him for a few minutes—I want to ask his advice."

Miss Mercer left the room, and presently returned, bringing Mr. Saunderson's compliments—would Miss Braye do him the honour to join him in the dining-room?

Mr. Saunderson sat in state in his favourite arm-chair, a large cigar in his mouth, a tumbler of toddy at his elbow. He rose and bowed very politely as his visitor entered, and brought an arm-chair to the corner of the cheery hearth for her. It seemed to Margaret that the steward had a very pretty idea of how to make himself comfortable of an evening.

"I hope I am not intruding upon your privacy, Mr. Saunderson?" said Margaret, as she took the chair which the steward offered her.

Mr. Saunderson treated his visitor and himself to another courtly bow.

"Not at all, Miss Braye, not at all!" he hastened to reply. "No, indeed! I was just saying to myself that you would feel lonely, miss, all by yourself. If at any time it would be a relief to your feelings to indulge in conversation with me, you have only to say the word and I am at your service. Evening," continued Mr. Saunderson, waving his large, fat hand comprehensively, "is with me a period of well-earned repose. I am a hard-working man during the day-time, and when my day's work is done I like to take my ease by my own fireside. I hope you have no objection to tobacco, miss?"

"Oh, none at all, Mr. Saunderson!" replied Margaret. "Yes, I did want to have a little conversation with you. You are, of course, fully acquainted with all these recent sad events?"

Mr. Saunderson sighed.

"Unfortunately, miss, I am," he answered. "Sad events they are! I scarcely realise them. I have been connected with the fortunes of the family and the estates ever since I was a boy, for my father was steward before me, and I never thought to see such a catastrophe. Ah, yes—sad indeed!"

"I am quite sure, Mr. Saunderson, that you do not believe for a moment in Lord Marchester's guilt—it is preposterous to think of such a thing!" said Margaret.

Mr. Saunderson shook his head solemnly, and sipped his toddy, bowing in his visitor's direction as he did so.

"No, Miss Braye, no, I do not," he replied with fervour. "But you speak of Mr. Gerald as Lord Marchester—haven't you heard the latest news?"

"No, what is it?" asked Margaret.

The steward swayed his somewhat corpulent form from side to side, and rolled his head on his plump shoulders.

"Ah!" he said. "It's a sad story, miss. There's an old saying that one should never say aught but what's good of those who are departed, but I cannot but feel that the late Lord Marchester treated me with duplicity—yes, nothing less than duplicity, which is a thing I never could bear in man or woman. You never can tell what human nature is!"

"I do not understand," said Margaret.

Mr. Saunderson groaned.

"The late Lord Marchester was married, miss," he said. "Married unbeknown to anybody—even to me and to Mr. Deckenham, the solicitor from London, both of us old and tried servants."

"Married?" exclaimed Margaret in great surprise. "Why, his brother did not know that."

"As I said, miss, not even me nor Mr. Deckenham knew it, though we were his late lordship's right hands in a way of speaking," said Mr. Saunderson. "No, Mr. Gerald certainly did not know it— until this afternoon."

"But to whom was Lord Marchester married?" asked Margaret.

"Ah, you may well ask that, miss!" sighed Mr. Saunderson. "He was secretly married six years ago, so it appears, to an Italian girl, the sister of that man Peter Vasari, his valet, of whom I have no opinion at all, and never had. He it was that made it all known this afternoon, and I understand that he produced and exhibited papers and documents to Mr. Deckenham and Mr. Gerald which proved that his story was true."

"And is there a son?" inquired Margaret.

"There is, miss. A boy five years old, living with his mother in London. And of course, he is the real Lord Marchester," replied Mr. Saunderson. "I understand, too, that in a will drawn up for the late Lord Marchester by a local attorney, and duly signed and attested, this man Vasari is made the young peer's guardian until he is twenty-one years of age. We all know what that means," concluded the steward mournfully. "The man that was just a valet, a lackey, will be master—master of Marchester Royal."

Margaret was very much astonished, and said so, and Mr. Saunderson shook his head more mournfully than ever.

"Yes, miss, you never can tell what to expect in this wicked world," he said. "I've never had such a shock. Of course, there'll be an end of my stewardship—me and Vasari never did get on, for I've very little opinion of foreigners, and think they should keep

to their own countries, and we've had words more than
once, and he's a revengeful fellow. However, I'm
getting on in years, and I shall be glad to retire.
There's one thing, I'm thankful for, Miss Braye, and
that is that that Italian fellow can't turn me out of
this house. I've got him there!"

"Oh?" said Margaret, who scarcely comprehended
Mr. Saunderson's meaning.

"Yes, miss. This house and the land on which it is
built, and the orchard, garden, and two adjacent fields
are my property," said Mr. Saunderson with pride.
"You see, miss, they form a sort of what they call a
buffer state between the Marchester Royal estate and
the Marchester Abbey property, now your respected
father's. Some years ago, the man who owned this
bit of property—he was a little farmer living in a
tumble-down old house that stood where this house
now stands—wanted to sell and go away to another
part of England where his daughter lived, and he
was going to put the property up to auction. However, I persuaded him to sell it to me by private treaty,
and when I'd got it I pulled the old house down and
built this, with all the latest improvements. And out
of it no Peter Vasaris nor Peter anything else can
turn me!" concluded Mr. Saunderson triumphantly.

"That is nice for you," said Margaret, who, thinking of other things, had only just heard sufficient of
the steward's discourse to understand his meaning. "I
suppose things would have been different if Mr. Wintour had succeeded to the title and estates?" she
added.

"Oh, vastly different miss," replied the steward.
"The family always had implicit faith and confidence
in me."

Margaret remained silent for a moment or two,

thinking over the sudden and curious vagaries of fortune.

"Mr. Saunderson," she said at last, "I don't know much about legal matters—will Mr. Wintour be taken before the magistrates?"

"He will, miss," replied Mr. Saunderson, shaking his head.

"And what will they do?" she asked.

"Why, miss, they will hear the evidence brought forward against him, and then they'll commit him for trial at York Assizes," answered Mr. Saunderson. "At least, they'll commit him if they think the evidence justifies them in doing so."

"And do you think they will consider the evidence strong enough?"

Mr. Saunderson shook his head more solemnly than ever.

"I'm afraid I do, miss," he said. "You see, there's the fact that the pistol which the policeman found, and with which, according to the doctor, the murder was probably committed, was Mr. Gerald's property, though, of course, he says it must have been stolen out of his rooms. Then there's your respected father's, Sir Thomas's evidence, and his woodman, and the evidence of those two labourers, who saw Mr. Gerald leave the library by one of the windows. Ah, I'm afraid the magistrates will find it their duty to send him for trial, miss! You see," concluded Mr. Saunderson, with an air of profound wisdom, "you see, miss, that'll shift the responsibility from their shoulders on to somebody's else—which is what country magistrates always like."

"Will he have to remain in prison until his trial, then?" asked Margaret.

"I'm afraid he will, miss, I'm afraid he will," replied the steward. "Murder, you see, is a very serious charge. Yes, I don't think they'd admit anybody to bail when murder is the charge."

"When will they bring him before the magistrate?" asked Margaret. "And where?"

"I should say to-morrow morning, miss, at Market Fordham," replied Mr. Saunderson. "Let's see—this is Thursday—yes, the bench sits to-morrow. They may get through the case, on the present evidence, to-morrow; they may order a remand."

"I shall go to Market Fordham to-morrow," said Margaret. "I suppose I could get into the court?"

Mr. Saunderson coughed—a cough of respectful deprecation of Margaret's proposal.

"Well, of course, it is not for me to suggest anything to you, miss," he said. "But if I were you, I shouldn't."

"But why not, Mr. Saunderson?"

"Well, miss, it would be a painful thing to all concerned if you were present," said the steward. "You would not like to hear your father give evidence, neither would he like to see you there. And I should say that Mr. Gerald himself, miss——"

"Ah, but I want to see him!" exclaimed Margaret. "I must see him, Mr. Saunderson. I mean to do all in my power to clear him of this abominable charge, and I must see him personally. There are so many things I must know."

"Well, miss," counselled Mr. Saunderson, "Mr. Gerald, of course, will have Mr. Deckenham's advice, and you may be sure he'll leave no stone unturned in his behalf. If I might advise you, I wouldn't go to-morrow, for there'll be nothing but confusion and bustling about—a police-court's no nice place for a young lady. But I'll tell you what, miss—I shall be

going, of course, and I'll take you a letter to Mr.
Gerald and engage to bring one back from him, and
if he is committed to York Castle or remanded here
I'll arrange for you to visit him. I can easily do that,
for I know all the magistrates on the bench. You'll
have much more chance of talking quietly to him in
that way than you would have to-morrow."

So Margaret allowed herself to be persuaded by
Mr. Saunderson, and she spent the remainder of the
evening in writing a long letter to Gerald Wintour
in which she told him of her own doings, of what
she intended to do, and of her unalterable faith and
belief in him and her conviction that all would come
right. This she gave to Mr. Saunderson in the morning with strict injunctions to deliver it into no other
hands than those for which it was intended. And
Mr. Saunderson promised solemnly and departed in
his governess-cart, leaving his lady lodger to spend
a very anxious day.

It was late in the evening when Mr. Saunderson
returned, and he looked tired as he drove into his
little stable-yard. Margaret, who had been on the
look-out for him since the middle of the afternoon, ran
to meet him. His face was rather more solemn than
usual, and her heart sank at sight of it.

"Well, Mr. Saunderson?" she said, expectantly.
"Please tell me—quickly."

"Remanded, miss," answered Mr. Saunderson, "remanded until Tuesday next. If you'll come into the
parlour, miss, I'll tell you all about it."

He threw his reins to the man-of-all-work who
looked after his garden and his stable, and led the
way to the house and the parlour, where, before
entering upon his story, he mixed himself a glass of
whisky and water, remarking that it had been a very

trying day, and that he was much fatigued, and further adding that he was truly thankful that Miss Braye had not gone, for the court had been that full that you couldn't have squeezed an atomy into it. Then, having swallowed half the whisky and water, he pronounced himself better, and fishing in his breast pocket, brought out a note in Gerald's handwriting and duly handed it over to Margaret.

"And as to what was done, miss," he said, "well, I'm sorry to say that the evidence as put before the magistrates did seem very strong. Mr. Deckenham tried to shake the witnesses all he could, but it was no good. Your father, Sir Thomas, was very bitter, miss, very bitter; they had to check him once from the bench. It was a long business, miss, and the magistrates, I understand, were decided to commit him for trial when something new cropped up."

"In his favour?" asked Margaret anxiously.

"Ah, nobody'll know that until Tuesday, miss," replied Mr. Saunderson. "At five o'clock came a telegram from a famous firm of gun-makers in London saying that they could give highly-important evidence in the case, and asking the police to communicate with them. So, of course, the magistrates adjourned—until Tuesday."

"I shall go on Tuesday, Mr. Saunderson," said Margaret. "Don't try to persuade me not to go—the waiting for news to-day has been too awful. I must go!"

Then she went away to read his letter, and to wonder how the man she loved was to be cleared of this awful charge. Tuesday seemed a long, long way off—and when Tuesday came would this new evidence be for him or against him—which?

XIV: COMMITTED FOR TRIAL

CHAPTER XIV

Committed for Trial

DURING the next few days no development of any particular importance took place in what was now known all over the country as the Marchester Royal Mystery.

The murdered man was interred in the family vault in Marchester churchyard, and thousands of people from all round the countryside thronged the appoaches and the village street, probably more out of curiosity to see the dead peer's widow, whose romantic story everybody now knew, than out of respect to the dead peer himself. Certainly they saw little of her, for though she followed her husband's remains to the grave, she was so heavily veiled that nothing could be seen of her features. But the crowds saw that she was a woman of fine figure and a commanding presence, who moved with the subtle grace of the Italian, and they wondered why the late Lord Marchester had kept her hidden away so long.

There was no obscuring veil, however, to hide the new peer from their sight—a fine, sturdy boy of five years old, too young to realise what the ceremony really meant, who stared boldly at the crowds as he passed them, and was declared by many to have the real old Wintour look.

Nor was Mr. Pietro Vasari unseen—his sister on his arm, his nephew holding his other hand, the ex-valet, immaculately clothed in mourning garments of the deepest hue, moved at the head of the procession with dignity and impressiveness. There was the consciousness of power in the lofty glances which he cast around him.

Inspector Skarratt, returned by that time from London, watched the funeral obsequies with observant eyes. He said to himself that whatever else Vasari might be or might be proved to be, he was a consummate man of the world and thoroughly master of himself. His port and behaviour were perfect; he had instantly stepped into his post as guardian to a youthful peer of the realm as if to the manner born. Inspector Skarratt remarked to himself that Vasari would make no mistakes—he would play his part with infinite credit to himself, being much too crafty to commit errors. No one would have reason to complain of him.

"All the same," said Inspector Skarratt, "I don't believe in him, and if I find what I believe I shall find I'll hang him yet. He's a much more likely man than Gerald Wintour."

Then he left the churchyard and went away to scheme and plan, and to collect information. On returning to the district he had not gone back to Marchester Royal, but had taken rooms in the village, feeling that this arrangement would leave him more to himself. Nor had he come down single-handed—two young men, ostensibly of the tourist class, had travelled from King's Cross in the same train, and were now following out his instructions. One was staying in a neighbouring village which had some slight fame as an inland watering-place; the other had put up at the Marchester Arms, giving himself out to be an artist who wished to stay a while in the neighbourhood for the purpose of sketching the old castles and religious houses in its immediate vicinity. Both these

young men rode much about the country on bicycles,
and each was helping Inspector Skarratt to solve a
question which bothered him very much—where did
Pietro Vasari spend the night which intervened between his departure from Whitby and his appearance
at Marchester Royal?

The rooms which Inspector Skarratt had taken for
himself were in an old house tenanted by the widow
of a farmer—an old house standing well away from
the village, and having the great advantage of being
approached from a quiet by-lane. Here he received
the reports of his assistants, who usually came to him
at night, and here he did a good deal of writing, and
a great deal more thinking.

Going straight to his rooms from the funeral ceremony, which took place on the Saturday afternoon
following the murder, Inspector Skarratt found a
bicycle leaning underneath his window, and recognised
it as the property of one of his assistants. He went
into the house and discovered the man who was staying at the little spa comfortably settled in the easiest
arm-chair which the room afforded.

"Good-afternoon, Burton," said Inspector Skarratt,
carefully closing the old oak door of the room.
"Well? Anything?"

Burton, a smart, keen-eyed fellow, who looked anything but a detective in his well-fitting Norfolk jacket
and riding-breeches, rose with alacrity.

"Well, I don't know whether I haven't got something definite, sir," he said. "Anyway, I thought it
well to ride straight here and tell you of it. I'll just
spread out my map on the table—then you can follow
me."

He spread out a large ordnance survey-map of
the district as he spoke, and taking up a pen-holder

from a desk close by, prepared to point certain things out to Inspector Skarratt.

"It struck me this morning," he said, tapping the map with the pen-holder, "that if the man whose movements you are anxious to trace that night came here, he might approach the district by conveyance from some place situated a fair way off. Now you see, sir, here we are—here's Marchester. You see, it's set in what one may call a diamond-shaped frame of railways, and there's at least one town on each of the four sides of the frame that's a posting town, and that could be approached from the direction of Whitby, by changing here or there. I thought I'd try these towns, just to see if I could hear of anybody having engaged a trap in any of them last Tuesday evening. I went to Great Bywold first, and, as luck would have it, I hit on something straight off. Last Tuesday evening, about eight o'clock, a man, who carried no luggage, walked into the hotel-yard near the station, and asked if he could have a conveyance to take him to Wiltonthorpe—that's the village, as you see, sir, at the farther side of Marchester Royal Park. He was driven to the cross-roads there, outside the village, and there he dismissed and paid the driver, remarking that he was a bit cramped, and would walk the rest of the way to get the stiffness out of his legs. The driver thinks they would arrive at the cross-roads about twenty minutes past nine. From the cross-roads to Marchester Royal the distance through the park and the woods is within a mile and a quarter. This may be the man, but unfortunately——"

"Well?" said Inspector Skarratt, seeing that Burton hesitated. "Well?"

"Unfortunately, sir, the only person who saw or noticed him was the man who drove him, and he is not over bright or observant. He describes his fare as a man with a thick, black beard and moustache."

"Might be false," said the Inspector. "Did the driver say in what direction his fare went when he set him down?"

"Yes—towards the village, Wiltonthorpe," replied Burton.

"Very well, go to Wiltonthorpe and find if you can hear anything of such a man. Let me know later," said Inspector Skarratt.

He sat staring at a map of his own when Burton had gone, speculating and theorising.

It would have been an easy matter for Vasari on leaving Whitby to alter his journey in several directions, and to have finally turned up in disguise at Great Bywold. It would be dusk by the time the conveyance set him down at the cross-roads outside Wiltonthorpe, and anyone knowing the district as he did would have no difficulty in reaching Marchester Royal through park and woods by pathways which at that hour would be in absolute solitude. Yes—Vasari's whereabouts on that fatal night must be finally ascertained.

But there was one fact in this mysterious case which Inspector Skarratt confessed himself utterly unable to understand. He had thought of it over and over again, and he could get no nearer to any clear solution.

Why was that particular duelling-pistol used in committing the crime?

This was beyond Inspector Skarratt, and he confessed it readily. Why use that pistol when any modern revolver would have effected the murderer's purpose just as well? There was some significance attached to that pistol—what was it?

"Well, I shall have to hear what these gun-makers say on Tuesday," he said to himself. "They may throw some light on the matter."

The magistrates' court at Market Fordham was packed when that Tuesday morning came. People of all degrees had trooped in from every quarter of the countryside; the market-square in front of the Town Hall was as crowded from one side to the other as if the occasion had been that of the annual Statutes Hiring Fair.

Inspector Skarratt, from his coign of vantage, looked round the court and felt himself whimsically speculative as to why all these people should be so frantically anxious to see a fellow-being charged with the commission of the most heinous of crimes.

To him, following the exercise of his profession as he did, with keen interest, there was something strange in the expression of the faces which looked down from the gallery or were dimly seen in the dark recesses beneath it. There were several fashionable women of the county family class on the bench; they were armed with scent-bottles and lorgnettes, and something in their faces made the Inspector think of old engravings which he had seen in print-shops—engravings of eighteenth century squires sitting round a cockpit watching two feathered bipeds tear each other to death. . . .

There was a rustle and a commotion in the court—Inspector Skarratt, who had been making notes, looked up and saw Miss Braye, attended by Mr. Saunderson, advancing to a seat near the solicitor's table—a seat next to that occupied by Mr. Deckenham, who, evidently expecting her, shook hands warmly with her and seemed to speak some reassuring words to her. She was very pale, but perfectly com-

posed, and, after glancing round the Court, she entered
into an animated conversation with the old solicitor
on one side, and with Mr. Saunderson on the other.

The women on the bench fixed their lorgnettes upon
her; she took no heed. Nor did she betray any consciousness of her father's presence. Sir Thomas
Braye, a monument of Spartan virtue, faced her from
the other side of the well of the court; once her eyes
swept his face with cold indifference and turned away
to look at other things.

Never in the history of police proceedings at Market Fordham had there been such a full bench of
magistrates as there was that morning. When they
filed in, led by their chairman, a well-known sporting
peer, who looked as if he would much rather have
been lying in a ditch with a broken leg than occupying his present position, there proved to be so many
of them that the curious and inquisitive ladies who
had been favoured with seats under the insignia of
justice had to move to the rear. One of the local
police-inspectors, sitting next to Inspector Skarratt, remarked *sotto voce,* that he never remembered seeing
so many magistrates gathered together before, except
of course, at Quarter Sessions. He added to that that
—also of course—it was not often they had such an interesting case as this seemed to be about to prove.

And then, amidst a sudden hush, Gerald Wintour
was in the dock, and the attention of everybody was
centred on the man upon whom such strange and
mysterious vicissitudes of fortune had fallen in such
an incredibly short space of time. He himself showed
no consciousness of the curious glances turned upon
him; he bowed formally to the magistrates and took
the seat which the chairman indicated by a word and
a nod.

Margaret Braye, leaning forward over the solicitors' table, scarcely heard the few words in which the barrister who had been sent down by the Treasury reopened the case. She was all impatience to hear the evidence of the gunsmiths, whose telegram had caused the remand of the previous Thursday—would that evidence help Gerald, or would it not?

"Your worships will have it in recollection," began the barrister, "that——"

Another sense of commotion, of curiosity amongst the crowded assemblage. From a door on one side of the bench an official conducted Signor Pietro Vasari, clad in immaculate black broadcloth and equally immaculate white linen, and carrying a glossy silk hat and gold-mounted umbrella. The ex-valet tip-toed to a seat facing Margaret Braye at the solicitors' table —his manner was quiet and full of respect to the court and his surroundings.

"—that on Thursday last a telegram was received by the police here from Messrs. Webb & Britford, gun-makers, of the Haymarket, London, which was to the effect that they believed they could throw some light on the matter of the old duelling-pistol with which it is practically certain the late Lord Marchester was shot, and your worships adjourned the proceedings until to-day in consequence. I now propose to put the senior member of the firm into the witness-box—call Alexander John Webb."

A smartly-dressed, keen-eyed, business-looking man stepped into the box, and was duly sworn. He acknowledged himself as Alexander John Webb, senior partner of the firm of Webb & Britford, gun-smiths and makers of firearms, of the Haymarket, London.

"Your firm is one of the oldest-established in England, Mr. Webb."

"It is. It was established in the year 1731."

"You consider yourselves experts in anything re-
lating to guns, firearms, pistols, revolvers, and so
on?"

"We consider that we have a just claim to be considered experts—because of our long experience."

"Just so. Oblige me by looking at this pistol.
What is it?"

"It is an old duelling-pistol, made, without doubt,
by Andrea del Sarte, a famous Italian gunsmith of
Milan, who died about 1785. Here is his well-known
mark—on the side of the butt."

"Mr. Webb, have you ever seen that pistol before?"

In the dead silence which followed Inspector Skarratt quietly took out his notebook and his pencil. Like
everybody else he listened for all he was worth to
the expert's answer.

"Yes—I have!"

"When and where have you seen it? Tell the court
the circumstances in your own words."

"Very good, sir. This pistol was delivered at our
establishment early in April last. It came by parcel
post, packed in cotton-wool in a cigar box, which I
produce—this is it. It had been posted at the Burling-
ton House post-office in Piccadilly, that morning. It
was accompanied by a typewritten letter which I also
produce—this letter. The letter simply requests us
to put the pistol in working order, and to hold it until
instructions are sent for its delivery. It is signed
Gerald Wintour, and the address given is 105a,
Jermyn Street, S. W."

There was such a buzz of excitement over this announcement that the chairman was obliged to call for
order. The prosecuting barrister spoke.

"You recognised the name—the signature?"

"Oh, quite well, though we had never done any work for Mr. Wintour before."

"Please continue your statement."

"We repaired the pistol—that is, we put it in working order. About three weeks ago—that is, on the 27th April—we received another typewritten letter with the same signature, instructing us to send the pistol to Mr. Wintour by return of post, the address given being Marchester Royal, Market Fordham, Yorkshire. This we did, the same day. Since then we have heard nothing of the pistol until these proceedings."

"On your oath, Mr. Webb, are you positively certain that the pistol you now hold in your hands is the one of which you have been speaking?"

"I am absolutely certain. If you wish for proof, here is my private mark upon it."

The prosecuting barrister sat down—Mr. Webb stepped out of the witness-box. Mr. Deckenham was about to rise when he felt a note thrust into his hand. He opened it mechanically and read:

"On no account ask a single question or do anything—I have a clue—SKARRATT."

And Mr. Deckenham passed the note on to Gerald Wintour, and sat down again.

Five minutes later Gerald Wintour heard himself formally committed for trial at the ensuing York Assizes. He made no remark.

As the court cleared amidst a whirl of excited comment, Margaret Braye found Inspector Skarratt at her side. He addressed her with deep respect.

"Miss Braye," he said. "I must see you and Mr. Wintour at once, with Mr. Deckenham. Come this way, Mr. Deckenham—come this way, Miss Braye."

XV: INSPECTOR SKARRATT IS BUSY

CHAPTER XV

Inspector Skarratt is Busy

IT was soon apparent that Inspector Skarratt, fore-
seeing certain eventualities, had already made arrangements with the local authorities for the interview
of which he spoke. Within a few minutes he and
his two companions found themselves face to face with
Gerald Wintour in a quiet room at the back of the
Town Hall, where, the Chief Constable was gracious
enough to inform them, they might remain undisturbed
for half an hour. There were two policemen in attendance on the prisoner; the Chief Constable was
further inclined towards graciousness by ordering
them to remain outside the door.

The man who had just been committed for trial
seemed calmer than ever. He and Margaret em-
braced each other in silence; then Gerald gave
his hand to Mr. Deckenham and to Inspector
Skarratt. He unrolled the crumbled note which the
Inspector had passed to Mr. Deckenham, and the latter had passed on to the prisoner. He looked from it
to Inspector Skarratt with a puzzled air.

"I'm sure you had some good reason for writing
this, Inspector," he said. "Otherwise I wanted Mr.
Deckenham to put a few questions. You say you have
a clue—does that mean that you have reason to suspect some person other than myself of my brother's
murder?"

"It does, sir," said Inspector Skarratt.

"Good reason?" asked Gerald.

"I believe it to be an excellent reason, sir. But at present I don't want to discuss it. I have hit on a trail, and I am following it up; I believe I shall have a good deal of valuable information presently. And that is the reason—and I want to impress this upon you, Miss Braye, and upon you, Mr. Deckenham— why for the present I do not wish to do anything to direct suspicion from you. It may seem a hard thing to do, but for the present you must be content to lie under that suspicion. I honestly believe that before your trial comes off at York I shall be able to clear you by producing the real culprit. That is why I begged Mr. Deckenham not to ask any questions. Otherwise, of course, there are certain questions which are obvious."

"Well—did you send any typewritten letter with your signature attached to Messrs. Webb & Britford?"

"Never!"

"Then I may add to my notes in this case that your signature to those letters—purporting to be yours, rather—was a forgery?"

"Most certainly."

"That we can establish at the trial. You saw the signature, didn't you, Mr. Deckenham?"

The old solicitor sighed and shook his head.

"Yes," he answered, "and so did Miss Braye. They're marvellous—I should have said it was your handwriting, Mr. Wintour."

"So should I," said Margaret. "Do you think you ever scribbled your name on any sheets of typewritten paper, and left them lying about, Gerald?"

Gerald Wintour smiled.

"No, never!" he said. "The signatures, however clever they may be, are forgeries, and their cleverness only serves to show what a clever scoundrel he is or scoundrels they are who has or have worked up this plot. For plot it is, without doubt—an abominable plot!"

"Just tell me one or two things more, Mr. Wintour," said Inspector Skarratt, still busy with his note-book, which he kept in a peculiar shorthand only translatable by himself. "Have you a typewriting machine?"

"I have."

"Where is it—at your chambers or your rooms?"

"As a matter of fact I have two—one at my chambers, one in Jermyn Street."

"What makes are they?"

"Both Remingtons."

"I suppose there's a clerk at your chambers, isn't there, Mr. Wintour?"

"Oh, yes—I share him with a fellow barrister, Mr. Sinclair."

"Very good. Now another question—on what date did you arrive at Marchester Royal?"

After thinking for a few moments, Gerald replied that it was on the 25th April.

"That was two days before the second typewritten letter was received in London by Webb & Britford?"

"I suppose it was."

Inspector Skarratt turned to Mr. Deckenham.

"The most remarkable thing about this pistol business is the daring of the man, whoever he is, who engineered it," he said. "First of all, he seems to have been absolutely determined that the crime should be committed with this particular weapon. Then he takes elaborate pains to connect Mr. Wintour with the repairing of the pistol—I am going, of course, on the hypothesis that the real culprit stole that pistol out of Mr. Wintour's rooms——"

Gerald started.

"Ah, so you, too, have formed that conclusion?" he said.

"Certainly," replied Inspector Skarratt. "Well, now, look at his daring in having the parcel, openly addressed to Mr. Wintour, at Marchester Royal. One fact, since we hold Mr. Wintour is innocent, is plain—that parcel was intercepted. And the man who intercepted it, whoever he may be, is the murderer. We must find him. That parcel can be traced to a certain point—the point where it was duly delivered at Marchester Royal. Now—who got it?"

"I suppose we can get some information on that point?" observed Mr. Deckenham. "Mountford, I should think, could tell us something about the arrangements for letters and parcels."

"I can do that myself," said Gerald. "There is only one delivery of parcels a day at Marchester Royal—about nine o'clock in the morning, an hour after the first delivery of letters."

"How many deliveries of letters are there, then?" inquired Inspector Skarratt.

"Two—one at eight, one at four in the afternoon."

"Are there usually a good many parcels delivered at Marchester Royal, Mr. Wintour?"

Gerald Wintour considered this question.

"Well," he replied, "you must remember that for some years I have only been an occasional visitor at Marchester Royal, so I cannot speak positively as to the average number of parcels received there. I should say from what I have seen that a good many arrived each day—my brother did a good deal of what one might call small shopping from London."

"Just so," said Inspector Skarratt. "Now, I wonder if you could tell me something respecting which

I don't want to make any inquiries at Marchester Royal. Do you know to whom parcels are delivered, and what is done with them by the person who receives them?"

"Yes," replied Gerald, readily enough. "I can inform you on those points quite easily. They are received by either the footman or the under-footman, whichever happens to be in the hall. Anything for the household they take to the persons to whom the parcel, or parcels, is addressed; anything for my brother or his guests is placed on a table in the inner hall. Parcels for my brother, for instance, would be fetched by his man, Vasari, and opened by him; if there were any guests there—well, I suppose the footman might take their parcels to their rooms or let them take them themselves."

"Did you ever have any parcels sent to Marchester Royal, Mr. Wintour?"

"Never anything much besides an occasional book from my booksellers or some small articles which I needed from town."

"Anybody in the house could have appropriated any parcel lying on that table in the inner hall?"

"Oh, I should say so—yes."

"Well, you never received any parcel from Webb & Britford, did you, because you never gave them any instructions to send one? At the same time, it is certain, without a possibility of doubt, that Webb & Britford did address to you a parcel at Marchester Royal, which parcel contained the duelling-pistol with which your brother was shot. Now, there can be very little doubt—none, really—that that parcel was delivered at Marchester Royal; things don't go wrong very often in the Post Office—only now and then. Since the probability is practically assured that it was delivered at the door, and since it is certain that you never had it, it is quite obvious that somebody in the house immediately appropriated it. I am going to find out, Mr. Wintour, who did appropriate that parcel—when I have found out the thief I shall also have found out your brother's murderer."

Gerald Wintour looked long and earnestly at the detective.

"I wish you would tell me, Inspector, if you suspect any particular person?" he said.

"Frankly I do," answered Inspector Skarratt. "But at present I do not intend to say whom I suspect. I am at work. I've learnt a good deal from what you tell me about the parcels, and now I've no more to ask you, sir. But I want to give you and Mr. Deckenham some advice—keep as quiet as you can about your line of defence until the trial comes off at York Assizes. What counsel do you propose to instruct, Mr. Deckenham?"

Mr. Deckenham shook his head and sighed.

"Really!" he said. "Really—I hadn't thought of that so far. We've never been mixed up with criminal matters in our practice, and I'm so bewildered and troubled that I scarcely know what—"

"Yes, but that sort of feeling is no good, sir," interrupted Inspector Skarratt. "You have to think of your client here. Remember, there's a strong *prima facie* case against him, and it will take some upsetting. I suggest that you retain Sir Andrew Kenrick at once. He's the man—as I'm sure Mr. Wintour will readily agree."

"Yes, I quite agree," said Gerald.

"Very good," assented Mr. Deckenham. "And we'd better have Mr. Palethorpe as well."

"That's good, too," said Inspector Skarratt.

"Well, that's all I've got to say—I'd just like a word or two with you outside, Mr. Deckenham, if you don't mind. I thought perhaps the two young people would like a few minutes together," he added, when they had left the cell. "They're sure to have something to say to each other."

Mr. Deckenham wiped his forehead, and sighed more profoundly than ever.

"Ah!" he said. "It's a very sad affair—I'm terribly upset by it. Do you really mean that you suspect somebody? I haven't seen or heard anything that has given me the slightest clue."

"Aye, but I have, sir," replied the Inspector, smiling. "Leave it to me, Mr. Deckenham. I'll make those two young people happy yet."

Inside the cell the two young people were in each other's arms.

"You won't lose hope or courage, Gerald?" said Margaret, after a long silence.

"No, dear—not for one moment. It is all a most remarkable mystery to me, but I expect the problem to be solved. I believe that man Skarratt is genuinely anxious to save me, and that he has some clue; he is a smart, clever fellow. But never mind that now— I want to know about you, Margaret, dearest. I noticed that though your father was in court just now, you never seemed to acknowledge his presence, and, stranger than all, that you sat by and were in apparently close conversation with Mr. Saunderson. What does that mean?"

Margaret gave him a brief account of what had happened between herself and her father, and of her arrangements with the steward.

"I am perfectly comfortable, Gerald," she said. "Mr. Saunderson is thoughtfulness itself, and his housekeeper already understands all my needs and requirements. I shall not leave the neighbourhood until this trouble is over, and then——"

"Yes—and then?" he said, seeing that she paused. "What then?"

"Then I suppose we shall be married and go away to India to your appointment," she answered quietly. "I shall be glad to go, dear."

When these two parted, five minutes later, Margaret found Inspector Skarratt waiting in the corridor. He lifted his hat politely.

"I should like to have a few minutes' conversation with you, Miss Braye," he said. "The churchyard is close by here—do you mind turning in there for a little while? I promised Mr. Saunderson that you will meet him in the market-place in half an hour."

Margaret assented to this proposal readily, and they left the Town Hall and went into the tree-shaded churchyard together.

"Miss Braye," said Inspector Skarratt, "I am known amongst my colleagues as being something of an impulsive man. I have been even called decidedly rash, not to say eccentric. I want to do something now which some people would call both rash and impulsive, but which I believe to be a wise thing to do —a very wise thing."

"Yes, Mr. Skarratt?" said Margaret, wonderingly. "May I ask what it is?"

"Yes, I want to take you into my confidence."

"To take me—into your confidence? But—why?"

"There are two reasons, and both good, Miss Braye," replied Inspector Skarratt. "One is an obvious one—that it is always well to confide in some second person (granted that you can trust that person) ; the other, that I particularly wish to confide in you."

"But why in me?" asked Margaret.

"I have intuitions," answered the detective. "I rather believe in my intuitions. I feel that I shall do well to confide in you. First of all, I am assured of your honesty and sincerity; second—and most important—you want to save the man you love. Thirdly, you may be useful to me."

"You may confide in me, then, Mr. Skarratt. I shall never reveal to anyone anything you may tell me, unless you give me permission to tell my husband of it—later, when all this is over."

"That of course I would, Miss Braye,"—heartily, "Thank you. Very well—I suspect Pietro Vasari of being the murderer of the late Lord Marchester, and I hope to bring him to justice. The proof of Vasari's guilt will be the proofs of Mr. Wintour's innocence."

"But—oh, that is a dreadful theory, Mr. Skarratt! The murderer of his sister's husband! Do you mean it? And he so—well, you know how sincerely grieved he seemed to be this morning, in a quiet, self-possessed way. Ah, that seems a dreadful thing indeed!"

"Miss Braye, if you had seen and known as much of crime as I have, you would be surprised at nothing!" said the Inspector. "One of the coldest-blooded, most callous murderers I ever knew was a benevolent-looking old gentleman whom you would not have thought capable of hurting a fly, and Vasari is scarcely that. But never mind that—such is my theory. I want you to help me. May I ask—have you ever been in Italy, and can you speak Italian?"

"I have been in Italy often, and I do speak Italian, Mr. Skarratt."

"If I want you to go over to Antignano, near

Naples, to make a few enquiries for me, will you go, Miss Braye? It is for Mr. Wintour's sake?"

"Do you think me capable of doing what you wish?"

"Certainly—the very person to do it!"

"Then, of course, yes, I will go—at any time."

"That's right," said Inspector Skarratt. "I shall let you know. Now I will go home to my lodgings. I expect news. Thank you, Miss Braye."

When the Inspector reached his lodgings he found a very dirty envelope lying on his table, which had been delivered by the afternoon post. The thin, creased, whitey-brown sheet inside bore the following scrawl in pencil;

"Guverner,—If so be as you wants to know a bit about that afare at the big house, come to Dead Man's Tree in Middle Spinney to-nite at ten. Don't be afeard."

XVI: THE POACHER

CHAPTER XVI

The Poacher

INSPECTOR SKARRATT was not the man to dis-
regard any clue, however slight, or of whatever
doubtful character as regards its origin, and he at once
determined to keep the appointment made for him by
the writer of the illiterate scrawl which lay before
him. And after darkness had set in over the village
and its orchards and coppices, he slipped out of his
room and went off in the direction of the rendezvous,
the exact situation of which he had readily ascertained
from his own private copy of the ordnance map for
that district.

It was very quiet, and very dark in the woods which
the Inspector traversed—so quiet that the faint rustle
of the leaves stirred by the winds, or the sharp crackle
of a dry twig snapping under his feet in the narrow
paths, seemed to make echoes in the deep silence.

If Inspector Skarratt had been a man of over-
abundant imagination, he might have fancied all manner of things in that nocturnal ramble, for to the
fanciful nothing is so productive of uncanny imagin-
ings, not to say fears and qualms, as a dark night and
a thick wood. There were whisperings and murmur-
ings, ghostly and elusive, all round him, and once or
twice an owl uttered its mournful plaint in some far-
off recess. Inspector Skarratt paid no heed to anything except to keep on the tortuous, scarcely-developed
track which would lead him to his unknown corres-
pondent.

He came to the appointed meeting-place exactly as the clock in Marchester church-tower struck half-past ten. He found himself in a tiny clearing in the midst of which stood what seemed to be, so far as the darkness would allow him to make out, an ancient oak which appeared to have been struck by lightning.

There was a rattling of metal in the branches of this tree, whose leafless, skeleton-like form he saw outlined dimly against the dark sky above, and after listening carefully to it for a minute or two he came to the conclusion that it proceeded from something in the nature of chains or of loose bars of iron linked together.

"Very likely somebody was hanged in chains in this old tree many a long year ago," mused Inspector Skarratt. "It's just the sort of place they'd choose. Now, I wonder if this chap's going to be punctual?"

He leant back against the gnarled trunk of the oak, and for a moment thought of lighting a cigar, but refrained on reflecting that its aroma would extend far in that atmosphere and might bring observation upon him which neither he—and presumably the man he expected to meet—would care to have. And as he made the heroic determination to deny himself of tobacco, he heard the faintest crackle of a snapped twig, the merest rattle of leaves, behind him, and then a man's voice spoke in a hoarse whisper:

"Guv'nor!"

"Well?" replied Inspector Skarratt also in a whisper.

"Are yer alone? Y'ain't got nobody with yer—no cops, guv'nor?"

"I am entirely alone," answered Inspector Skarratt. "Are you?"

A laugh, as hoarse as the man's voice, was the reply to this.

"Not very likely I should have anybody with me, guv'nor!" said the unseen. "I don't know anybody as I could have with me. But as you're alone and evidently disposed to treat me square, I'll come out and we'll begin our bit of talk, though keep your voice down, guv'nor, for there's keepers about in these woods, and now along o' this murder there may be pleecemen, too, and I can assure you, guv'nor, I don't want to have no truck with either of 'em."

A human shape had come out of the brushwood—that of a big, burly man, of whom Inspector Skarratt could see little except that he possessed very broad shoulders and uncommonly long arms, and slouched rather than walked. He came up to the tree, and, leaning one hand on it, approached his face close to the inspector's, and tried to see it in the darkness.

"Yes, that's you, guv'nor," he said, in his hoarse, throaty whisper. "I seen you when you was down here two year ago about the disappearance of them shiners; seen you more than once at that time, I did."

"Who are you?" demanded Inspector Skarratt.

"Well, guv'nor, if you want my full monicker, it's a bit of a rum 'un," answered the man, with another hoarse laugh. "It's Wellington Nelson Cooper, as every policeman round here knows—my old dad, d'ye see, has been both soldier and sailor in his day, and he'd a great admiration for them two distinguished heroes as he called me after."

"Well, what are you?" asked the detective.

"Like many another man, guv'nor," replied Cooper, with a chuckle, "I've two trades. To the world I'm a hedger and ditcher, and a smart hand at it, too, when I like to work, which I don't always. To myself, I'm a poacher—and a smarter hand at that than at hedging and ditching, which is saying a good deal. I ain't never been copped yet—and I don't mean to be, what's more."

"What have you got to tell me?" asked Inspector Skarratt.

"What I've got to tell you, guv'nor," replied Cooper, "I'm not going to tell you here. If you'll trust me you shall come to no harm, and I, in return, shall expect you to keep a bit of a secret which I wouldn't like letting out for as much gold as there is in the Bank of England, for it would spoil my pet diversion. Is it a bargain, guv'nor?"

"It is," replied Inspector Skarratt.

"Then follow me," said the poacher. "Don't say a word until I give you leave, and walk as if you were a cat stepping on a Turkey carpet. This way, guv'-nor—this way."

Cooper slipped into the brushwood again, and the detective followed him, to find his feet treading a narrow pathway which wound away in a direction at right angles to that by which he had approached the meeting-place.

The undergrowth through which they penetrated was thick and low; here and there they were obliged to bend almost double in order to pass beneath the branches. The poacher, in spite of his ungainly slouch and heavily-fashioned figure, moved along with a silence and rapidity which astonished his companion. Now and then he paused, putting a hand behind him to keep Inspector Skarratt back—it was evident that during these pauses he was listening intently.

They proceeded in this fashion, alternately pressing forward, alternately pausing, for what the detective judged to be half a mile; then the poacher stopped longer than usual. He turned and approached his lips close to Inspector Skarratt's ear.

"There's a grass lane to be crossed here, guv'-nor," he whispered, "and it's just about the time the keepers come along it. Keep quiet a bit."

Inspector Skarratt became motionless. Some minutes passed—then Cooper tapped his companion on the arm.

"They're coming," he said in a scarcely audible whisper.

The Inspector heard nothing just then, but he presently heard the thud of heavy footsteps, evidently falling upon the grass. He recognised distinctly the sound of two men, walking quickly and in step, and the scent of strong, acrid tobacco, was wafted to his nostrils.

"Easy enough to outwit that lot," said Cooper. "You wouldn't catch me smoking when I'm on my little job. Come on, guv'nor."

Having crossed the grass road, the poacher led his companion through more devious paths beneath the brushwood for some distance. The ground began to fall away; they at last made a steep descent, and came out on what seemed to be a natural terrace on the edge of the wood. Somewhere far beneath him in the darkness Inspector Skarratt heard the brawling of a river.

"You'll have to get on your hands and knees, guv'-nor, for a few yards," whispered the poacher, dropping to the ground himself. "Follow me."

It seemed to Inspector Skarratt that they squirmed through a very thick cluster of bramble-bushes, then beneath an equally thick carpet of bracken, then into a narrow passage, the floor of which, much to his relief, was covered with fine sand.

"What's this?" he inquired of Cooper, whose boots he could feel.

"It's a cave, guv'nor, which is only known to me," replied the poacher. "Don't you be afeared—you're all right. It's only a yard or so farther—there, now you can get on to your feet."

Inspector Skarratt gladly resumed a perpendicular position. As he rose to his feet Cooper struck a light and applied it to a lanthorn; in its yellow glare the detective saw that they were standing in a natural cave, some ten feet in height and fifteen in length, and breadth, the walls of which were of grey rock. The interior bore many evidences of occupancy and showed distinctly the calling of its occupant. Nets hung festooned from the rough walls; snares of all sorts stood on the ledges; all the paraphernalia of the poacher's trade was there. There was a rude couch formed of old cushions and rugs on one side of the cave, and near it was a roughly-fashioned cupboard. Cooper pointed to each in succession.

"Sit you down, guv'nor," he said. "You can smoke here, for nobody would smell it outside—we're too far in. And if you'd like anything to eat and drink I've victuals and liquor in the cupboard there. I always keep cheese and bread and a meat pie and a bottle of rum here—they come in handy."

Inspector Skarratt declined meat or drink, but accepted the invitation to sit down and to smoke. The poacher having mixed himself a stiff dose of rum and water in a cracked tumbler, took a hearty pull at it, and sitting down on the sand-strewn floor near the Inspector, took out a well-blackened clay pipe and filled it with loose tobacco, which he extracted from his waistcoat pocket. Inspector Skarratt let him take his own time in telling what he had to tell; it was a principle of his never to hurry any man.

"Well, guv'nor, about this here murder business," said Cooper, when he had got his pipe well alight. "I can tell you something that in my opinion will more than likely be useful to you, and I'll begin at the beginning. You must know, guv'nor, that I live with my old mother and a sister of mine in a cottage not so very far away from where those two men live what gave their evidence about Mr. Gerald coming out of the libr'y window on the night of the murder; in fact, they're my nearest neighbours. Now, of course, I've been a poacher for years, especially since I got to know of this cave, the secret of which was given to me by an old chap on his death-bed, as was an old hand at the game himself. I don't come out every night—it depends on the seasons—but when I do I gen'rally make for this cave by a short cut through the grounds and gardens at Marchester Royal. And that's what I did on the night that the young lord was done for."

Cooper paused to take another pull at his rum and water and to press the tobacco into the bowl of his pipe.

"It was getting on to half-past ten when I left home that night," he continued. "I slipped across the park and through the spinney, and across that there Eyetalian garden, dodging from bush to bush. There wasn't a light to be seen anywhere on that side of the house, however, but in the libr'y windows, what was all lighted. Well, I was creeping along under the terrace wall, between it and them laurel bushes, when I heard somebody coming along in the opposite direction, and presently in the light from the libr'y I catches sight of them two neighbours of mine, as was taking a short cut, too. Now, I'd no mind that they should see me, so I dodges as sharp as a weasel behind a thick bush. Just then I heard a sharp click on the terrace, and peeping round, I sees Mr. Gerald, just exactly as they said, come out of one of the libr'y windows and walk along the terrace to the right. These here two chaps they bob their heads down until he'd gone out of view; then they scuttled along past me—never seeing me, mind ye, guv'nor—and went off in the spinney direction."

"Their evidence, then, was quite true?" asked Inspector Skarratt.

"True as we're sitting here, guv'nor," replied Cooper. "Oh, yes, true enough. Well, now I goes on—the other way. I wasn't going to this cave, though—what I was after that night was to visit some snares that I'd set. I might be about an hour going round them snares—I got precious little out of them that night, guv'nor!—and then I went back by the same way I'd come. Well, now, guv'nor, you must follow me close as regards what I see on my way home. D'yer know which Low Bottom Wood is?"

"Yes—the wood that bounds the park on the side you were returning from," replied Inspector Skarratt.

"You're right, guv'nor," said the poacher. "Very well, I was going through Low Bottom Wood towards that part, and had just got to within a few yards of the stile between the wood and the park, when I hears somebody coming from the direction of the house. Whoever it was was walking at a rare lick—seemed to be running, in fact. Nat'rally, I took good care to lay low, but, being of a curious and inquiring nature about folks who are out at that time o' night, I also took just as good care to be as near to that stile

as I could get with safety to myself. In a minute
up comes a man, panting and blowing as if he was
in the violentest hurry. He tumbled over that stile
more than climbed it proper, and he said something
that sounded like swearing, but I couldn't understand
it, because it was in one of them foreign languages."

"A foreign language?"

"Yes, guv'nor, a foreign language, and I know
which foreign language, too—Eyetalian. I knew it
'cause I've heard it spoken by the valet at the big
house, Peter Vasari. And it was Peter Vasari hisself,
guv'nor, as got over that there stile in such a mort
of a hurry."

"How do you know that, seeing that it was so
dark?" asked the Inspector.

"Because, guv'nor, as soon as the man got over
the stile, he stopped and struck a light. He sat down
on the step of the stile for a minute and pulled out a
railway guide—one o' them little penny books that
they sell at Market Fordham. And, of course, I saw
his face plain enough as he held the match to the
book, and I never saw a man look in such a way in my
born days. He was white as a mork! And I saw
something else, guv'nor—worse than that!"

"Well?" said Inspector Skarratt.

Cooper leant nearer to his listener and spoke in a
lower voice.

"Blood!" he said. "Blood, guv'nor—on his
fingers."

"You're sure of that?"

"As sure as that I see yer, guv'nor, a-sitting there
before me. And see, here's the proof!"

Cooper suddenly dived a hand into his breast-
pocket and produced a dirty envelope, from which he
brought out a small local time-table, interleaved with

blank pages. This he passed over to the Inspector. "Look at that, guv'nor," he said. "You'll find bloodmarks on every page that he touched. He'd piled up two or three wax matches to see by on the step of the stile, and he was in that hurry to get the right page that he kept wetting his finger and thumb —guv'nor there was blood on all his fingers!"

"What did he do in the end?" asked Inspector Skarratt.

"Said something that sounded very bad in Eyetalian, guv'nor, flung this here little book away, and rushed off down the path as if the Old 'un had been at his heels," replied Cooper.

"Could he have got to any railway station that way?"

"He could, guv'nor, that path takes into the road for Long Belford, three miles off—it's a short cut."

"What did you do?"

"Waited until he'd clean gone, guv'nor; then sought and found the little book and went home," answered the poacher.

Inspector Skarratt put the time-table in his pocket; knocked off the ashes of his cigar, and rose.

"Let's be going," he said. "It's late, and I must go to London first thing in the morning. In my absence, Cooper—not a word to any person living of what you have told me!"

XVII: THE TWISTED SEMI-COLON

CHAPTER XVII

The Twisted Semi-Colon

LATE as it was when Inspector Skarratt left the poacher, and tired out as he was by the events of the day, his mind was busily occupied as he walked home through the silence of the gloomy woods. It seemed to him that the chain of evidence against Pietro was becoming stronger. He saw no reason to doubt the truth of Cooper's statement; it was impossible to deny that it fitted in with what had been told him by his assistant, Burton, with regard to the Italian's movements on the night of the murder. Just to refresh his memory he ran over the points against Vasari, checking them off on his fingers as he walked along.

First, no one could deny that, in view of Vasari's relationship to the late Lord Marchester, and of the terms of the will executed by the dead peer, the ex-valet was placed for at any rate sixteen years in a position of great influence, which he could most certainly turn to his own personal advantage in several ways.

Secondly, it was not true, as he had alleged, that he left Whitby on the morning after the murder.

Thirdly, it was true beyond doubt that he did leave Whitby in the afternoon of the day on which the murder was committed and returned to the neighbourhood of Marchester Royal, acting in such a fashion as to give reasonable grounds for suspicion.

Fourthly, if Cooper's evidence were strictly veracious, there could be no doubt whatever that Vasari came from Marchester Royal a very short time after the murder, according to evidence, had been committed; that he was in a state of considerable agitation, and that his fingers were stained with blood, which stains had been transferred to the pages of the little local time-table which Inspector Skarratt carried carefully in his inner pocket.

Fifthly, Vasari by reason of his visit to Gerald Wintour's rooms in Jermyn Street, had had access to the case of old duelling-pistols.

Sixthly, Vasari, by reason of his position in the household at Marchester Royal, had the opportunity of intercepting any parcel which would, in his knowledge, arrive at a certain hour on a certain day, and could therefore easily secure the pistol.

Now the question as to why that particular pistol was used, when any modern revolver would have answered the murderer's purpose just as well, was by this time causing less concern to Inspector Skarratt than it had done even a few hours before.

He was reconstructing for himself his own theory and suggestion of the crime, and it seemed to him that if Vasari did commit it he carried out his purpose in such a fashion as to throw the blame, with deliberate intent, on Gerald Wintour. He would know that, found guilty of such a crime, Gerald Wintour would certainly suffer the extreme penalty of the law—no jury would have any sympathy with so brutal and

callous a case of fraticide. And, with the death of
Gerald Wintour, all obstacles to Vasari's undisputed
sway at Marchester Royal would be removed.

True, by the provisions of the dead man's will, no
one but Vasari and the widowed peeress could exercise
any supervision over the youthful successor during
the time of his minority; nevertheless, Gerald Wintour
was his uncle, and public opinion would have been
with him had he claimed an uncle's right to counsel
and advise.

No—if Vasari had done this, Vasari had good
reason to wish Gerald Wintour swept clean away from
his path.

Before going to bed that night, Inspector Skarratt
decided on a plan of action, and he was up betimes in
the morning to put it into execution.

After breakfast he walked over to the station to
catch an early train for Market Fordham and York.
While he was getting his ticket, the brougham from
Marchester Royal drew up at the station entrance,
and Vasari and Mr. Deckenham descended from it.
Inspector Skarratt, joining them, quickly perceived
that the punctilious solicitor was by no means pleased
to have had the ex-valet in his company. Frigidly
polite, his manner was cold and formal, and he seemed
relieved to see the detective.

"Are you going to town, Inspector?" he inquired.
"If so, we will travel together."

"I am going first to Market Fordham," replied
Inspector Skarratt, "and I may be detained there for
several hours. Then I am going on to London."

Vasari, who seemed in no way abashed by the
solicitor's cold manner towards him, smiled, showing
his white teeth.

"All in connection with the case, Mr. Inspector?" he said.

"All in connection with the case, Mr. Vasari," replied Inspector Skarratt.

"I hope you are arriving at some solution of the mystery," said Vasari. "But, of course, you gentlemen of the police are so very guarded that no mystery is as mysterious as you are. You have nothing to tell us, I suppose?"

"No," answered the Inspector quietly. "I have nothing to tell you—yet."

Vasari shrugged his shoulders. His moustache curled a little.

"Let us hope you will have better fortune than you had with the diamond necklace two years ago," he said, with an almost imperceptible sneer.

"Let us hope I shall," said Inspector Skarratt.

Then the local train came up, and Mr. Deckenham and the Inspector got into an empty compartment. And in the hurry of departure each contrived to avoid shaking hands with Vasari, whose black eyes glittered dangerously as he responded to their curt nods.

"I hate that fellow!" exclaimed Mr. Deckenham, as the train moved off.

"Yes?" said Inspector Skarratt interrogatively.

"Can't endure him! Why, I don't know—case of Dr. Fell, I suppose—no reason, whatever, except that I can't bear him near me," said the Solicitor, mopping his forehead. "He irritates me—gets on my nerves."

"Have you seen his sister?" inquired Inspector Skarratt.

"Lady Marchester? Oh, yes—twice. A very handsome Italian, with good manners, and, I should say, not merely very much under Vasari's influence, but almost entirely under his thumb. It's a queer,

queer business!" sighed Mr. Deckenham. "What
have you done, Skarratt? You were right to say
nothing before Vasari."

"Well, Mr. Deckenham," replied the Inspector,
"I don't mind telling you that I've formed a theory
of my own as to the real murderer, and that I've
already gathered together some very important evidence in support of it. I'm going to Market Fordham
in pursuit of more, and then on to town. I suppose
you'll follow my suggestion as to counsel for Mr.
Wintour?"

"Oh, yes, yes!" answered Mr. Deckenham. "I
wired about it last night, and I shall have a consultation at once—very likely this afternoon."

"Well, I hope that trial will come to a summary
end—if it's ever started," said Inspector Skarratt.

"You feel pretty confident about your theory,
then?" said the solicitor.

"Yes—so far I do," replied Inspector Skarratt.
"Of course, one may be mistaken. I suppose there's
no doubt, Mr. Deckenham, that the marriage of the
late Lord Marchester was quite legal, and that Vasari
is duly appointed joint guardian with the mother of
the young peer?"

"Oh, none!" replied Mr. Deckenham. "None!
No, it's all legal—Vasari, I should imagine, took good
care to see to that."

"It gives him a great deal of power," said the
Inspector reflectively. "He'll practically be lord and
master of Marchester Royal until the young lord
comes of age, won't he?"

Mr. Deckenham groaned, and threw up his hands.

"He'll be able to do just what he pleases," he
answered. "There will be great changes—great
changes!"

"I should say from what I have seen," remarked Inspector Skarratt, "that there is no love lost between Vasari and Mr. Saunderson."

"Oh, he'll get rid of Saunderson," replied the solicitor, "that goes without saying. But that won't make any great difference to Saunderson—he's a well-to-do man, Saunderson—owns his own house and land. Oh, Saunderson won't care, except for the natural feeling about the severing of a very old connection with the family."

Inspector Skarratt, calling to mind the undoubted agitation which the steward had shown on hearing the news of the late peer's secret marriage, was not so sure that Mr. Deckenham was right in this supposition, but, as the train just then carried them into Market Fordham, he made no reply.

"I suppose you'll call on me in town?" said Mr. Deckenham, as they shook hands.

"Very likely to-morrow morning," answered the Inspector.

He walked quickly away from the station into the little market-town, and made his way to the police-office, where he found the Chief Constable.

"I want you to let me see the typewritten letters which purported to be sent by Mr. Gerald Wintour to Messrs. Webb & Britford," he said.

"Oh, certainly. They're locked up here with the rest of the papers!" replied the Chief Constable. "I noticed you said 'purported'—do you think the signature's a forgery, then?"

"Well, it hasn't been established that it isn't, has it?" said the Inspector, with one of his good-humoured smiles.

The Chief Constable, who was not given to humour, seemed to be somewhat taken aback by this answer.

"I never heard that its genuineness was ever in question," he said. "I'm very well acquainted with Mr. Gerald Wintour's handwriting, and I should say that this signature is genuine enough. Here are the two letters," he continued, as a clerk entered with a sheaf of documents, "and here are some signatures of Mr. Wintour which we've collected for comparison. I don't see any reason to doubt the two sent to the gun-makers."

Inspector Skarratt bent over the documents which the Chief Constable placed on the table at his side, and compared them with several letters attached to them.

"These letters," said the Chief Constable, "we got from tradesmen in the town. You see, although Mr. Gerald Wintour lived in London he did a good deal of trade here in Market Fordham—always got his clothes and his boots here, you see, and so I thought it a wise course to take to collect some of his signatures. I don't see any difference in these signatures —do you?"

Inspector Skarratt looked carefully at the various documents before replying to this direct question.

"Well," he said at last, tapping the two typewritten letters, "there's no doubt that if the written signatures to these things are forgeries they're the work of an uncommonly clever hand. But doesn't it strike you that it's rather a curious feature of this business that Mr. Wintour should have taken the trouble to type-write these two letters to Webb & Britford, when, so far as one can judge, he invariably wrote his letters and orders to other tradesmen in holograph? You see, for instance, that all these letters to your local tradesmen are written with his own hands. Some of them are rather lengthy—look at that, giving particular instructions about some new boots—why didn't he use a typewriter for that? Or, rather, why did he use a typewriter in the case of Webb & Britford?"

The Chief Constable shook his head, and was plainly unable to reply.

"Of course, there's an obvious answer to that, in my opinion," said Inspector Skarratt. "It is, as you know, a much easier thing to forge a man's signature than a whole letter, in which a great many more characters would be made use of. Now, my theory is that if these two signatures to the Webb & Britford letters are forgeries, the forger made use of the typewriter because, though he felt sure of forging the signature of Mr. Wintour successfully, he was not so sure about forging a mass of his handwriting, which is, as you see, somewhat peculiar. No, sir, if Mr. Wintour were in the habit of writing his tradesmen's orders in holograph, he wouldn't have resorted to a typewriter just for these two particular letters."

"It's my belief," said the Chief Constable, "that you don't think him guilty, eh?"

"Well, frankly, I don't and never did," answered Inspector Skarratt. "And I don't mind telling you why. He's a clever man—do you really think that if he wanted to get his brother out of the way he'd have done it in this clumsy fashion? Why, detection was certain! The pistol was sure to be found, placed where it was; it was just as sure to be identified as his property; when the news of the murder got out, Webb & Britford were equally sure to come forward to tell what they knew. No—that's too clumsy work!"

"What do you think, then?" asked the Chief Constable, somewhat uneasily.

"I think that whoever the murderer is, he had as

much intention of getting rid of Mr. Wintour as he had of killing Lord Marchester," replied the Inspector. "He's a deep and subtle specimen of his sort, any way."

"Aye, but if he isn't Gerald Wintour, who is he?" asked the Chief Constable.

"That," answered Inspector Skarratt, with a dry smile, "is quite another matter."

Then he turned to a further examination of the two tyewritten letters, looking them over very narrowly. He held them up to the light, scrutinizing the watermark and making a mental note of the fact that it was "British Bond," with a monogram underneath. That, he knew, was a paper in very common use—you might find it in thousands of offices and private houses. There was little to help him there, and he turned to the contents of the letters. And suddenly, without uttering an exclamation or showing any sign of elation, Inspector Skarratt made a discovery which he knew to be of the highest importance.

The discovery was in the second of the two letters —that which gave instructions for the delivery of the pistol at Marchester Royal. In the one paragraph of which the communication consisted, use was made of a semi-colon—and the semi-colon was imperfect. Instead of the comma which formed its lower sign looking to the left, as a well-behaved comma should, it was turned to the right, thus: ؛

Inspector Skarratt did not draw the attention of the Chief Constable to this little matter. He presently handed the documents over to him, and taking farewell of him, after an interchange of a few common-places, betook himself to the station, and was soon on his way to York, there to catch the express for King's Cross.

It was not yet four o'clock when Inspector Skarratt found himself again in the Metropolis, and he decided to get the business which had brought him there over at once.

Taking a hansom, he drove to Gerald Wintour's chambers in the Temple, and, finding his clerk, asked him to let him see the typewriter of which Gerald had spoken. He examined every letter, sign, and figure carefully—each was in perfect order. There was no twisted semi-colon there.

He went away and drove to Jermyn Street. Gerald Wintour's valet took him into the study and produced the typewriter from its stand in a corner. Inspector Skarratt went as thoroughly over it as he had gone over that at the Temple. Again he discovered nothing —one of the capitals was a bit twisted, but the semi-colon was perfect.

Inspector Skarratt made a call at Scotland Yard that night, and another on Mr. Deckenham next morning, and then returned to Marchester. He went up to Marchester Royal before evening came on, and asking for Vasari, boldly demanded to see the type-writer which stood in the library.

"There is also one in the study," answered Vasari. "A new one, bought recently. You shall see them both. You are wondering if those letters were written on them, eh? But then, how is one to tell? One Remington is as like another Remington as two olives off the same tree are alike, eh?"

Inspector Skarratt made no answer to this proposition. He examined both typewriters carefully. The older one was somewhat out-of-date, and rather cranky, and it had several broken letters; the newer one was obviously brand-new, and had scarcely been used. In neither of them did the Inspector discover the twisted semi-colon which he was anxious to find.

XVIII: WHERE IS MR. COOPER?

CHAPTER XVIII

Where is Mr. Cooper?

RETURNING to his lodgings that evening from Marchester Royal, Inspector Skarratt frankly confessed to himself that the business of the twisted semi-colon was going to prove awkward. It was a distinct advantage to Gerald Wintour that the irregular mark of punctuation was not found on the keyboard of either of his machines; it would have been an equally distinct help in building up the chain of presumptive evidence against Vasari if it had been found to result from the use of one of the machines at Marchester Royal.

True, it could have been pointed out with justice that these machines were just as available to Gerald Wintour as to Vasari, but the Inspector felt that he was in possession of sufficient evidence to prove that Gerald Wintour never did make use of a typewriter in attending to his correspondence. No—it would have helped him considerably in working up his case against the Italian if he could have proved access to a machine with a twisted semi-colon.

His failure at Marchester Royal meant that he would have to share the secret of the semi-colon with somebody else. That somebody else, of course, would have to be the Press. Through the medium of the Press he would have to ask anybody who possessed a typewriter on the keyboard of which was a twisted semi-colon to communicate with him.

Inspector Skarratt was not greatly enamoured of

the Press, for he considered that pressmen, in their insatiable thirst for news, sometimes hampered the machinations of those who, like himself, had to labour secretly and quietly—moreover, he was not anxious that the local police should be informed of a discovery which, so far as he could see, they would never make for themselves.

He was still wondering what he could do in this matter and yet keep his secret to himself next morning, when his assistant, Burton, called on him. Burton wore a somewhat disconsolate look.

"Wherever Vasari passed the night after he left the trap which drove him from Great Bywold," he said, "I can't make out! I've visited every place in the district within the distance that a man could walk at night, and I haven't got a single clue. I've inquired of hundreds of people—nobody can tell me anything."

"Well, I can tell you something," said Inspector Skarratt. "Vasari was seen coming away from the direction of Marchester Royal between half-past ten and eleven that night. I have found out that much."

"Coming away from the place, eh?" said Burton. "And which way did he go?"

"Into the wood."

"Then he must have hidden himself in the woods," said Burton.

Inspector Skarratt, who was breakfasting, carved some cold ham with deliberate precision.

"What you want to find out," he said, "is where he was between the time he was certainly seen in the woods and the time he presented himself at Marchester Royal after the inquest. He must have been somewhere."

"What was the time exactly when he turned up at Marchester Royal?" inquired Burton.

"About three o'clock in the afternoon," replied Inspector Skarratt.

"Then that leaves exactly forty hours to be accounted for," said Burton. "There were the remaining hours of the night of the murder; the whole of the next day and of the next night; a considerable part of the day after that. He must have been somewhere!"

"Obviously," said the Inspector, with laconic emphasis.

"How did he arrive at Marchester Royal?" asked Burton. "Did he drive, or walk, or what?"

It suddenly occurred to Inspector Skarratt that upon this point he was in complete ignorance, and he made a mental note to the effect that he would find the matter out before the day was over.

"He couldn't have flown in," continued Burton, "at least, unobserved. And I expect he'd have luggage —must have had, since he'd been staying a fortnight at the seaside."

"Of course," said Inspector Skarratt, and began to blame himself for not remembering everything that he should have remembered. "You're quite right, Burton. Look here, go up to the station, and, if necessary—I'm afraid you'll have to do it—tell the station-master who you are—sent by me, you know. Find out how Vasari's luggage did come, and come back and tell me at one o'clock. In the meantime I'll find out how he arrived."

So Inspector Skarratt went in one direction and Burton in the other, and when tney met at one o'clock each had some information to impart.

"I've found out everything about Vasari's luggage," said Burton, in reply to the Inspector's question as to his doings. "It was sent on from Whitby direct to Marchester Station—a portmanteau and a bag— and arrived here on the evening of the murder—by the 8:37 train from York, to be exact. As there were no instructions about it, and it was simply addressed to its owner at Marchester Station, it remained there for two days, when, late in the day——"

"That would be the day of the inquest—and of Vasari's return," said Inspector Skarratt. "Well?"

"It was fetched away by one of the grooms from Marchester Royal, who came in a light cart, inquired for it, and paid the carriage—that was in the evening. I also found," continued Burton, "that Vasari was never seen at Marchester Station from the time he left there for Whitby until he drove there with you, and took a ticket for London."

"Anything else?" asked the Inspector.

"Nothing—except that the station-master won't say anything. I had to tell him what I was after, of course," replied Burton.

Inspector Skarratt nodded. He seemed to consider some matter for awhile, and once or twice he took a turn or two about the room, pulling at his moustache.

"It's a perfect mystery to me," he said at last, sitting down in an easy-chair and stretching his long legs, "a perfect mystery how Vasari got into that house on the afternoon of the inquest without anybody seeing him enter. I've made the most searching inquiries there, and there isn't a single soul from Mountford down to the scullery-maid who even saw him come in or approach the house! It's all the stranger, because the servants were in and about all the afternoon. And there are not so many entrances to that

house, after all—the front door, opening into the hall;
a door opening on the west front; another on the terrace; and the door of the kitchen and servants' hall.
No one saw him enter at any of these. It would seem
that he slipped in quite unobserved and came straight
to the study, where several of us were met at the
time."

"It's very possible," said Burton, "since Vasari's
such a genius at slipping about, that he knows more
ways than one of getting into that house without at-
tracting attention."

"Maybe," answered Inspector Skarratt. He rose
and began to pace about the room again. "Upon
my word!" he exclaimed after a time, "I really don't
know whether I won't arrest Vasari on what evidence
I have. Certainly, he doesn't seem likely to run
away, but if he got an inkling of what I'm after I
don't know what he might not do. · I'll think it over.
See here, Burton, you'd better stop and take your
dinner with me, because I might want you this afternoon. I shouldn't be a bit surprised if I have a wire
from the Yard before night. I left a complete *precis*
of the case against Vasari for the Treasury's consideration day before yesterday. I may hear something
to-day."

Inspector Skarratt's assistant was in no wise loth
to accept this invitation, and they presently sat down
to dine together. Before they had been plying knives
and forks many minutes, the daughter of the house
entered with a telegram. Inspector Skarratt looked
knowingly at his guest as he opened the buff envelope.
His quick eye took in the message in one glance.

"There's no answer," he said to the girl, as he
threw the flimsy sheet of paper over to Burton. "And
you can change these plates now, if you please."

Burton was looking at the message; it was very brief—three words only:—

"Yes—at once."

"That means take him, I suppose?" said Burton, handing the message back.

"Yes—I thought they'd direct that after what I told them. We'll get it over this afternoon," said Inspector Skarratt. "I shall want Wilson as well—you must go and find him."

"And the local policemen?" asked Burton.

"No!" answered Inspector Skarratt. "Three of us will be quite enough for him if he's inclined to be nasty. But I don't think he will be. Let's see now—you'd better order a cab, with a good horse, to come up to the top of the beech-avenue at Marchester Royal, and to be there at four o'clock promptly. We three will walk up and enter by the kitchen garden—I know how to get in quietly."

It was just upon four o'clock when old Mountford, who was enjoying a quiet nap in the butler's pantry, was startled, first by a knock at the door, and then by the entrance of Inspector Skarratt, who came quickly across the floor to him.

"Where's Mr. Vasari?" he inquired.

"Dear me, dear me! How you made me jump!" exclaimed the butler. "Why, in the study, I believe —he's always in there now, writing and figuring. Shall I tell him you're here, Inspector?"

"No, thank you," replied Inspector Skarratt. "See here, Mountford, I and my men are going to take Vasari away, and we want to do it quietly. So you can just say that we're leaving the house on business, eh?—I don't want the servants to make a fuss just now—they'll know what's happened soon enough."

Mountford gasped and stared.

"God bless my soul!" he exclaimed at last. "You don't mean that—that—"

Inspector Skarratt nodded. He went to the door, followed by the astonished old butler, beckoned to Burton and Wilson, and led them towards the study. Mountford, growing more astonished every moment, tottered in their wake until they reached the door, where he stopped, placing one hand on the wall for support, and stared wide-eyed, as they passed within.

Vasari, unceremoniously interrupted in the act of writing, looked up from the desk at which he sat, and stared at Inspector Skarratt, and at the two men behind him, who in mufti, looked like tourists or visitors to the neighbourhood. He gave the three one keen look and laid his pen aside.

"Well, Inspector Skarratt?" he said.

There was something very cool and self-possessed in the tone in which the Italian spoke, and the three detectives were quick to notice it.

"Mr. Vasari," said the Inspector, "I shall have to ask you to come with me to Market Fordham. I have had instructions from London to arrest you and—"

"On the charge of murdering my late-brother-in-law, I suppose, Mr. Skarratt?" interrupted Vasari, with a sneer. "I can quite believe it. And, of course, on information supplied by you. Very good— but let me tell you that you are making what you call—is it a mare's nest?—no, a mistake as big as that you have found a mare's nest. Come, come!— now, just let us converse amicably, good Mr. Skarratt, for a few moments—I am quite prepared to go with you anywhere, and to meet and defend any charge you bring against me. But we shall do no harm by a little conversation. Why do you suspect me?"

"I am not bound to tell you that, Mr. Vasari, but, as you say, there will be no harm in conversing amicably. If you can clear yourself of this charge no one will be better pleased than I—I have never wished harm to an innocent man. Does it not strike you that your movements about the date of the murder were somewhat—well, mysterious?"

Vasari regarded Inspector Skarratt with a more concentrated attention; it seemed to the three men watching him that a new expression came into his eyes.

"Well?" he said. "Mysterious, you say. Well, then?"

"You allowed it to be supposed that you arrived here on the afternoon of the inquest direct from Whitby," continued Inspector Skarratt. "The truth is that you left Whitby two days before, and on the day of your departure travelled to Great Bywold, where, that evening, you hired a conveyance and were driven to the cross-roads on the other side of the woods between here and Marchester Abbey. That night you were seen coming away from this house a short time after the murder was committed. Those are—"

Vasari interrupted Inspector Skarratt with a gesture.

"Those are, as you say, or were going to say, incriminating facts," he said. "And I perceive that there is nothing for me to do but answer them—as I shall. I am wise enough to be aware that Inspector Skarratt has what he thinks some good cards up his sleeve in addition to these. Well—so has Pietro Vasari, and one which is the master card. Good Mr. Skarratt, I am at your service. Two things I request —one that I may pack a bag of necessities; the other that I may just inform my sister, Lady Marchester, that I shall be away on business until to-morrow afternoon, when, Mr. Skarratt, I will bet you a thousand pounds to a sixpenny-piece I shall certainly return."

"You may do both things in my presence, Mr. Vasari," said Inspector Skarratt, ignoring the concluding portion of his prisoner's remarks.

"Oh, pardon!" said Vasari. "There is yet a third —that I may order the brougham to take us to Market Fordham, whither I suppose, you intend to convey me?"

"There is no need," replied Inspector Skarratt, "we have a cab waiting at the top of the avenue."

"Then if you will come with me—" said Vasari, bowing.

Inspector Skarratt did go with him, and kept a sharp eye upon him until he had safely landed him in the cells at Market Fordham an hour and a half later, with the preliminaries over, and everybody at the local police headquarters thoroughly mystified. And then, with the knowledge of what he would have to do to-morrow, when his prisoner would be brought up before the magistrates, he drove back with Burton and Wilson to Marchester, and leaving them there set off on foot to find Mr. Wellington Nelson Cooper, whose presence at Market Fordham on the morrow he particularly desired.

The poacher's cottage proved to be in a somewhat lonely and deserted spot, and although it was only half-past eight when the Inspector got to its door, its outward appearance seemed to denote that all its inhabitants had already retired to bed, for there was not a sign of life about the house.

Inspector Skarratt had knocked a score of times before one of the little upper windows was unclosed, and the strident voice of an unseen woman was heard, demanding who it was that roused decent people out of their beds at that time of night, to which Inspector

Skarratt, to whom it was quite plain that the shades of evening were not yet fallen, replied mildly that he did not wish to disturb anybody, but wanted to see Mr. Cooper. Where was he?

"And I'm sure that I don't know where our Wellington is or is not!" answered the voice. "Yesterday morning he did what he hasn't done for many years —he dressed himself up in his best clothes and my poor father's old top hat, and he said he was going to Leeds or to Scarborough, or to some other merry-making place to have a day out, and that he'd be home at night, for certain. But he never came, and he hasn't come to-day neither. And, pray, who are you that wants our Wellington?"

"Oh, I'm a friend of his!" answered the Inspector suavely. "I suppose you're his sister?"

"Yes, I'm his sister, young man, as everybody round this country knows—you can't be of these parts, else you'd know that."

"Well, will he be home to-night? If he is, tell him to come down to-morrow morning first thing to see Mr. Burton at the inn, on business—there's some money for him. And here, I'll put five shillings for you yourself under the door, to remind you—it's very important Mr. Burton should see him first thing in the morning," said the Inspector.

But in spite of these blandishments, and of the palm-oil, no Mr. Cooper appeared next morning, and Burton, speeding away on his bicycle to find him, had to report that he had not yet returned to his cottage, and that his sister was getting anxious about him. At the station they discovered that no Mr. Cooper had travelled by train for a long time. Where was he, then? And he was Inspector Skarratt's principal witness!

XIX: THE FINGER-PRINT

CHAPTER XIX

The Finger-Print

THERE had been no attempt on the part of the authorities to conceal the fact of Vasari's arrest, and the news spreading rapidly through the town of Market Fordham and the surrounding villages, and all over the country by means of the newspapers, there was quite as large a crowd in and around the Town Hall next morning as when Gerald Wintour appeared there to undergo magisterial inquiry on the same charge.

To the vast majority of people in the neighbourhood the news of this startling development seemed incredible—most folk had come to the conclusion that Gerald Wintour had murdered his brother in a sudden fit of temper or resentment, or jealousy brought on by the angry remarks of Sir Thomas Braye, and could scarcely believe their ears when they heard or read that the famous Scotland Yard detective had fixed upon the ex-valet as the late Lord Marchester's real assassin.

The magistrates who crowded the bench, the people who filled the court to overflowing, stared at Inspector Skarratt as he sat talking earnestly to the barrister who had travelled down during the night to represent the Treasury, and wondered if he had really solved the mystery. There were not wanting those (for provincialism invariably cherishes a good conceit of itself) who wagged their heads and said openly that smart as Scotland Yard might be they would back their own local police against any Londoner.

And, if the truth is to be told, Inspector Skarratt himself was by no means happy. It was nearly time for the sitting—a special one, hastily convened—to begin, and so far Mr. Wellington Nelson Cooper had not arrived. Wilson was keeping an anxious lookout for him in the purlieus of the Town Hall; Burton was cycling backwards and forwards about the highway leading from Marchester in the hope of meeting him.

Inspector Skarratt and the barrister from the Treasury were inclined to do no more that day than give formal evidence of arrest and apply for a remand, but they had already received a mysterious hint that not only would the defence resist this cause most strenuously, but would insist on establishing the prisoner's innocence beyond doubt there and then.

And that Vasari was going to fight was made evident when his solicitor—the man who had been employed to draw up the late Lord Marchester's will—came bustling into court accompanied by a noted barrister of the North-Eastern circuit, who in his time had restored a good many doubtful characters to their friends and their relations by sheer pertinacity and eloquence, and a curious trick of working on the feelings of jurymen—especially of his own country.

"By George, we've got Pilchard against us!" whispered the barrister from the Treasury. "Now we shall have something pretty."

Inspector Skarratt paid no attention to this remark, nor to the gentleman who caused it. He knew Mr. Pilchard by reputation, and at any other time would have been very much interested in meeting him; just then there was nobody in the world that he so much

wanted to meet as Wellington Nelson Cooper. And
Cooper, unlike the two great heroes whose names he
bore, was not there when he was wanted.

Wilson came to the door of the court-house two or
three times and shook his head significantly, meaning
to indicate to his chief that so far Mr. Cooper had not
presented himself. The last time he came in this way
Inspector Skarratt beckoned to him.

"Get a horse and trap as quickly as you can and
drive out to Cooper's cottage," he said. "Pick up
Burton on the way. If Cooper is there, bring him
back with you. Don't lose any time—get the fastest
horse you can find."

He turned as Wilson went off, and found that the
magistrates were crowding on to the bench; there
were quite as many of them as when Gerald Wintour
was brought before them. Their faces, like those of
the people in court, betrayed a wondering curiosity,
which deepened considerably when Vasari was placed
in the dock. What were they going to hear?

Vasari, carefully and fashionably attired in mourning garments, made a picturesque figure as he faced
the court. His olive cheeks were neither flushed nor
pale, and his black eyes sparkled with something very
like defiance as they swept a glance at Inspector Skarratt and his companion. If he were a guilty scoundrel,
thought some who watched him, he was a consum-
mately bold one. He stood there an incarnation of
injured innocence, and the way in which he folded
his arms and faced his accusers was superb in its unconscious acting.

Before the proceedings had been opened five minutes, the gentleman from the Treasury and Mr. Pilchard were at grips.

The prosecuting counsel wished to confine the

doings of that day to mere formal evidence of arrest and to an application for a remand. Mr. Pilchard, with great animation, not unmixed with indignation, protested against any such course. His client, he said, had a complete answer to the charge, and could prove his innocence within a few minutes by the mouths of thoroughly reputable witnesses. He demanded that the prosecution should produce what evidence they had against him—whatever it was, contemptuously added Mr. Pilchard, it would be torn to shreds. A gross blunder had been made by the so-called skilful detectives sent down—quite unnecessarily, in his opinion—from Scotland Yard, and it was only just to his client to have that blunder rectified. He strenuously opposed any request for a remand— let them hear what there was against them there and then, concluded Mr. Pilchard, with one of his well-known outbursts of oratory. And Mr. Pilchard apparently carried the magistrates with him, for they, in spite of energetic protests from the authorities, announced their intention of hearing what evidence the prosecution had to bring forward.

"Sheer inquisitiveness on the part of Justice Shallow!" whispered the prosecuting counsel, as he laid his papers in order. "I hope that witness of yours is going to turn up, Skarratt—we shall look well if he doesn't. However, here goes!"

There was a breathless silence in court as the keen-eyed, sharp featured barrister got on his legs and faced the bench.

It would be within the recollection of their worships, he said, that the late Lord Marchester was recently found mysteriously murdered, and that his brother, the Honourable Gerald Wintour, had been charged with the crime, and had been committed for

trial by that very bench. He, the speaker, now appeared, on behalf of the Treasury, to prosecute the
man in the dock, Pietro Vasari on the same charge.
This was an unusual event in the history of criminal
procedure, but he believed that he would be able to
show that the real culprit was not the gentleman now
awaiting trial in York Castle, but the man before him.

That man, Pietro Vasari, was a native of Antignano, near Naples, in Italy, and was understood to be
about forty years of age. About seven years ago
Vasari entered the service of the late Lord Marchester, whom, some little time afterwards, he accompanied to Italy in the capacity of confidential servant.
There, Lord Marchester made the acquaintance of
Vasari's sister, whom he subsequently married. That
marriage was kept secret, and was never revealed
until Vasari himself made it known after the murder
of the man who was both his employer and his brother-
in-law.

It was then found—a fact of the greatest significance—that the deceased peer's untimely end had
placed the valet in a position of vast influence and
importance; it was, indeed, useless to deny that Vasari,
by Lord Marchester's death, gained financially and
socially. From being a mere serving-man he became
guardian and trustee of a peer of the realm, and,
virtually, master of Marchester Royal. Could anyone
doubt that here was a motive for the commission of
the crime with which he was charged? Let them now
consider what Vasari's movements and actions were
at the time of the murder.

About a fortnight previously Vasari had not been
well, and he went to Whitby to recuperate. He had
ostensibly travelled direct from Whitby when he presented himself at Marchester Royal on the afternoon

of the inquest. But he had not come from Whitby. He left Whitby two days before that.

On the day of the murder—which, they would remember, took place at or about half-past ten o'clock at night—Vasari left Whitby early in the afternoon, and instead of travelling direct to York, and thence to Marchester, he took a somewhat circuitous route to Great Bywold, where, as further evidence would show, he engaged a horse and trap, in which he was driven across country to a point within two miles of Marchester Royal. There he left his conveyance, telling the driver that he would walk the remainder of his way, but not saying what that way was, and having paid his fare, he disappeared into the woods in the direction of his employer's house.

Now, it was then twilight, and, so far as the driver could recollect, about nine o'clock. About twenty or fifteen minutes to eleven a man named Cooper, who happened to be crossing one of the woods close to Marchester Royal, heard footsteps approaching hurriedly across the adjacent park. He hid himself behind a stile, to which a man presently came up in the darkness. This man, who was breathing hard, struck a light after crossing the stile, and with its help consulted a small local time-table. The concealed eye-witness, Cooper, recognised the man as Vasari. He also saw that he was very much agitated, very pale, and most significant fact of all—that his fingers were blood-stained. It seemed to Cooper that he was trying to extract some information from the time-table, and that, failing to get it, he flung the book away amongst the brushwood before disappearing at a swift pace along the path through the wood. Cooper, waiting until the coast was clear, secured the time-table.

"And that time-table," said counsel, giving full dramatic effect, "stained here and there with blood, and one page bearing an unmistakable finger-print, we shall produce!"

Vasari, upon whom all eyes were turned at this juncture, smiled—it seemed to the more observant of those who watched him that it was a smile of triumph, the smile of a man who knows something secret, and enjoys his knowledge. And they began to have some doubts.

The prosecuting counsel quickly brought his opening statement to an end. He showed how Vasari could have obtained the pistol with which the murder was held by expert evidence to have been committed, and how it was in his interest to throw suspicion on the brother of the dead man. He had all to gain by the deaths of both brothers. And with a reference to a deep-laid and cunningly devised scheme such as could only be hatched in a nature fortunately not much known in these northern latitudes, but common in those of which the prisoner was a native, counsel ended his speech, and proceeded to call his witnesses.

Thanks to a profuse use of the telegraph wires, Inspector Skarratt had collected a number of witnesses together. There was a considerable body of evidence to bear out counsel's statement.

One by one witnesses went into the box—Inspector Skaratt himself; the head-waiter and hall-porter from the Whitby Hotel; a porter from Whitby station; the man who drove Vasari from Great Bywold to the cross-roads; Gerald Wintour's valet from Jermyn Street. But no Wellington Nelson Cooper appeared on the scene, and Inspector Skarratt grew anxious and the Treasury Counsel fidgety.

"If they would only grant an adjournment," he said,

"we might find the fellow, but I'm certain they won't now. Hello, here's Lemercier—you sent for him, I suppose?"

"Yes," said Inspector Skarratt, beckoning to a dapper-looking little man in sober black, who had just entered the court, and was trying to force a way through the crowd. "I want him to examine the finger-print in this time-table."

The famous expert made his way to Inspector Skarratt's side, shook hands with him and the barrister, unbuttoned his coat, sat down, and looked about him. The barrister went on—and came to an end of his witnesses, Mr. Cooper being still absent. He began to hint at an adjournment. Mr. Pilchard, watchful and eager, was instantly on his feet, protesting.

"I shall oppose any adjournment tooth and nail, your worships!" he exclaimed. "We want to know all that may be brought against us to the very full, and then we will answer this abominable charge in a very few minutes in such a complete and satisfactory fashion that my client will leave this court without the slightest stain upon his character. But, your worships, we are so confident of our success that we do not wish to be unduly hard upon our opponents. We understand their most important witness has not yet presented himself. Well, let me suggest something which may ocupy the time of the court profitably—I see there my friend Mr. Lemercier, of Scotland Yard, whom I shrewdly suspect to have come amongst us poor bucolics in connection with the finger-print which is so clearly impressed upon a blank page of the local railway-guide we have heard of. I suggest that Mr. Lemercier should retire with the prisoner to some convenient apartment, and should take the impression of his fingers and compare them with that in the book—and in the meantime your worships will perhaps adjourn for lunch? I have no doubt that Mr. Lemercier has been brought here by the prosecution—I have no doubt, either, that he will prove a very valuable—a most valuable—witness for the defence, and will demonstrate to you that wherever else that mark in the time-table came from it certainly did not come from the fingers of Mr. Vasari."

There was some consultation amongst the magistrates, and then the chairman, addressing the Treasury counsel, said he supposed the course suggested by Mr. Pilchard would be agreeable to the prosecution? But at that moment there was a commotion at the back of the court, and presently Burton and Wilson appeared, conducting Mr. Wellington Nelson Cooper, at sight of whom Inspector Skarratt was more than exceeding glad.

"Here's our man," he exclaimed to the prosecuting counsel. "Let's get him into the box at once. I'd no reason to doubt his tale; it seemed straight enough, told to me."

Mr. Cooper, once in the witness-box, told just as straightforward a story as when he had entertained the Inspector in his cave. He also made an interesting figure. He wore a very old-fashioned black-tailed coat and white cord trousers, tight in the leg, a voluminous Belcher handkerchief encircled his throat, and in his gnarled, powerful hands he carried a rusty top-hat, very high in the crown and curly in the brim. He was sober after a fashion, but had evidently been rejoicing, and he looked round the court with a leer that was half cunning and half mischievous.

The poacher's evidence, in reply to the questions of the prosecuting counsel, was in entire accord with the story he had told to Inspector Skarratt. He answered every question readily, proving himeslf a good witness by giving plain affirmatives and negatives.

His testimony plainly told upon the court, for he was very exact as to dates and times, and had a certain air of simplicity in his bearing and answers which contrasted curiously with the look of slyness in his eyes. Vasari watched him with burning eyes all the time; Cooper, however, with the exception of one glance, never turned in the direction of the dock.

Mr. Pilchard was in one of his well-known moods when he rose to cross-examine Mr. Cooper. He regarded him with an air of something mixed up with that sort of benevolence which a cat sometimes seems to show towards the mouse it is going to torture and kill, and of a saddened pity that anyone should be so naughtily disposed.

"And what were you doing in the woods at that time?" he inquired blandly.

"Having a walk round, sir," replied Cooper.

"A bit late, wasn't it—half-past ten—for a working man, who goes to bed early, as I suppose you do?"

"It were a fine night, sir."

"Oh, I see! You're fond of walking in the woods on fine nights. Are the walks public in those woods?"

"On the paths, sir."

"Of course. You never go off the paths, I'm sure."

"No, sir."

"Not to do a bit of poaching, eh?"

"Me, sir? No, sir! I'm a hedger and ditcher."

"I'm sure you'd make a good fencer," said Mr. Pilchard. "That'll do—I don't think we need bother much with you, Cooper."

With that the case for the prosecution came to an

end, and the court adjourned, the finger-prints expert being instructed to take an impression of the prisoner's fingers during the interval, and to compare them with the stains in the book.

Inspector Skarratt and his prosecuting counsel went across the market-place for lunch—each was somewhat puzzled by the cocksureness of Mr. Pilchard and the triumphant defiance of Vasari.

"I wonder what they're going to set up—I'm expecting a surprise," said the barrister.

One surprise greeted them as soon as they re-entered the court. At the solicitors' table, chatting smilingly and vivaciously with Mr. Pilchard, sat a handsome, elegantly-dressed woman of about thirty-five years of age; next to her, a boy, obviously her son, and apparently fourteen or fifteen years old; next to him, staring round the court and twirling a glazed peaked cap in his hands, a young man who was unmistakably a chauffeur. Close by, talking quietly to Vasari's solicitor, sat an old clergyman.

XX: PROVING AN ALIBI

CHAPTER XX

Proving an Alibi

WHILE Inspector Skarratt and his Treasury counsel were speculating on the identity of these strangers, the magistrates re-entered, and Vasari once more appeared in the dock. He bowed politely to the bench, and then nodded and smiled in unusually friendly fashion to the strangers sitting by Mr. Pilchard, who on their part returned his greeting with equal cordiality.

"Witnesses for the defence, I'll lay a sovereign to a lemon!" whispered the prosecuting counsel. "Skarratt—you've been off it! They're going to prove an *alibi.*"

That Mr. Pilchard was very confident as regards his task was at once evident. He rose in his grandest manner and spoke in his finest tones.

"Your worships," he said, "the case which we have to meet is so weak, so flimsy; the answer which we have to make to it so complete, so strong, that I shall not trouble your worships with any poor words of mine, but shall put certain witnesses of the most unimpeachable integrity in the witness-box, who will speedily prove to you that at the hour on which the murder of the unfortunate Lord Marchester took place, my client was not near Marchester Royal, but was, in fact, at the ancient and beautiful city of St. Godminster, whither, your worships, he had sped on a mission as widely removed from the loathsome crime of homicide as the heavens from the earth. If

243

I may quote the words of the glorious Swan of Avon,
I will say:

"'Mark now, how a plain tale will put you down!'

"Your worships, I will not waste your time, so
valuable, yet so freely given in the service of your
Crown and country, nor will I harrow the feelings of
my opponents, though they have not scrupled to
lacerate those of the respectable and worthy gentleman whom you will presently acquit—no, I will proceed to business. Call Monsieur Eugene Lemercier.
. . . M. Lemercier, you are one of the most
famous experts in the world on the question of identi-
fications by means of finger-prints?"

"I believe I am considered to be so."

"You have examined the finger-print on the blank
page of the local railway time-table which was handed
to you by the prosecution prior to the adjournment?"

"I have."

"And you have taken impressions of the fingers of
the prisoner?"

"Yes."

"And compared them with that in the book?"

"Yes."

"In your opinion was the print in the book made
by Mr. Vasari?"

"No, most decidedly. There is no single point of
any one of Mr. Vasari's fingers which resembles that
on the blank page of the book. That print is from
the finger of a man of much greater physique—it is
coarser, heavier."

"You have no doubt?"

"Not the slightest!"

"Indeed, you would stake your professional reputation upon your opinion?"

"I would, willingly."

"I thank you, Mr. Lemercier." Mr. Pilchard
bowed in his grandest manner, and as the expert left
the box, turned to the bench. "Your worships, I
shall now avail myself of that wise provision recently
placed upon our statute-books—I shall, in short, put
the prisoner in the box to give evidence on his own
behalf. Call Pietro Vasari."

The accused, thus dramatically summoned, made a
dramatic exit from the dock, and a dramatic entrance
into the witness-box. He took the oath with a great
show of solemnity, and faced his interrogator with a
proud and confident mien, replying to the preliminary
formal questions in staccato-like monosyllables. Yes
—he was Pietro Vasari, an Italian subject, of Antignano, near Naples, thirty-nine years of age, now of
independent means.

"During the last seven years you were employed
by the late Lord Marchester in a very confidential
capacity?"

"Yes—a most confidential capacity."

"And for six of those years, in point of fact, you
had been his brother-in-law?"

"Yes."

"You were on good terms?"

"On the very best of terms, sir."

"And at the time of his death there was no difference between you?"

"Certainly, none!"

"Mr. Vasari, take this small railway guide in your
hand, and look at it. Is it your property?"

"It is."

"You remember purchasing it?"

"I do."

"When and where was that?"

"It was on the platform at Market Fordham, when

I was changing trains there on my way from Marchester to Whitby over three weeks ago."

"What did you do with it then?"

"Kept it in a waistcoat pocket for reference. It has one or two pencil notes on it, which are mine."

"Mr. Vasari, can you remember when you last had that book in your possession?"

"I can—distinctly."

"When, then, and where?"

"About nine o'clock in the evening of the day on which I left Whitby—the day on which, as I afterwards discovered, Lord Marchester was murdered. As to the exact place, it was at White's Spinney, a little way from the cross-roads near there."

"What were you doing there?"

"I was on my way to meet friends."

"You had an appointment?"

"Yes."

"What made you look at the little railway-guide just then?"

"I wanted to find out if I could how far St. Godminster was from that point. As I could not find out I threw the book away, it being useless to me. I then went through White's Spinney, crossed the fields at the other side, and came out at the second milestone on the road between Market Fordham and St. Godminster—my rendezvous."

"There you met your friends?"

"I did."

"What did you do then?"

"I entered their motor-car and drove with them to St. Godminster."

"And there you stayed the night?"

"Yes—at the St. Godminster Arms."

"Now, Mr. Vasari, I think an interesting event

took place in the parish church of St. Godminster next morning with which you were closely concerned. What was it?"

"I was married."

Amidst the buzz of excitement which this answer roused, Mr. Pilchard raised his voice.

"You were married. Very good. Now, Mr. Vasari, what happened between your leaving the church and your presenting yourself at Marchester Royal next day? Tell the court briefly in your own way."

"Willingly. My wife, her son, and myself breakfasted with friends of hers in St. Godminster, with whom she had stayed the night. We then motored to Harrogate and stayed at the Imperial Hotel. The following morning we heard of the tragedy at Marchester Royal, but not until rather late, as we had gone out for an early drive. My wife's chauffeur, somewhat later, drove me over to Marchester Royal, and put me down at the Italian garden entrance. I walked unobserved into the house, and went straight to the study."

"Thank you, Mr. Vasari. I have nothing more to ask."

Mr. Pilchard turned to the prosecuting counsel. But that gentleman, who had listened to the prisoner's evidence with great attention, showed no disposition to ask any questions, and Mr. Pilchard first beamed upon the lady who sat by his side, and then spoke in very mellifluous accents.

"Call Mary Isabella Vasari!"

The lady rose amidst the hushed whisperings of the court, and gracefully advancing to the witness box, obeyed the usher's instructions to take off her right-hand glove, an operation which occupied some little time, during which she was the object of much curiosity and admiration. Once in the box and duly sworn, she admitted that she was now the wife of the last witness, and until her marriage with him the widow of the late Anthony Richard Formby, of Holly Lodge, near Marchester Royal, owner of racehorses.

"I think, madam," said Mr. Pilchard in his most dulcet tones, "that you had been engaged to be married to Mr. Vasari for nearly a year before the recent interesting event was celebrated?"

"Yes."

"And you both desired to keep the engagement secret?"

"Well, it was known to a very few trusted friends."

"Quite so. And you both wished to be married very quietly?"

"Yes."

"And by an old friend of your family—Canon Saffrey, at St. Godminster."

"Yes."

"And you arranged that on the eve of the marriage Mr. Vasari was to meet you at the second milestone on the St. Godminster road, and drive with you and your son to that town, where the wedding was to be celebrated next morning?"

"Yes."

"And he did so meet you?"

"Yes."

"At nine o'clock?"

"To be exact it was nearly ten minutes past—we were a little late."

"You have heard your husband's evidence as to your subsequent movements—you corroborate it in full?"

"Oh, certainly!"

Mr. Pilchard bowed low, and looked again at the prosecuting counsel. And once more the prosecuting counsel had nothing to say.

There was, indeed, no good to come from questioning any of Mr. Pilchard's witnesses. A more complete *alibi* could not have been set up.

It was certain that on the day on which Lord Marchester met his death Vasari was at Whitby at half-past two in the afternoon, at Great Bywold soon after six in the evening, at White's Spinney at nine o'clock, at St. Godminster at a quarter past ten.

Miles Anthony Formby, now his son-in-law, corroborated these facts as from nine o'clock onwards; Emil le Blanc, Mrs. Vasari's chauffeur, corroborated them from nine o'clock until three o'clock on the day of the inquest; Canon Saffrey, vicar of Holy Cross, St. Godminster, proved that Vasari arrived at his house with his prospective bride and her son at a quarter past ten, and remained there until nearly midnight, when he, the canon, walked across the street with him and young Formby to the St. Godminster Arms, where they were to spend the night, and that he celebrated the marriage at nine o'clock next morning.

There were signs on the bench and in the court that everybody was satisfied, and Mr. Pilchard, magnanimous in his triumph, refrained from gloating over his adversaries, and contented himself by confidently asking their worships to dismiss the case—a case brought against one who by virtue of recent events, and by his marriage to one of the brightest ornaments of local society in the immediate neighbourhood of their salubrious and historical town—he referred to the lady who, now Mrs. Vasari, had long enjoyed a high reputation first as the wife, and then as the widow of their late esteemed fellow-townsman, that genial fellow and prince of sportsmen, Anthony Richard Formby—was, he felt sure, destined to attain considerable eminence in that district—not the least in honour nor in importance—of their famous county of broad acres.

There was an attempt at loud applause when Mr. Pilchard rolled out the last of his resounding vowels, but it died out as the chairman of the magistrates, who had already gathered the sense of his fellow-justices, spoke:

"The charge against Mr. Vasari is dismissed," he said, "and he, of course, leaves this court without the slightest stain upon his character. The evidence which has just been put before us is overwhelmingly conclusive as to his innocence of the charge preferred against him. At the same time, we do not agree with Mr. Pilchard in saying that this charge should never have been brought. It is impossible to deny that, granted a certain view of the case, Mr. Vasari's movements were extremely suspicious. We now know what made them appear so, and we are glad of the innocent cause. But the prosecution was perfectly right in having the matter investigated. Mr. Vasari, you are discharged."

"Clean off it there, Skarratt," observed the prosecuting counsel, as they elbowed their way through the crowds which thronged the corridors and the steps of the Town Hall. "It strikes me that man Cooper has deceived you. Now, where did he get hold of that time-table? Picked it up, of course, at the place where Vasari threw it away. But, having picked it up, what did he want to keep it for—and what on earth made him concoct the tale he told you? There's some queer mystery in all that, yet—in spite of Vasari's innocence."

"Yes," replied Inspector Skarratt laconically. "Yes."

He was feeling hurt and disappointed at the result of the magisterial investigation—not because Vasari's innocence had been proved, for he would have deeply regretted any miscarriage of justice, but because his theories had gone wrong, and he was as far off a solution of the whole difficult problem as ever. Now he would have to start his investigations all over again.

"Of course," said the barrister, "if the evidence of all these people were true—and there's no reasonable person would doubt its truth—your precious Mr. Cooper has committed perjury in swearing that he saw Vasari when Vasari was at the time miles upon miles away. I should keep an eye on him."

"I've got a man watching him," replied Inspector Skarratt, "and I'm going to get a warrant and a search-warrant too. I'll find out what his game has been, or what it is—you shall see!"

"Well, he's a sly fox, Skarratt," said the barrister. "A sly, sly fox!"

Then they parted, and Inspector Skarratt went off to the office of the magistrate's clerk. Outside it, angry and disconsolate, he met Burton.

"I was looking for you," said Burton. "That fellow's given me the slip."

Inspector Skarratt could not keep back an exclamation of annoyance.

"What, Cooper?" he said.

"Yes," replied Burton. "I followed him out of the court, when you gave me instructions about it. He talked to two or three groups of people when he got outside; then he went across to the Spread Eagle, and was there some time. When he left he went round to the Dog and Gun, in the narrow street behind the church, and I followed him in. There he gave me the slip, but how he did it I can't think, for I never had my eyes off him for a moment until——"

"Until you took them off," interrupted Inspector Skarratt. "Well, it's no use talking now. I'm going to get a warrant and a search-warrant—do you find Wilson, and then get a good horse and trap and be ready for me at the Crown. We must get hold of Cooper as quickly as we can."

Burton hurried off, and Inspector Skarratt turned into the Town Hall. He met Vasari and his wife and friends; the Italian smiled meaningly, and shook a forefinger.

"Ah, my friend Skarratt!" he said. "No more luck than with the diamonds, eh?"

"I am glad you are proved innocent," replied Skarratt.

He pushed on into the offices, and was some little time doing his business and getting out again. And at the door he met Margaret Braye, who looked troubled and anxious. She stopped him.

"Mr. Skarratt, may I see you—soon?" she asked. "To-night?"

The detective hesitated.

"It's of great importance," she said. "I—I've discovered something."

"Discovered something, Miss Braye? What is it?"

She looked round and lowered her voice to a whisper.

"It's the diamond necklace that was stolen from Marchester Royal two years ago," she said.

XXI: THE DIAMOND NECKLACE

CHAPTER XXI

The Diamond Necklace

IF Inspector Skarratt had been surprised, and, if the truth is to be spoken, not a little annoyed by the events of the day in respect to the Vasari case, he was something more than astonished by the news which Margaret Braye gave him in that whispered sentence.

The diamond necklace stolen from Marchester Royal two years ago! He could hardly believe his ears. Why, he himself had spent three months investigating that matter, and had eventually returned to London completely baffled.

True, he had a theory of his own as to the theft and its perpetrators, and had at times strengthened it by new evidence, but he felt at once that if Margaret had really found the missing valuable that theory had been a wrong one. That she could have found it seemed impossible to him. Few men of his age had had more experience of jewel robberies than Inspector Skarratt—that of Marchester Royal had been the toughest nut to crack which he had ever encountered.

The circumstances under which the diamond necklace had been stolen were peculiar. The necklace itself had a history. During the troublous times of the French Revolution of 1798 the Lord Marchester of that day happened to be in Paris when one of the most furious outbreaks against the aristocrats occurred. By a carefully arranged scheme, carried out at great risk and expense to himself, he contrived the escape to England of a certain nobleman of very high rank, who, in token of his gratitude, and knowing that Lord Marchester was about to be married, presented him with a magnificent necklace composed of one hundred diamonds of the finest quality, with an expression of the hope of its donor that it might be preserved as an heirloom in the family for ever. Unfortunately, the grandson of that Lord Marchester, father of the Lord Marchester whose murder had just caused such interest and speculation, was in his youth a good deal of the rake and a spendthrift, and in one of his revels or orgies he bestowed the precious necklace upon his favourite for the time being.

As ill-luck would have it, his two previous ancestors had made no provision in their wills for the proper protection of the necklace; it had never even occurred to their honest minds that any successor of theirs would be such a fool as to give away a valuable possession of such historic interest. Somehow, the necklace was recovered from the person to whom it had been presented—there was some mystery about that recovery, and not even Mr. Deckenham knew the exact truth about it. After its recovery it was jealously guarded in the strong room at Marchester Royal, and from that strong room it had been abstracted in the most mysterious and unaccountable fashion just two years before its then owner came to his equally mysterious end.

Then had come Inspector Skarratt's investigation of the affair, and his hopeless failure to find the thief or thieves. He had worked hard, done everything he could think of, and had been obliged to confess himself beaten so far as immediate practical results were concerned.

And now, if the girl's story were true, she had come across the thing which he had laboured so hard to find—without success! It struck him with a sense of grim irony that not all the work in the world can be so effective as mere chance sometimes is. For it could only have been by mere chance that Miss Braye had made this discovery—how else?

But had she made it? It seemed impossible—so impossible that he found it hard to credit the announcement, and stood staring at Margaret as if he had suddenly lost the power of speech. She saw the amazement in his eyes; it was a full minute before he found words.

"The diamond necklace stolen from Marchester Royal!" he exclaimed. "Impossible, Miss Braye!"

"I don't think so, Mr. Skarratt," replied Margaret quietly. "I am sure it is that necklace."

"What makes you think so?"

"Because I read the description at the time," replied Margaret. She glanced round her and lowered her voice again to a whisper. "It consists of a hundred very fine stones, set in old gold work," she said.

Inspector Skarratt's eyebrows went up, and he whistled.

"That's it," he said. "Good Heavens!"

"I want to tell you all about it," she said.

"And I want to hear all about it," he replied with emphasis. "But just at this minute I want to lay hands on that fellow Cooper. See here, Miss Braye, oblige me by walking a little in the churchyard, where we talked before—I'll join you there as soon as I've seen my men and made some arrangements. I'll be as quick as I can; please wait for me."

Margaret agreed to this proposal, and Inspector Skarratt, his head buzzing with all manner of new

ideas, hurried away to find Burton and Wilson and
to get aid of the Chief Constable, who, for once,
was somewhat amiable, and readily agreed that it was
highly desirable that hands should be laid upon Mr.
Wellington Nelson Cooper as soon as might be possible. The telegraph and telephone were set at work,
and it was quickly made impossible for the poacher
to get away from the district by train, while instructions were sent all round to the village police to watch
the roads.

Then Inspector Skarratt gave his own particular
aides-de-camp certain orders, and hurried away to
meet Miss Braye. A feeling of elation rose within
him—what if, through her, he should find the diamond
necklace, and through Cooper the actual murderer!
For he was now convinced that the poacher knew a
good deal more than he had told, and was playing
some strange game.

Striding swiftly across the market, his progress was
suddenly interrupted by Mr. Saunderson, who, looking unusually solemn, buttonholed him securely before
the Inspector was well aware of his bulky presence.

"Ah!" said the steward, shaking his head in his
gravest fashion. "I was afraid you were on the
wrong tack there, Inspector, in going after Vasari.
Not but what I wish it had been him instead of poor
Mr. Gerald—oh, yes, indeed! However, your intentions were good, and you did your best. We can't
all succeed—oh, dear, no! You'll have to try again,
Inspector."

"Yes—and I won't fail this time," said Inspector
Skarratt.

"Well, I wouldn't be too confident," said the steward, with another solemn shake of the head. "Young
men are apt to be over-confident. Now, that man

Cooper—oh, dear me, how he deceived you, Inspector! Ah, if you'd only come to me about Cooper I should have told you not to believe a word he said—I know what Cooper is—you don't."

"I shall know more in a few hours," answered Inspector Skarratt. "He can't have got far, and we've got a ring all round the country already."

"Going to arrest him?" said Mr. Saunderson. "Oh, indeed! Well I shouldn't pay over-much attention to anything that Cooper said if I were you, Inspector. You're a very clever young man, you know, but rash, rash, sir! I shouldn't like you to come off as poorly in this as you did in that little affair of the diamond necklace—no, indeed, I shouldn't."

Now Inspector Skarratt was wanting to get away, and he resented this last remark, and he suffered his temper to get the better of him. He twisted the lapel of his coat out of the steward's grasp.

"Mind I don't solve the mystery of the diamond necklace and Lord Marchester's murder at one and the same time, Mr. Saunderson!" he exclaimed. "I can put my hands on the diamond necklace within an hour if I want."

Then he turned and hurried off, leaving the steward to stare after him open-mouthed, and ultimately to take off his tall hat and stroke his head thoughtfully.

"Um!" he said. "An impetuous young man. Speaks before he thinks. Dear me!"

Then Mr. Saunderson turned away, and crossing the market-place entered the stable-yard of the inn which he patronised whenever business brought him to Market Fordham.

"You can get my pony and trap ready at once," he said to one of the hostlers. "And bring it round to the front door. And if that young lady, that sometimes drives with me should come and enquire, you can tell her that I've had to go a little farther into the country on urgent business, and that she can either wait for me here until six o'clock or take a fly or a cab, or something, home—just which is most agreeable to her."

Then Mr. Saunderson went into the house and sought the bar, and treated himself to a comfortable glass of whisky-and-soda, and very soon, with a large cigar between his lips, he was bowling homeward in the summer afternoon, a picture of great content to all whom he encountered.

"Ah, he's a rash young man is that!" soliloquised Mr. Saunderson, blowing blue spirals of smoke away into the hawthorn scented air. "He'll learn when he gets older what a beautiful thing it is to know when to hold one's tongue!"

At that moment Inspector Skarratt, pacing up and down a quiet corner of Market Fordham churchyard with Margaret Braye, was holding his tongue in the most approved fashion. He was listening with all his ears to a narrative which, had he heard it ten minutes sooner, would have prevented him from saying a word to the steward on the subject of either the diamond necklace or the murder.

"Let me hear all about it quickly, Miss Braye," he said as he joined her. "I must lose no time in following up Cooper, but I must hear about the diamond necklace, first. Tell me all—clearly."

"Well, Mr. Skarratt," began Margaret, "you know that I have been occupying rooms in Mr. Saunderson's house since I left my father's. You also know that Mr. Saunderson has a housekeeper——"

"Miss Mercer—tall, gaunt, curious woman—yes, I know her."

"Recently Miss Mercer, who is very faddy, has been spring-cleaning. She keeps a maid-servant, as a rule. During her spring-cleaning she has had the assistance of a woman who lives in a neighbouring cottage. This morning, about eleven o'clock, when there was no one in the house but Miss Mercer and myself, Mr. Saunderson having driven in here soon after breakfast, Miss Mercer, who happened to come to my room for some purpose, complained to me that her charwoman had not yet arrived. She seemed very much upset about the woman's late arrival, because, she said, she had planned out certain work for the day, which should have been commenced at nine o'clock.

"About half an hour later the charwoman entered my sitting-room in a state of great agitation, saying that she had just arrived, and had found Miss Mercer lying on the kitchen floor, and she thought she was dead. I ran there as quickly as possible, and found that she had fainted. Now, I had never had any actual experience of a fainting person before, but I knew that brandy was a restorative, and I went to Mr. Saunderson's parlour to get some. There was no brandy in the sideboard cellaret, however, so I went to a cupboard in one corner of the room, from which I have seen him take spirits and cigar-boxes at different times.

"On opening the door I found that the cupboard was full of quite a variety of things—a number of bottles, piles of cigar-boxes, old tea-caddies, and at least half a dozen silver teapots. At first I did not see any brandy, but presently I caught sight of some at the back of a shelf. In reaching for a bottle I had to make use of a footstool, and just as I had grasped the bottle my foot slipped, and I pulled over some of the things in the cupboard, and they fell with a crash to the floor.

"Naturally, as Miss Mercer was so ill, I did not stop to pick the things up there and then—I ran back to the kitchen, and with the aid of the brandy the charwoman and I brought Miss Mercer round. When she was quite recovered I returned to the parlour to repair the damage which I had inadvertently caused. I found that I had not broken anything—no bottles had fallen, but two of the teapots had been knocked down, together with several cigar-boxes. One of these cigar-boxes had burst on coming in contact with the floor, and lay face downwards over a lot of loose cigars. I picked it up, and from beneath it, mixed up with more cigars, dropped a magnificent diamond necklace!"

Inspector Skarratt drew a deep breath, and said "Ah!" Then he nodded his head, once, twice, thrice.

"Just so!" he said. "Please continue, Miss Braye."

"Well," said Margaret, "you may imagine, Mr. Skarratt, what astonishment I felt on seeing such a valuable thing concealed in a box of cigars. What could it be doing there, and whose was it? These were the first thoughts which crossed my mind. I picked it up and examined it. Now, I know something of diamonds, and I was instantly aware that the necklace was of great value—immense value."

"If it's the necklace, Miss Braye, it's reckoned to be worth seventy-five thousand pounds," said the Inspector.

"I quite believe it," said Margaret. "Well, I carried it over to the window to examine it—and it suddenly flashed upon me. 'Why, this must be the famous Trecintrot necklace, which was stolen from Marchester Royal under such mysterious circumstances two years ago!' Then I began to count the stones—there were just one hundred of them, and the gold work is French of the Louis Quatorze period."

"That's it!" exclaimed Inspector Skarratt. "That's it! You've found it. And I'm a fool—an awful fool!"

Margaret looked an inquiry.

"Just now," groaned the Inspector, who manifestly desired to punch his own head. "Just now I met Saunderson in the market-place, and because he twitted me with my failure as regards the diamond case and the charge against Vasari, I was ass enough to lose my temper and to tell him that I could put my hands on the diamonds in an hour's time. Fool that I was!"

"But—I don't quite understand!" said Margaret.

"He'd smell a rat and be off," replied Inspector Skarratt. "Off at once, to see if mine were an empty boast, or if the diamonds were safe in his cigar box. By the by, does he know you're in Market Fordham?"

"Oh, yes—I came in by train, but I met him near the Town Hall half an hour ago, and he asked me to meet him at the Three Tuns, at half-past four and ride home with him," answered Margaret.

"Ah, then he wouldn't suspect anything! I wonder if he saw us talking together—later on?" said Inspector Skarratt.

"Yes, he did," replied Margaret. "He was on the steps of the Town Hall, just behind you while we spoke."

Inspector Skarratt burst into activity.

"Then come along, Miss Braye!" he exclaimed. "He'll have put two-and-two together after that foolish remark of mine, and he'll be off. Come with me, first to the Three Tuns. And tell me," he continued, as he hurried her away from the churchyard, "tell me what you did with the necklace?"

"I placed it in the cigar-box again," replied Margaret, "covered it with the cigars in order, and put the box back in the cupboard with all the other things, arranging them in the same order in which I had found them, so far as I could remember it."

"You could tell the box again?"

"Oh, yes! The cigars were Henry Clay, and the quality Maduro."

They hurried down to the Three Tuns Inn, and after some searching about, found the hostler who had attended to Mr. Saunderson, and received that gentleman's message to Miss Braye.

"Just so," said Inspector Skarratt, with an almost imperceptible wink at his companion. "Of course you'll have a fly at once, eh, Miss Braye?"

Miss Braye said she would, and the Inspector ordered the best landau and fastest couple of horses, and insisted on their being ready in ten minutes. Then he and Miss Braye went across to the Town Hall and astonished the Chief Constable with the latter's story.

A little later, now armed with an additional warrant, and accompanied by Miss Braye, the Chief Constable, and Burton, Inspector Skarratt set out in pursuit of the steward. The horses were good ones, and the driver an experienced man, who scented adventures. They got over the ground towards Marchester Royal in excellent time and without accident.

But Mr. Saunderson had had twenty-five minutes' good start, and when they reached his house he was gone. And so was the famous diamond necklace.

XXII: THE RIDING WHIP

CHAPTER XXII

The Riding Whip

THE only human being readily discoverable when the police officials and Margaret Braye entered Mr. Saunderson's house, was the charwoman of whom Margaret had spoken to Inspector Skarratt. She, appearing at the front door in answer to a loud knock, showed every sign of having been interrupted in the act of white-washing—splashed from head to foot with great blotches of whitewash, she looked as if she had been caught in a sudden snowstorm. Brush in hand, and sleeves rolled high above her red elbows, she stood in the doorway staring at the interrupters of her task as if they had been ghosts.

"Is Mr. Saunderson at home?" demanded the Chief Constable.

The woman looked up and down the hall as if she scarcely knew whether to answer this question in the affirmative or negative.

"Well, really, sir," she said, glancing at Margaret as if she wondered what Miss Braye could be doing in the company of these gentlemen. "Really, sir, I can't rightly say. He was here, was Mr. Saunderson, some twenty minutes since, but whether he's here now or not I don't know."

"Where did you see him?" asked Inspector Skarratt.

"See him, sir? Why, sir, I'm whitewashing the wash-kitchen, and he came in from the stable-yard through here, and he says, says he; 'Where's Miss

Mercer!' he says, short-like. 'Why, sir,' I says, 'Miss Mercer, she's a-lying down, her not being over and above well, and having had a fainting fit this morning. Shall I get you some tea, sir?' I says, thinking that a cup of tea was what he wanted. 'No,' he says, 'I don't want any—and don't disturb Miss Mercer.' And with that he went into the kitchen and into the hall here, and I haven't set eyes on him since. But I don't think Mr. Saunderson's in the dining-room, sir, 'cause I see the door's wide open."

"Come along," said the Chief Constable, and walked without ceremony into the house.

"Is this the dining-room?" he asked.

Margaret nodded, and the entire search party went inside, the charwoman hanging on their skirts with a sense of wonder on her splashed face.

"Yes, sir, that's the dining-room," she said, feeling it incumbent upon her to say something. "Leastways, Mr. Saunderson calls it the parlour."

Mr. Saunderson was not in the parlour. But there were evidences that someone had just been there. A spirit-case stood on the table, a decanter containing whisky had been taken out of it; the stopper of the decanter had not been replaced; a glass, recently used, stood by a syphon of soda-water. And on the other end of the table, its contents spread over the table in confusion, was a cigar-box, on the end of which was the word, branded on in black letters—*Maduro*.

"He's off with it!" exclaimed Inspector Skarratt, picking up the box. "This is the box, I expect, Miss Braye?"

"Yes," said Margaret, "that's the box."

"He's got twenty minutes' start," said the Inspector. "Less, really—he'd be here a few minutes—he'd be sure to have some papers to get. Ah—look there!"

He pointed as he spoke to a small safe which stood in one corner of the room. The door stood wide open —inside was a jumble of papers. Some hand had evidently sought and found what was wanted, and, satisfied with what it got, had left the rest for anybody to examine.

"Time enough to look into that after," said the Inspector. "Let's see if we can get on his track. Here—hasn't he got a stable-yard or something at the back, and a groom, or a gardener?"

The charwoman, now thoroughly mystified, chimed in with alacrity;

"There's Thomas Booth, sir, as fettles up the garden, and sees to the pony, and feeds the pigs, and such," she cried. "But Thomas isn't about just now, 'cause the master gave him leave to go to Market Fordham to hear Mr. Vasari tried for his life, and he hasn't come back, hasn't Thomas and——"

"Stay here, Burton," said Inspector Skarratt, and led the way from the room. "The woman says he entered from the back—he must have driven in at the back and slipped round there again after he'd secured what he wanted. Let's see if we can trace any wheel marks and find out which way he's gone."

Followed by the Chief Constable and Margaret, Inspector Skarratt made his way through a kitchen garden to Mr. Saunderson's modest stable-yard. And at the entrance thereto he paused and uttered a gasp of astonishment. For there, tied up to a ring in the stable-wall, was Mr. Saunderson's fast trotting pony, and attached to it was its usual appendage, Mr. Saunderson's governess-car!

"Good Heavens!" exclaimed the Chief Constable. "He's set off on foot! Well, that ought to make it easier for us."

Inspector Skarratt darted a quick glance at the Chief Constable and another—of a different nature —at Margaret Braye.

"On the contrary," he said dismally, "that makes it all the harder for us."

"How so?" demanded the Chief Constable.

"First, because a man in a horse and trap is much easier to follow than a man on foot," answered the Inspector. "And second, because it shows what a wily and subtle old fox we've got to deal with. Come, let's have a look round the house."

"We'd better rouse the housekeeper and see if she knows anything," suggested the Chief Constable.

"Let me go to her then, please," said Margaret. "She was not well when I left here this morning, and a sudden shock might alarm her."

"Anything you wish, Miss Braye," answered the Chief Constable gallantly. "I'm sure you'll do it better than we should. Of course, the good lady will have to be put in possession of the true state of affairs, sooner or later."

However, there was no need for Margaret to exercise her well-meant offices. On re-entering the parlour they found Miss Mercer, gaunt, white, spectral, confronting Burton, who, big and athletic as he was, looked at that moment as if he would much prefer an hour in a lion's cage to five minutes with Mr. Saunderson's housekeeper. He turned to the others with an appealing look.

"This lady, sir——" he began.

But Miss Mercer had already faced round on the Chief Constable and his companions.

"Who are you?" she demanded. "Who *are* you? What right have you to come into Mr. Saunderson's house without his leave, especially when he is away from home? Who are you, I say?"

The Chief Constable lifted a hand in deprecating fashion, and assumed his suavest manner.

"My dear madam," he said soothingly. "My dear madam—I am sure we are very sorry to give any lady an annoyance, but duty, madam, duty, you know is duty. As to who we are—well, we are police officers. I am the Chief Constable of this division, and this gentleman is Inspector Skarratt——"

"I know him," interrupted Miss Mercer, looking fixedly at the Inspector. "Well, what do you want?"

"To be plain, Miss Mercer, we want Mr. Saunderson," answered Inspector Skarratt. "We hold a warrant for his arrest—and for searching this house too."

They were all watching her intently, and they saw her turn still paler. Her hand went, involuntarily, to her heart.

"What for?" she said, in a voice which had suddenly grown hoarse.

"On a charge of stealing the diamond necklace from Marchester Royal two years ago," answered Inspector Skarratt.

The woman slipped into the nearest chair and burst into a peal of laughter which made the three men and the other woman start with fear.

"What!" she said. "The Trecintrot necklace! Benjamin Saunderson! So he got it? Well—well—well! Then, after all, there is such a thing as poetic justice. Oh, ho, ho! Benjamin Saunderson and the Trecintrot necklace!"

And again she laughed—laughed like a madwoman.

Inspector Skarratt turned to the Chief Constable and whispered.

"This woman knows something," he said. Then, raising his voice and going nearer to the housekeeper, he continued: "Come, Miss Mercer, there's no doubt that Saunderson's got the necklace. He's had it hidden here; it was discovered this morning; he got a hint" (here the Inspector felt a longing to kick himself again) "that it had been discovered, and he came home half an hour ago, secured it, and has made off with it. Can't you help us to lay hands on him?"

Miss Mercer suddenly became calm and stared at her questioner.

"Why should I help you?" she asked.

"Why shouldn't you? You're no relation of his, I suppose?"

Miss Mercer became stonier than ever.

"What has that to do with you?" she demanded. "If Benjamin Saunderson has got away with even five minutes' start you'll never catch him!"

She rose from her chair and went towards the door, but with her hand upon it turned and looked at Margaret Braye.

"I suppose it was you who found the Trecintrot necklace?" she said. "Yes—I see it was. I might have guessed it. I shouldn't advise you to stay in this house, to-night, young woman—Benjamin Saunderson has a long arm. Other people have—strong fingers."

Then she left the room, and they heard her climbing the stairs, muttering to herself. Those left behind looked at each other, and the Chief Constable mopped his forehead and shook his head.

"There's more in this than's seen on the surface," he remarked, with an air of profound sagacity. "It's one of the most surprising things I have ever known—I always considered Mr. Saunderson to be a most respectable man."

"I believe the late Charles Peace was esteemed a
highly-respectable man, and a worthy citizen, in certain districts in which it was his interest to pose in that
way," remarked Inspector Skarratt, who was beginning to look around the room rather narrowly.
"Wasn't he?"

"Charles Peace!" exclaimed the Chief Constable.
"Charles Peace! Oh, come now, Charles Peace was
a bird of a very different feather. But you always
had queer ideas, Skarratt! Well, look here—what do
you propose to do now? Miss Braye—after what
that woman said, let me advise you—I've daughters
of my own older than you—do let me advise you not
to stay in this house to-night. You don't know what
mightn't happen. Eh, Skarratt?"

"I think Miss Braye would know how to take care
of herself," answered Inspector Skarratt. "But I
should certainly counsel her to take your advice. As
to what I propose to do—well, I propose to have a
look round this house—in a leisurely fashion."

"Will that do any good?" said the Chief Constable.
"He's putting distance between himself and us, you
know, every minute we delay."

"Never mind," replied the Inspector, "he can't have
gone very far, and, do you know, you gave definite
instructions before leaving Market Fordham about
watching the stations for him as well as for Cooper.
But I'll tell you what you might do, if you will, and
that's step across to Marchester Royal and get Mountford to allow you the use of their telephone and get
some extra help here. It's very evident that Saunderson has escaped to the woods, meaning when night
falls to get away to some railway station across country. What do you think?"

If the truth is to be told, the Chief Constable had

for some moments been regarding the whisky decanter and the syphon of soda-water with longing eyes. He felt—having had a very hard day—that a little refreshment would do him no harm, and it was somewhat trying to a man who felt like that to see such refreshment within actual reach and be unable, because of the conventions of civilised life, to lay hands upon it. And he knew that if he went across to Marchester Royal—a mere three hundred yards' walk—old Mountford in his quiet little pantry would press hospitality upon him to the last degree.

"I think you're right, Skarratt," he said, embracing the suggestion with alacrity, "I'll go over at once. How many men do you want? I may have to get some from Great Bywold. Our forces are not over strong here, you know."

"I should much prefer that you would use your own judgment," answered Inspector Skarratt. "You know this district better than I do. Don't you think we ought to search the woods?"

"We'll cover every inch of them before sunset!" responded the Chief Constable. He marched to the door and turned back again. "I may be a little time in getting on the telephone all round," he said. "You'll know where I am when you want me."

"Oh, yes!" replied Inspector Skarratt.

He waited until the Chief Constable had left the house, and had been seen striding across the park in the direction of Marchester Royal, and then turned to Burton.

"Burton," he said, "just go and have a thoroughly careful look round all the out-buildings here—gardens, stables, anything. Keep your eyes open."

Burton nodded, said nothing, and left the room.

Inspector Skarratt, when he had gone, looked at Margaret Braye and smiled.

"It will be a tremendous relief to you, Miss Braye, when Mr. Gerald Wintour is a free man—cleared of the charge that hangs over him?" he said.

"Relief?"

"Oh, I knew that—know it more now by the tone of your voice. You—love him so much?"

"I do!" she replied, with as much simplicity as surprise. "Of course I do!"

Inspector Skarratt looked at her with great admiration.

"He is a very fortunate man, Miss Braye," he said. "And he'll owe his life to you—no, not perhaps directly to you, but to mere chance or Fate, or, if you like to call it so, to Providence, of which you are the instrument. Ah, it's a strange thing—Chance!"

"Mr. Skarratt, what do you mean? What have I done?"

"You've done, Miss Braye—or, to be exact, you've been the means of doing—what I haven't been able to do with all my experience. Chance! Chance! No—it must be, as my good old mother—God bless her!—says—Divine Providence. If you hadn't found that necklace this morning, I shouldn't have been in this house this afternoon, and if I hadn't been in this house this afternoon, I shouldn't have seen *this!*"

He stepped across to the cupboard in which Margaret had found the diamond necklace and from a corner of it drew out—a riding whip. He held it towards Margaret, but drew it away as she was about to take it from him.

"Don't touch it, Miss Braye—it's been handled by a murderer! Don't you remember that, at the inquest on Lord Marchester, old Mountford testified that on examining the house to see if anything had been stolen he missed only one thing—a riding whip which had belonged to the dead man's father? This is the whip and you see where it has been found. I saw it as soon as I looked into that cupboard—and knew what it signified."

Margaret, scarcely comprehending, stared at the whip, and at the speaker. Inspector Skarratt went on, placing the whip on the table.

"Miss Braye—Chance! No—Providence! You've heard of—but no, I won't trouble you any more with reflections. You see that typewriter over there in that corner, with its cover off? Did you notice that while I was strolling about the room just now I bent over it, apparently in purposeless curiosity? Aye? Well, in those two letters purporting to be sent to Webb & Britford by Mr. Gerald Wintour, there was a mis-formed semi-colon. I've searched for that semi-colon on several typewriters. See, here it is—on Benjamin Saunderson's. Do you see it? Chance—no, Miss Braye, it's stern, implacable Justice!"

"Mr. Skarratt, you don't mean—you don't mean——"

"I mean, Miss Braye, that within a week your lover shall be a free man! Let's get hold of Saunderson, and—what's that?"

A clicking sound caused both to wheel round suddenly—to find themselves confronted by Miss Mercer, who was covering them with a wicked-looking revolver.

XXIII: BENEATH DEAD MAN'S TREE

CHAPTER XXIII

Beneath Dead Man's Tree

NEITHER Margaret Braye nor her sharer in this unpleasant situation was constitutionally inclined to nervousness—she, a healthy, high spirited girl, had never known fear in her life. Inspector Skarratt had looked death in the face too often to jump at the renewal of a nodding acquaintanceship with it.

But the very bravest of us cannot avoid a certain feeling as of cold water running down the spine if we suddenly find ourselves looking into the barrel of a revolver held in a steady hand—especially if that steady hand belong to a woman whom if not entirely mad, is sufficiently so as to be merciless and murderous. And Margaret Braye and Inspector Skarratt, faced with the prospect of finding bullets singing their way into some part of them, felt a mutual thrill which made them exchange a flashing glance before they turned again to confront the white-faced, blazing-eyed woman who barred the only way from the room.

"Keep cool!" whispered Inspector Skarratt. "She's mad!"

Miss Mercer smiled—her disorder had sharpened her sense of hearing.

"Am I?" she said. "It wouldn't be any wonder if I were, considering all I've gone through in my time. But I'm not mad—any more than you are!"

"Then I think you had better put that revolver down, Miss Mercer," said the Inspector. "It's a dangerous thing to play with firearms, you know."

The woman sneered.

"Yes—to *play* with them!" she said. "But I don't play with them—I use them. I can hit the middle pip in a five of hearts nine times out of ten shots—and I'll put a bullet through heart or brain of either of you two if you move."

Inspector Skarratt laughed.

"I've heard people boast before," he said quietly, picking up one of the cigars which lay strewn about the table, just as they had been tumbled, anyway, out of the box, and placing it between his lips. "See here, Miss Mercer, I'll light this cigar and turn sideways to you. Let me see you put it out—a mere touch of a bullet at the end will do it."

"Mr. Skarratt—" began Margaret. He stopped her with a look, lighted the cigar, and turned with his profile cut clear against the wall behind. "Now, Miss Mercer," he said, "try your skill."

Margaret turned away as the shot rang out; turned back half afraid of what she might see. But there stood Inspector Skarratt, smilingly examining the cigar, the extreme end of which had been cut off as cleanly as if by a sharp knife.

"That's very clever of you, Miss Mercer," he said. "You're an expert, and I see we're quite at your mercy. Now—what do you want?"

The woman glared at him.

"Anything I want I can have—with this in my hand," she said. "I wish I'd had it this morning when she," pointing her revolver at Margaret, "was spying about—I'd have shot her. And I don't know that I won't do it now—only I don't want to spoil the carpet—it's nearly new, and there isn't a stain on it."

"Utterly mad!" said Inspector Skarratt to himself.

"Yes," he continued aloud, "it would be a pity to spoil either carpet or furniture, and besides, it wouldn't be a nice thing to do, would it? You see—ah!"

For the last few seconds he had been attentively looking past the woman in the doorway as if he expected to see something behind her in the hall, and Margaret, following his glance, suddenly saw Burton emerge as from the earth or the sky, immediately in Miss Mercer's rear. There was a spring, a scuffle, a revolver shot rang out again, and then the two men and the mad woman were mixed up in a struggle which turned Margaret sick.

"Phew!" said Inspector Skarratt, as he and Burton rose after making Miss Mercer secure. "I'd rather tackle half a dozen sane men than one mad woman! I'm sorry to have frightened you so, Miss Braye, but that little trick with the cigar was the only thing to save us. You see, I knew Burton here wouldn't go out of earshot of me—I gave him a particular sign which signifies that he was not to do so—and our only chance of escaping murder, or serious injury, was in Burton knowing that we were in danger. I knew that the sound of a shot would alarm him, and that he would come at once. And well—there you are!"

"But—suppose she had shot you?" said Margaret. "Think—only the length of a cigar!"

"Ah, but I knew she wouldn't!" replied Inspector Skarratt, smiling and shaking his head. "I'd been watching her. Her hand was as steady as a rock, and so was her eye—poor thing!" he continued, casting a pitying glance at the housekeeper, who, safely secured, lay on the sofa on which he and Burton had placed her, and was glaring stonily at all three. "I daresay she can tell me something—but now, Burton, we must be moving. Run over to the house and get the Chief Constable, and some help—we must have this woman removed. Then we must be hot foot after both Saunderson and Cooper—I have an idea now where we shall find both. Miss Braye, you mustn't stay in this house—if it is impossible to return to your father, let me advise you to go down to the Marchester Arms, or better still, to some hotel at York. You'll have news to take personally to Mr. Gerald Wintour within a few hours, and you may as well be on the spot."

"You really think that, Mr. Skarratt? Oh, if I were sure! But——"

"Well, Miss Braye?"

"I believe you think that—it seems an awful thing to say—that Saunderson is the murderer!" she said in a whisper, glancing at the woman on the couch.

"I am sure that he is concerned—the probability is that the actual murderer, the man who committed the actual crime, is Cooper," answered Inspector Skarratt. "But we shall lay hands on them—now, Miss Braye, if there's anything you want to get, make your preparations, because I want to see you safely off these premises before I leave them. We will commandeer Saunderson's governess-car and pony and one of the Marchester Royal grooms must drive you to the station. Take my advice and go to York—it will surprise me if I do not send or bring you news there before this time to-morrow."

"It will make me very happy if it is good news, Mr. Skarratt," replied Margaret.

She hurried away to make her preparations, and Inspector Skarratt, paying no further heed to the figure on the couch, occupied himself in doing certain things which betokened some forethought on his part.

Looking about the various litter on Mr. Saunderson's desk, he found several large sticks of sealing-wax; taking one of these and a candle from the mantelpiece he went outside into the garden and sealed up all the windows, impressing upon each seal the device of his own signet-ring. The table he left exactly as he and his companions had found it; the riding-whip he restored to its place in the cupboard; the typewriter he covered over with a sheet of paper, the edges of which he sealed down exactly as he had sealed the windows. And then, just as he had completed these tasks, and as Margaret Braye came downstairs, quite a crowd of curious and excited people came rushing over the park from Marchester Royal—Vasari, the Chief Constable, Burton, footmen, grooms, gardeners, with old Mountford puffing and panting in the rear.

Inspector Skarratt would let none of them, except Burton and the Chief Constable (to whom he briefly explained what he had discovered and what had happened), enter the parlour. They carried Miss Mercer out and laid her in the drawing-room, where her eyes made amends for the obstinate silence of her voice. Then followed a busy time.

After sealing up the door of the parlour, Inspector Skarratt and the Chief Constable made a thorough search of the house, and locking it up left it in charge of the local policeman and two of the gardeners from Marchester Royal until further help came from Market Fordham.

The charwoman went home to tell wonderful things to her neighbours; Miss Mercer was removed in a brougham fetched from the Marchester Royal stables to the village lock-up for examination by a doctor; and Margaret Braye, Thomas Booth having arrived just when he was wanted, was driven off by that much-surprised man-of-all-work to Marchester

Station, there to catch the evening train for York.

"Where shall I find you, Miss Braye?" asked Inspector Skarratt, as she was about to drive away. "There is sure to be news."

"At the North-Eastern Hotel, Mr. Skarratt," she answered. Then, lowering her voice, she said: "I hope you—no one—will run any risks . . . such as that you ran this afternoon."

Inspector Skarratt smiled, bowed, and raised his hat. Thomas Booth whipped up the fast-trotting pony—in a moment the governess-car was out of sight. The Inspector turned to the Chief Constable.

"Now, then, for Cooper and Saunderson," he said. "I have a strong idea where we shall find one or the other—possibly both. I suppose you will come along with Burton and myself—it's over roughish country."

The Chief Constable, who had been very comfortable indeed in Mountford's pantry until Burton disturbed him, answered that he, of course, would go anywhere and do anything, but doubted the wisdom of exploring the woods now that it was drawing near to twilight. The Marchester Royal woods, he remarked, were noted for thickness of their undergrowth and their labyrinthine character, and it would be difficult to penetrate them in the dark.

"Where we're going," said Inspector Skarratt, "it will make very little difference whether it's light or dark. As a matter of fact it never is light there."

"Well, we'll get off while there is some light anyway," said the Chief Constable. "I'm sure I haven't the least notion where we're going, so I shall trust to you, Skarratt."

"If Inspector Skarratt has no objection to my doing so, I should like to accompany you," said Vasari, who had been a silent observer of the recent proceedings, and was accompanied by his newly-acquired son-in-law, "What do you say, Inspector?"

"I haven't the slightest objection, Mr. Vasari—the more the merrier, and, to tell you the truth, I shall be glad of as much help as we can get. I hope you bear me no ill-will, sir, for my part in proceeding against you," said Inspector Skarratt.

Vasari showed his white teeth, this time not unpleasantly, and waved his hands, which were nearly as white.

"Oh, no, no," he said magnanimously. "It is over —done with. A natural suspicion. You are on the right track now, eh?" he continued, drawing the Inspector aside. "You are not making another mare's nest, eh?"

"I don't think there's much mistake this time, Mr. Vasari," answered Inspector Skarratt triumphantly. "I've hit on the right clue, I do believe, but I'll tell you honestly, it's been by what's commonly called good-luck. You see, there were two or three things I hadn't quite solved in your case—if the authorities hadn't hurried me on I should have left you alone for a while, in fact, until I had more information. An important thing was—where were those letters to Webb & Britford, the gunsmiths, typed? I know now—they were typed in the house we have just left!"

"*Cospetto!*" exclaimed Vasari. "You do not mean that?"

"They were, beyond doubt. Another matter—robbery was certainly not the motive of the murder of Lord Marchester, yet something was stolen from the house that night."

"Ah, yes, the old riding-whip which belonged to my late brother-in-law's father."

"That riding-whip is in the house we have just left,"

said Inspector Skarratt. "And, Mr. Vasari, so, this morning, was the famous diamond necklace which was stolen from Marchester Royal two years ago."

"I am astonished beyond astonishment!" said the Italian. "Then you think that Saunderson——"

"I think, Mr. Vasari, that we are about to hear, or to find out, the solution of as deep a plot as ever occurred in any of the histories of your Italian societies—your Decisi, your Vardarelli, your Carbonari, and the like," replied Inspector Skarratt. "To me, indeed, it seems to have been a sort of vendetta which brought about the murder of your brother-in-law."

"A vendetta!" exclaimed Vasari, much surprised. "What, in this England of yours?"

"Aye, in this England of ours," answered the Inspector. "And in my opinion the murder of the other week is connected with the theft of the diamond necklace two years ago. Look at two or three facts and tell me, if you can, what they point to. The diamond necklace had a history—it is found, after two years, in the possession of Saunderson. Saunderson's housekeeper, hearing that he has it, says that there is, then, after all, such a thing as poetic justice. In Saunderson's cupboard is found the riding whip stolen from the house on the night of the murder. The murder was committed with a weapon which has a history, and was carefully abstracted from the possession of its rightful owner. Whoever planned or committed the murder—seeing that it was not you, Mr. Vasari, if you'll excuse me for mentioning it—laid a deep and subtle scheme to connect Mr. Gerald Wintour with it, and if that scheme had prospered, and if your brother-in-law had not happened to have become your brother-in-law, the Wintour family would have been—what? Utterly extinct!

"Now, then, what we want to get at is this—what was the motive for the wiping out of the two brothers (for if Gerald Wintour were found guilty he would most certainly be hanged) in this way? I say, it is of the nature of a vendetta?"

Vasari was too much surprised to reply to this. They were now crossing the Italian garden at Marchester Royal on their way to the woods, and he suggested that they should have some refreshment before proceeding farther. Inspector Skarratt made no objection; he was tired, physically, for once, and he knew that a few minutes' delay would make no difference if his theory were correct. Besides, he wanted to ask Mountford a question, and after he had had a drink in the library, he followed the old man out into the hall, and drew him into a quiet corner.

"You've been a long time in this family, Mountford?" he said.

The old man smiled and sighed.

"Yes, sir—and seen a many changes in it!" he answered.

"Of course you'll remember the Saunderson's connection with it well?" asked Inspector Skarratt.

"Oh, very well, sir! I knew this Saunderson's father before him."

"Well, now, did you ever hear of any feud, any quarrel, any misunderstanding that ever existed between the family and the Saundersons?"

"Never, Mr. Skarratt! Never, sir! Never heard word or breath of such a thing."

"Always amicable relations, eh?"

"Always, sir, so far as I ever saw," answered Mountford, who seemed troubled that any question of misunderstanding between the Marchesters and their people should ever be hinted at. "No—they were always on good terms."

"Do you remember Miss Mercer coming to Saunderson's house?" inquired the Inspector, suddenly.

Mountford started.

"Why, yes, Mr. Skarratt, I do, now you mention it," he replied. "She came to Saunderson just after the old lord—this little lord's grandfather—was married. That's eight-and-twenty years ago. Oh, I remember that very well!"

"I suppose you knew nothing about her, any of you?"

"No, sir, why should we? We heard she was some relation of Saunderson's, I think. He lived in the village then—he hadn't bought that place nor built his house on it in those days."

Inspector Skarratt went back to his small posse in the dining-room, and presently led them through the woods in the direction of Dead Man's Tree, and the cave in which he and Cooper had held their conference. He had an intuitive feeling that he would find one or both of the men he wanted at the cave; he had reason for so much of that feeling as warranted him in going there.

But they never reached the cave. Coming to the little clearing in which stood Dead Man's Tree, young Formby, who, with a boy's zest, was pressing forward, suddenly stopped and turned a whitening face to those behind him.

"There's a man lying here in the path—and I think he's dead!" he whispered.

XXIV: SAUNDERSON'S CAVE

CHAPTER XXIV

Saunderson's Cave

MR. WELLINGTON NELSON COOPER lay
staring up at the network of leaves outlined
against the twilight sky, but his eyes saw nothing.
There was a tiny rivulet of blood running from one
corner of his mouth, and his left hand was convul-
sively pressed over a certain spot in the near neighbourhood of his heart, and concealed an even tinier
trickle of the life fluid which was flowing faster within
than without.

He lay so still, this suddenly stricken-down bit of
humanity, that those who followed close upon the
boy's footsteps, and found him staring at the body,
felt as if they were suddenly brought into the presence of death, and became almost as still as the thing
before them until one of their number, bending over
the stricken man, looked up at the rest and said he
was still alive.

"Where's the nearest cottage?" inquired the Chief
Constable. "We must get him there at once, and
fetch a doctor and a magistrate; he looks to me like
dying, and we must have his depositions if possible."

One of the men who had accompanied them from
Marchester Royal said that the nearest house was the
south lodge, half a mile away.

"We'd better not move him yet?" said Inspector
Skarratt. "Has no one any brandy?"

It turned out that the Chief Constable had a pocket-
flask, which he had asked Mountford to fill for him

before leaving the house, no one ever knowing, he remarked, what might not be wanted on occasions of this sort, and after some of its contents had been administered to Cooper he showed some signs of returning consciousness, and finally opened his eyes and recognised Inspector Skarratt, who was kneeling by him.

"Now then, my man," said the Inspector. "Can you speak? Who shot you?"

The poacher's lips moved feebly, and Inspector Skarratt gave him more brandy, and bent nearer to him. Cooper's voice came in a whisper.

"Ben Saunderson did it, guv'nor!" he said. "You see, I knew something about Ben, and after what happened to-day I came across him here in the wood, and we had words, and I collared him, and then he shook himself off and drew a revolver and left me for dead. I'm done for, guv'nor—I know!"

"Let's hope not," said Inspector Skarratt. He turned to the Chief Constable. "Let one of your men fetch a doctor," he continued, "and send someone to the house for something to carry him on—though I'm afraid it's not much good. Here, Cooper, take another sip of this—there. Now, which way did Saunderson go?"

Cooper made another effort.

"You know that there cave of mine, guv'nor—where I took you? Well, there's another cave like it, about thirty yards along the valley side. Saunderson knows the secret of that, but he doesn't know that I know. I've watched him enter it when he didn't know I was anywhere about. He'll hide there until he can get away through the woods. I've been in that cave, guv'nor—he's got things hidden away there, and I've seen him come out of it disguised.

Thirty yards away from my spot it is, agoing east-
wards along the valley. You can't miss it if you
count the yards. There's a big Scotch fir close by it,
and the cave itself is hidden like mine, behind bushes."

Inspector Skarratt told him to remain quiet and to
save his strength. He turned to Burton and gave
him careful instructions how to reach the valley of
which Cooper had just spoken, and sent him off with
most of the party to keep a strict watch around the
place until he joined them. He, the Chief Constable,
and Vasari remained with the wounded man, and Inspector Skarratt gave him more brandy—he felt sure
that Cooper was dying, and there were certain things
he wanted to know before death took place. And
Cooper himself was anxious to speak—painfully anxious. He fought hard for breath wherewith to get
out what was on his mind.

"I'll tell you about the night of the murder,
guv'nor," he panted out at brief intervals. "That
there what I told you about Mr. Vasari wasn't true—
at least, not all true. You see, I did see him that
night right enough. That was how I got hold of
the little book."

Inspector Skarratt motioned Vasari to draw nearer.
The Italian had caught Cooper's last words, and
looked puzzled by them.

"But that there blood, guv'nor, what was on the
book, now—well, it wasn't off Vasari's fingers. That
chap as gave evidence to-day—the little Frenchy chap
—he was right. It was my fingers as was blood-
stained—mine. That's why I cut and run from the
court at Market Fordham, 'cause I thought perhaps
the beaks 'ud give orders to have my finger-pictures
taken."

He seemed about to collapse here, but presently revived and went on:

"And I'll tell you all about how I got that there blood on my fingers," he continued. "You see, I'd gone out early that night, guv'nor, and as it was early I took a stroll round about the roads and footpaths, promiscuous-like, so as not to get across with any keepers if I chanced to meet 'em. That was how I came to be in White's Spinney when Mr. Vasari was there. I saw him chuck the time-table away, and as I passed the spot when he'd gone I picked it up and put it in my pocket. I've always had a trick of disliking to see anything wasted, and I saw there were lots o' pages in it that wasn't written on. And——"

"Take your time, my man," said Inspector Skarratt.

"I want to get it over, guv'nor, 'cause I'm done for," continued the poacher, with a great effort. "After Mr. Vasari had gone off one way I went the other—went home, and didn't set out again till past ten. Then things happens as I told yer, guv'nor, 'cepting that when I turned back from the woods I had got very nearly to the house when I heard a shot. It wasn't a gunshot—I knew that—I knew, too, that it was fired inside the house. When I came up to the terrace all was in darkness. I climbed up over the balustrade and went up to the libr'y window—to tell you the truth, guv'nor, I've often peeped in there o' nights, and never been seen. Well, I felt at the windows, and came to the one that was unfastened, and I pushed it open and went in—on tip-toe. And I give you my word, guv'nor, it was for nothing but curiosity."

Again he had to pause, and again he rallied and went on.

"The room was all in darkness, guv'nor, and I put

out my hand in it, feeling for anything that might come in the way. And before you could say, 'Jack Robinson' I felt my fingers touch a man's head—and the hair was wet and sticky. I knew that head was the head of a dead man, and I was out of that room and over the terrace and in the Eyetalian garden in a jiffy. And that was where Benjamin Saunderson caught me!"

"Caught you?" exclaimed Inspector Skarratt.

"Yes, guv'nor, caught me! I'd just dropped down to the level of the garden when I felt a heavy hand catch my arm, and before I could do anything a match was struck on the balustrade, and there was Benjamin Saunderson a-staring at me—and at my hand. There was blood on it, guv'nor—we both saw it before the match went out."

" 'What's this you're after, Cooper?' he says. 'There's blood on your hand.'

"And then I thought of what a fix I should be in if I were found there, and what it 'ud mean, and I says:

" 'Before A'mighty God, Mr. Saunderson,' I says, 'I didn't do it!'

" 'Do what?' he says.

" 'I don't know,' says I, 'but there's a man lying on a sofa, just inside the libr'y window, and there's blood on his head.'

" 'What were you doing there?' he asks.

" 'Only curiosity, Mr. Saunderson,' I says. 'I heard the sound of a shot from the inside, and I felt the window open and just stepped in.'

" 'Is whoever it is dead?' he says.

" 'He felt stiff,' says I.

"Then he didn't speak for some time.

" 'You'd best get off, Cooper,' he says. 'If you're

caught about you'll swing for this—nobody'll believe you.'

" 'Don't give me away, Mr. Saunderson,' I says.

" 'No,' he says. 'I won't give you away—but you keep a quiet tongue in your head, at any rate till I give you leave to speak.'

"And of course, I promised, for I knew very well that if somebody had been murdered and Saunderson gave me away I shouldn't have a dog's chance."

The poacher's voice was growing weaker and Inspector Skarratt again made him rest, and gave him more brandy. It was after a longer interval than before that he was able to speak again, and his strength was now obviously failing.

"He went one way, telling me to mind and follow his advice, and I went home," he said. "But I got frightened, 'cause I was afraid of him. It was me made them bloodstains in the book—I got in a right fear when I got home, and I turned the book over to see if there was a train handy very early in the morning to run away by. Then I thought I'd wait until I heard who it was whose head I'd felt in the darkness. Next day I saw Saunderson, and again he told me to keep mum. But after that I got into a sort o' fright again, and as I didn't see Saunderson I fixed up that tale about the Eyetalian, 'cause I'd a grudge against him, and I knew it 'ud 'ang well together, 'cause yer see he was in the neighbourhood that night and——"

"He's going," said the Chief Constable.

A curious change suddenly came over Cooper's ashen-grey face, and his head rolled to one side. But just as nature seemed to be giving way, she reasserted herself in one great effort—the dying man turned his eyes full on Inspector Skarratt and jerked out a few last words.

"All the same, I don't believe it was Saunderson as did it, after all!" he said, and shut his eyes wearily. "I believe——"

"He's gone now!" said the Chief Constable.

Inspector Skarratt rose to his feet and stood looking thoughtfully at the dead man.

"Yes, he's gone," he said. "I wonder what he was going to say. We shall never know that now. I wish those men of yours would come—I want to be after Saunderson."

"Whether Saunderson murdered Lord Marchester or not, it's certain he shot this poor chap," said the Chief Constable. "It'll be a ticklish business to take him, Skarratt—especially if he's hiding in a cave with a narrow entrance. Why, he'd settle the lot of us, posted in such a position! Best starve him out, I should say."

"Or smoke him out," suggested Vasari. "Once I knew of men—brigands—who were hiding in a cave in the Catalonian mountains. You could not get at them, and they had many days' provisions. But, cospetto!—they were glad enough to crawl out into the blessed sunlight and the fresh air after they had been smoked out by the soldiers."

Inspector Skarratt, who was looking extremely thoughtful, nodded his head.

"Both excellent plans, gentlemen," he said, "if we were sure that Saunderson would be found in the cave which this poor chap spoke of. But I don't expect to find him there, though we'll make sure, of course. I'm afraid we may have some bother about getting hold of him—after all we've heard of his wiliness."

"I don't see how he's going to leave the district,"

said the Chief Constable. "By this time there'll be a perfect network all round him, and every station for miles round will be under observation."

"And Mr. Saunderson is not a man who can easily escape observation," remarked Vasari.

"Well, we shall see," said Inspector Skarratt, who seemed inclined to despondency. "But there's no doubt that Saunderson is an old fox, and he'll know more about running to earth than we do. Here they are, coming back—now, let's get the body away and go on to the cave."

It was almost dusk when they left the scene of the poacher's death, and quite so when they reached the valley and heard the rivulet brawling over the stones far beneath them. The Chief Constable shivered a little in the gloom—and thought regretfully of Mountford's comfortable pantry.

"We may as well look for a needle in a bottle of hay as search for anyone in these woods at this time, and in this light," he said. "You could hide a whole regiment of soldiers here."

"Well, we'll try that cave," said Inspector Skarratt. "First, let's find out if Burton's seen or heard anything."

He gave a peculiar low whistle, and within a moment Burton appeared as if from nowhere.

"Heard or seen anything, Burton?" asked the Inspector.

"Nothing, sir. I've been at both ends of this ledge; two patrolling above it, and two posted just beneath. Of course, one can't see now—it was twilight when we came—but I've made out that it would be next to impossible for anybody to climb down these crags and rocks to the valley. Anybody who came here would have to leave by this patch, one end or the

other, or go back the way they came—by the woods,"
answered Burton.

"Just so," said Inspector Skarratt.

He walked forward along the narrow, shelving
path, followed by the rest, until he saw the top of
a tall Scotch fir outlined against the sky above them.

"Here's the place," he said. "The entrance will be
at the rear of this clump of brambles. Give me one
of those bicycle lamps that you brought from the
house—I'm going in."

"You're doing a very risky thing, Skarratt," said
the Chief Constable, peering at the narrow entrance
which the Inspector presently revealed to them. "It's
like going into a drain pipe! What chance have you
if he's armed?"

"None," replied Inspector Skarratt. "But I don't
believe I shall find him there. However, I may find
something. Stand clear."

Getting on his hands and knees, with the bicycle
lamp held in front of him, he crawled into the narrow, tunnel-like entrance to the cave, and wormed his
way along. The opening was something like that by
which he and Cooper had gained the latter's strong-
hold, but of longer extent. As he penetrated further
inside, he listened intently for any sound—none came
to his ears. And then the cavity widened out, and he
sprang to his feet, and holding the lamp over his
head, cast its powerful light into the gloom around
him.

The cave was as empty as it was silent. It was not
so roomy as that which he had visited in company
with the poacher, and in a second he had seen into
every corner. In that second, too, he had seen that
Saunderson had been there—had been there without

doubt—had been there very recently. The evidences were as plain as they were curious.

For there, thrown anyhow on the sanded floor of the cave, evidently torn off and thrown aside in a great hurry, were the clothes with which those who knew the steward were fully familiar—the drab breeches and leggings, the pepper-and-salt cut-away coat and vest. There was his hat, lowish in the crown, broadish in the brim; there was his eminently respectable white stock. He had got out of those garments and into others with the rapidity of a quick-change artist.

But into what others? At any other time Inspector Skarratt would have laughed at a certain obvious answer to this question. Cooper had spoken of seeing disguises in this cave—looking about him the Inspector saw, lying about on ledges in the rock, a good many articles of outdoor clothing suitable to the proper apparelling of ladies of something more than middle age. There were bonnets—of the poke order —there were veils; there were cloaks; there were gowns—yes, and there were wigs, grey and black. Inspector Skarratt began to understand.

"Clever!" he said.

He looked round once more. There were several things he would have liked to examine, but he had no time to do so, then. Still, he glanced at a small iron box, which had evidently been dug up from the floor of the cave. Its lid lay wide open, and inside were numerous loose papers and some old pocket-books. He did not trouble to touch them—he knew there would be nothing left that could be of use to him at that moment.

The small company waiting outside, their ears alert for the sound of shots or a struggle, were greatly

surprised to see Inspector Skarratt's lamp gleaming
on the floor of the tunnel into which he had crawled
a brief three minutes before. He jumped to his feet
and knocked the dust from his clothes.

"Which is the nearest railway station to this
point?" he demanded. "Quick, somebody!"

A local man spoke.

"Willowmoor—a mile away. I know a short cut,
sir."

"Then take me by it as quick as we can go. You
come, Burton. The rest of you"—he turned to the
Chief Constable—"go back to Market Fordham.
There's nothing to do here. I wish I'd a motor-car
at disposal."

Young Formby pushed his way out.

"I can run across the wood to our place and get our
motor and meet you at Willowmoor Station," he said,
"do it in half an hour!"

"Good!" said the Inspector. "I'll expect you.
Now, come on, you—come on, Burton."

And without more ado he set off, urging his companions to their best pace. Those left behind, igno-
rant of what had happened, heard the three men
hurrying away along the stony path.

They were all three strong, athletic men, and they
made their way over the rough country to Willowmoor Station within twenty minutes, in spite of having
to cross two difficult ravines and to thread a wood.
Breathless and panting, Inspector Skarratt burst into
the little booking-office, half startling the collector
to death.

"How long is it since the last train left for York?"
he asked.

"Half an hour ago, sir."

"She'll be there, then?"

"Ought to have been in seven minutes ago, sir. She was on time here."

"Ring them up and see if she is in," said Inspector Skarratt.

The man set the telephone to work, and the Inspector got his breath. In two minutes the collector turned round from the receiver.

"In six minutes ago, sir."

Inspector Skarratt frowned.

"Did you book the passengers by that train?" he asked.

"Yes, sir."

"Did you notice them particularly?"

"Yes, sir, because we've had a message asking us to look out for Mr. Saunderson of Marchester Royal."

"You didn't see him?"

"No, sir, not at all."

"Did you see a tall woman, veiled, with a big cloak or travelling coat, who booked for York?"

"Oh, yes, sir—I've seen her before somewhere—cook at one of the big houses hereabouts, isn't she?"

Inspector Skarratt made no answer to this. He turned and walked out into the road. The lights of a motor-car were coming up to the station—young Formby had been speedier than he had promised. The Inspector motioned his two companions inside and took his seat by Formby.

"Now then!" he said. "Let her go—all she's worth—for York Station."

XXV: THE SETTLING DAY

CHAPTER XXV

The Settling Day

THE ladies' first-class waiting-room on the main platform of the great railway station at York that evening was very quiet. Just about that time there were no big, roaring-engined expresses going north or south; such occupants of the waiting-room as were in it were waiting for local trains, or, perforce, possessing their souls in patience until one or the other of the night mails was due to carry them on longer journeys. Some dozed, some chatted in whispers; some read books or newspapers; some nibbled at biscuits or buns; all looked as if they would be heartily glad when the period of necessary detention came to an end.

There was one lady, sitting a little apart from any other, in the darkest part of a not too well-lighted room, who was doing nothing, unless, indeed she was dozing behind the very thick veil which she wore.

She was a tall, heavily-built, masculine-looking lady this, who, from apparent sense of fitness, adopted a semi-masculine style of attire. She wore a long, loosely-made lady's ulster, which completely enveloped her from shoulder to foot; her head was surmounted by a mushroom-shaped hat which came well down over her face and her back hair, and was supplemented by the heavy veil aforesaid.

Round her shoulders was a strap, to which was attached a stout reticule or satchel of solid black leather; resting on the seat by her side was a somewhat similar satchel, larger in size. A substantial umbrella rested against her knees. If she had been furnished with a pair of field-glasses instead of the small satchel, she might have passed very well for a racing woman going homewards from some meeting.

The two men who came cautiously to the windows of the waiting-room and took surreptitious peeps within were not long in seeing this lady.

"That's him, Burton!" whispered Inspector Skarratt, utterly regardless of his grammar at this culminating moment. "And a very well-thought-out make-up too! Now, then, the question is—how to get him with the least fuss? We don't want any revolver shots straying about amongst these ladies. Hello, he's on the move. Get round the corner, Burton!"

The disguised Mr. Saunderson slowly rose, and, picking up his satchel, moved towards the door. Once outside he paced along with a capital imitation of female dignity—of the large and classic style—to the door of the first-class refreshment room, which is situated, as all travellers know, in the corner of the main platform. As the tall form vanished within the swing doors which separate the room from the lobby, Inspector Skarratt and his companion stepped over to the latter and took up a position right and left.

"Get them on him as he comes out, Burton," whispered the Inspector.

And five minutes later Mr. Saunderson, emerging, found his arms grasped on either side in a powerful grip, which left him defenceless, his bag shaken from his hand, and his wrists suddenly fettered by something very cold, and very smooth, and very hard. He squirmed once—and stood still.

Inspector Skarratt, without ceremony, tore off the thick veil, and nodded at the well-known features.

"Come along quietly, Mr. Saunderson," he said. "It's no use—we've got you."

And Mr. Saunderson recognised the futility of resistance and suffered himself to be led to a four-wheeled cab, in which he and his captors presently drove away, young Formby, in a state of high delight and excitement, cheerfully following behind at a pace which was in vivid contrast to that at which they had approached the Minster city.

"Well, you've not given us much trouble, after all, Saunderson," said Inspector Skarratt, gleefully rubbing his hands. "It's wonderful what a bit of luck does! If I hadn't visited that cave of yours and seen your wardrobe——"

"How did you find your way there?" growled Saunderson. "No one ever saw me enter or leave it, I know."

"There, my friend, you're wrong," answered Inspector Skarratt. "Cooper saw you, more than once, and explored it for himself. And, by the by, Cooper's dead, and I shall charge you with his murder—as well as with some other things. I'm afraid you're in for a good deal, you know."

Saunderson growled again, and relapsed into a sullen silence, which he preserved until they arrived at the police station, where he was presently safely incarcerated and thoroughly searched, with the result that the diamond necklace, a bundle of foreign securities representing a vast sum, and certain other matters (including a revolver) came to light. From the nature of the securities and the particulars upon them, it was very evident that the steward had contemplated taking up his residence in climes beyond the sea, and had sent a very handsome, not to say considerable fortune in advance of his arrival.

Inspector Skarratt went to the telephone and got into communication with the police at Market Fordham, and told them that he had arrested Saunderson, and should bring him over first thing in the morning. In reply, the Chief Constable sent him news which made him repair once more to Saunderson's cell.

"Look here, Saunderson," he said, "I've just heard some news from Market Fordham which you had better be put in possession of. I may as well tell you first that this afternoon your housekeeper was arrested for trying to shoot Miss Braye and myself."

Saunderson made no reply.

"She was taken to Market Fordham and locked up," said the Inspector. "And—she's taken her life. Poisoned herself. They must have been very careless in searching her."

Still Saunderson made no answer. He sat staring at the ceiling for a long time. At last he spoke.

"You're certain that's the truth?" he said.

"Quite certain. I have been in conversation with the doctor as well as the superintendent," answered Inspector Skarratt. "She was found dead at eight o'clock."

Saunderson said nothing to this, and the Inspector presently went away and left him alone. But within five minutes a policeman came to tell him that Saunderson wanted him, and he once more went to the prisoner's cell.

"Look here," said Saunderson, "if you'll get pen and paper and put it down I'll make a statement."

Inspector Skarratt looked thoughtfully at him.

THE SETTLING DAY   309

"Just as you like," he said. "But I warn you that——"

Saunderson waved his hand impatiently.

"Oh, I know all that!" he said. "Use it against me as much as you like. The game's up, and I may as well out with it. If I'd got away as I certainly thought I should, you'd have never known anything —mark me, you wouldn't! But I suppose I'm safely caged, now eh?"

The Inspector smiled.

"You'll be hanged within six weeks," he said frankly.

"Then I may as well speak," said Saunderson. "Get the writing materials."

Inspector Skarratt fetched Burton and the police-superintendent in charge, and the latter prepared to take down the prisoner's statement. At his earnest request they let him have a cigar, and he took three or four meditative pulls at it before he began his narrative.

"I'll tell you the exact truth about the Marchester Royal affair," he said in a cool, hard voice. "It may surprise some people—perhaps there'll be other people who'll understand a bit. We're not all alike.

"The person who really shot young Lord Mar-chester was my late housekeeper, Miss Mercer, as she was called thereabouts, though that wasn't her real name, which was Elizabeth Maynard. She shot him as the result of a plot made between herself and myself—a plot which we'd arranged for some years. The motive of the plot and the murder which re-sulted was revenge, vengeance, hatred of the Mar-chester family. That's the fact.

"And that had its origin a long time back. It all sprang from the utter badness and selfishness and cruelty of this little Lord Marchester's grandfather—father of the man we killed. He and I were boys together—we were just about the same age—he living at the big house with his father, I at the steward's house with mine. Sometimes when he was at home from Eton I used to come across him. He was full of cruel tricks. Once he shot a pet dog of mine dead at my feet. He thought nothing of beating me with his hunting-crop until I was half silly. When we were about fifteen I went up to Marchester Royal one day to take a message—I met him on a pony at the gate which he ordered me to open. I refused, whereupon he jumped off his pony and beat me with his riding-whip over the head until I was senseless. That's the riding-whip which I took away with me from Marchester Royal the night that Elizabeth Maynard shot his son. I'd always meant to have it—when she and I had had our revenge.

"And that wasn't all of his violence. Once, being sent into the gun-room for something or other, I found him there. He ordered me to get out. I refused until I had got what I was sent for. He snatched up a pistol that was lying on a bench for cleaning, and flung it at me and cut my head open just above the ear. See—you can all look—there's the scar to this very day. It was that old pistol which Elizabeth Maynard used to shoot his son with—we knew, she and I, why it was used.

"He got better of that sort of monkey-cruelty when he went to Oxford, and then on the Continent. But his heart was as bad as ever, and as black. When he came to the title he was still young and my father was getting old. He retired, and, in spite of the fact that Lord Marchester and I had quarrelled so as lads, I was made steward. He always treated me as a steward, and never seemed to think that I should harbour any resentment. But I did—I hated him, and I meant to bide my time and pay him out.

"Then, when I was about thirty-five or so, came the worst. There was a young woman, Frances Maynard, the daughter of a well-to-do Somersetshire farmer, came on a visit to friends of theirs in Marchester village. I saw a good deal of her—and I fell in love with her. I believe she might have returned my affection—I'd good reasons for hoping so. Then he—my lord—got hold of her—and ruined her. She disappeared—it was a long time before anybody found her. During that time he gave her the famous Trecintrot necklace. It was got from her somehow by some of his friends, and after he'd safely recovered it he turned his back upon her.

"It was Elizabeth Maynard who found her at last. The old home in Somersetshire was broken up—the mother had died of grief, the father had drunk himself to death, trying to forget. When Elizabeth found her she was worse than dead—and soon afterwards she did die. It was a few years later that I met Elizabeth, and that she told me the story. I took her to live with me as my housekeeper—and we began to plot for our revenge.

"You may think that we were slow in taking it, and that we took it in a strange way at last, but we were careful and methodical. We wanted to stamp out the entire race. If there had ever been a chance of getting rid of my lord and his two sons all at once we'd have taken it. But we never had one. And the old lord died suddenly.

"Now, as to this affair. We'd had one bit of revenge by recovering the Trecintrot necklace, which by all rights was Elizabeth's it having been legally given to her sister. I got that easily enough one night when I was sitting with old Mountford, who went out of his pantry and left the doors of the strong-room and the safe open. Nobody ever suspected the good and faithful steward—I kept it in that cigar-box, where, of course, Miss Braye found it, for two years. Who'd ever have suspected me—or its whereabouts?

"As to killing young Lord Marchester, it was easy when well planned—it was just as easy, too, to implicate Mr. Gerald. I knew Lord Marchester's habits, of course, and how to approach the library unseen or unheard. I knew where Mr. Gerald kept the old pistol in London, and it was I who took it from his chambers—I often called there, of course. It was I who typed the letters, and forged his signature. It was an easy thing for me to get the old pistol when it came from the gunsmiths'. I'd an office in Marchester Royal, close to the hall, and I took good care that I was there early that morning, and that several parcels came, so that the footman couldn't be particular as to one. So far as we could see, the blame would fall on Mr. Gerald and he'd be hanged, and the last of the cursed family would be wiped out —and good riddance!

"We got the thing well over—Elizabeth was a dead shot. She ought to be—she'd practised enough. However, it's all gone wrong. I've always regretted that I didn't get Cooper away and shoot him dead that same night. However, I've got this satisfaction —I've depleted the family wealth. You're welcome to give them those foreign bonds—they represent nothing like the amount I've got out of the estate for years back, by skilful forgeries. And you can give my compliments to Vasari and tell him that wild horses wouldn't drag out of me where that money's safely

planted. Of course I shall never see any of it now,
more's the pity. It's luck, that's all!"

He ceased there, and when Inspector Skarratt
asked him if he had more to say, he merely shook
his head. He listened in silence as the police-superintendent read the statement over to him, and he signed
his name at the foot with a perfectly steady hand.

"There's an end of that!" he said. "What comes
next?"

As he turned away from the table, Burton, who
was watching him, saw the prisoner raise his handkerchief to his face and wipe his lips. He walked up
and down the cell for a moment, then sat down on
the bed—and swayed sideways. Inspector Skarratt
and Burton jumped up and ran to him. He looked
up at them with what seemed to be a mocking smile,
slid heavily out of their hands, and fell, face downwards—dead.

*   *   *   *   *   *   *

Whether Inspector Skarratt was glad or sorry that
Benjamin Saunderson and Elizabeth Maynard escaped
the gallows, he found it hard to decide. He had a
strong sense of justice, and he felt that in this case
there was a good deal to be said on both sides, and
that it would be a charitable thing to believe that the
wrongs under which those two had laboured had
turned both a little mad.

"There's nothing to thank me for, Miss Braye," he
said next morning, as he drove with Margaret from
the North-Eastern Hotel to York Castle, where she
was going to break the good news of the proof of
his innocence to Gerald Wintour, "nothing at all. It's
been a series of providential dispensations, as my old
mother would have said. And—I'm glad it's over.
Yesterday was a bit—wearing."

He helped her out of the cab at the prison gates, and then held out his hand.

"But you will come in with me to see Mr. Wintour?" she said in some surprise.

Inspector Skarratt shook his head.

"No, Miss Braye, thank you, I don't think I will," he answered. "You will be able to tell Mr. Wintour your good news—and—well, you see, I must go back to Market Fordham, and then I want to get off to London. There'll be something waiting for me there —sure enough!"

She looked at him for a moment, and then gave him her hand.

"Then, good-bye," she said.

"Good-bye, Miss Braye," said Inspector Skarratt, and lifted his hat and marched away.

"Um—well!" he said, half-way up the street. "There's an end of that, too! What's it to be next?"

THE END